THE REPUBLIC OF WHORES

Josef Škvorecký

THE REPUBLIC OF WHORES

A Fragment from the Time of the Cults

Translated from the Czech by Paul Wilson

THE ECCO PRESS

Originally published in 1971 as *Tankový Prapor*
by 68 Publishers Limited, Toronto

THE ECCO PRESS
100 West Broad Street
Hopewell, New Jersey 08525
Published in Canada in 1993 by
Alfred A. Knopf Canada, Toronto
Printed in the United States of America

FIRST AMERICAN EDITION

Library of Congress Cataloging-in-Publication Data

Skvorecký, Josef. 1924–
[Tankový prapor. English]
The Republic of whores : a fragment from the time of the cults /
Josef Škvorecký ; translated from the Czech by Paul Wilson.
—1st ed.
I. Wilson, Paul. II. Title.
PG5038.S527T313   1994
891.8'635—dc20   92-939856
p. cm.
ISBN 0-88001-371-0

*To Jarmila and Vladimír Emmer and to Na'da and Jan Michal,
who hid this in times of peril, and to reserve NCOs P.L.
Dorůžka and Stanislav Mareš, who were there.*

CONTENTS

1

AN ATTACK ON A HASTILY CONSTRUCTED ENEMY DEFENCE SYSTEM

At twenty-three forty-seven, exactly eighteen minutes later than called for in the operational orders, Captain Václav Matka — commander of the Seventh Tank Battalion of the Eighth Tank Division — checked the disposition of his armour at the point from which the attack was to be launched. He then stood for about five minutes beside the tank commanded by Sergeant Krajta, to watch the digging-in. The moon, half hidden beneath the autumn clouds, poured down its spectral light upon five soldiers who were hacking away at the petrified ground with dull pickaxes. Looming in the background, its steel proboscis raised to the luminescent sky, the tank seemed to be gazing dreamily up the valley to the slopes of Old Round-top, a hillside scored with the tracks of countless assaults.

At last the captain and his aide, bundled up in greatcoats, turned away and headed into the scattered trees and the night mists beyond the tank. Under his coat the captain wore a spotless pair of coveralls, still wrinkled from long storage in the commissariat. As he strode through the ghostly September night towards his staff car, he felt none of the poetry of this strange midnight moment and this strange situation. He was thinking, instead, what a fool he had been two years earlier when he'd left his cushy job as a political personnel officer at the state insurance agency. He'd got himself into some vague trouble, and the offer of a special ten-month training course with the armoured division, with a guaranteed commission at the end of it and a promise of rapid advancement, had looked good. At the time, he had not been aware of these night-time manoeuvres that took place week after week, weather notwithstanding, nor had he known of the many other discomforts.

When he came to the road, he shone his flashlight on the order sheet. "*2330 – 0400:* crews to position, dig in, and camouflage armoured vehicles. *0430:* preparations for the attack. *0450:* artillery ready. *Start time: 0500.*" This meant he could sleep until four-thirty. He should, of course, go from crew to crew to check their progress. But screw that. He switched his flashlight off and walked into a stand of shrubbery where the camouflaged staff vehicle was parked. Stretching to plant his foot on the Tatra's high running-board, he turned to his aide, who was also the battalion's educational officer.

"Hospodin," he said, "take a stroll and see if you can put a little wind up these lazy assholes. I'm going to hit the sack. I haven't had a decent sleep all week. There was that cultural conference on Monday, Tuesday the Party meeting lasted till three in the goddamn morning and then I was on duty, and Wednesday was officer-training day. Wake me up at four, Hospodin."

"Yes, sir, Comrade Captain," Lieutenant Hospodin said mockingly, cracking his heels together. When the door had slammed shut behind the captain, the lieutenant walked around to the cab and opened that door. The driver was snoring behind the wheel. Hospodin shook him awake.

"What's up?" the driver grumbled sleepily.

"Look," said the lieutenant, "I want you to give a hand to Tank Commander Smiřický. They've only got four men. And wake me up at a quarter to four."

"Fucking hell!" the driver muttered, then clambered down

out of the car. He was still a rookie, a first-year wonder in basic training, and a muffled obscenity was all the resistance he could muster. Outside, the cold air made him shudder. Meanwhile the lieutenant scrambled up into the driver's compartment and slammed the door behind him. A blanket appeared in the window as he wrapped himself up.

Private Holený shoved his hands in his pockets and trudged off, teeth chattering, in a northerly direction, towards a clump of shrubs that looked like stage props for an amateur theatre production. The distant clatter and ring of shovels and pickaxes on the hard earth carried to him on the silent night air. As Holený walked quickly through some tall grass, he could feel the dew soaking through the thin cloth of his summer trousers. His mood grew fouler.

The political division's staff car seemed to be floating at anchor in a cluster of bushes. Just as Holený walked past it, someone turned on a flashlight. He could see the silhouettes of two officer's caps against the illumination. Then the car door opened, the running-board creaked, and the caps disappeared inside.

"The sons of bitches!" thought Holený, and trotted on.

When he reached the spot where, according to the plan of disposition, Tank Commander Smiřický's crew should have been digging in a medium tank, all he could see in the darkness was what looked like a thicket. Then, without warning, a motor coughed and rumbled into life. The thicket began to move. It was a tank: Holený could now see its cannon at high elevation. The vehicle lurched forward and, suddenly blending with the foggy grey monotone of the grassy plain around it, disappeared from his sight. The motor fell silent.

Fascinated, Holený trotted over for a closer look at this magical phenomenon. Yes, the big iron beast was in there, all right, nestled hull down in a beautifully made pit. On each side of the pit there were neat mounds of earth, and the cannon was resting at regulation elevation over a model breastwork. Holený felt a deep respect for a crew that, despite being short a man (the front machine-gunner was in sick bay with a case of the clap), and in less time than the regs allowed, could dig such an enormous hole.

He walked over to the tank commander, who was just climbing down from the turret. When he spoke, Holený's tone was half friendly, half respectful, as one would expect from a subaltern. But it wasn't Holený's sense of duty that made him speak this way; it was honest admiration.

"Comrade Tank Commander, Lieutenant Hospodin sent me here to lend you a hand with the digging-in, but I see – "

"That khaki-haired little bag of shit!" came a voice from the driver's cockpit. A stocky man in greasy coveralls with corporal's chevrons on the chest emerged from the hatch and stepped out onto a mound of earth. "Does he think we'll turn ourselves ass-inside-out just because he says so? He can stick *that* where the sun don't shine, the brainless little cocksucker." Then the corporal turned to the tank commander and said, somewhat more politely, "So what do you think, Dannyboy? Didn't I tell you? The perfect pit. I knew that sweet little thing was here. I know this place like my own shit. I've taken this fucking hill at least five hundred times."

Sergeant-Major Smiřický – commander of the second tank of the first platoon of the First Squadron – looked around. "This is great, Andělín. I just hope they don't twig."

"The hell they will, man. And if they do, who gives a shit? Let the rookies work their asses off – not the boys of April." Corporal Andělín Střevlíček was serving an extra six months because in an attempt to ingratiate himself with Stalin, the commander-in-chief, General Čepička, had prolonged the military service of all soldiers drafted in 1950 to approach (though not equal) the great Soviet model. "I'm hitting the hay," announced the hapless warrior, and he started to walk off.

"Wait a minute," the tank commander called after him. "We've still got to do the camouflaging. Let's get it over with."

"Why can't Juraj and Holený do it? Hospodin sent him to help, didn't he?"

"Fuck the camouflage," came a voice from inside the tank. It was the gun loader, Juraj Bamza.

"Don't be a pain in the ass, Juraj," said the corporal. "Just do the goddamn camouflage, okay?"

"Will you get off my fucking back?"

"Come on, Juraj, don't be a cunt. You wouldn't want to leave the job to poor old Střevlíček, would you?" pleaded the corporal.

"Why don't we all just collectively shit on it?" proposed the loader.

"Juraj," said the tank commander, "we've got to put some stuff on it, so they'll stay off our backs."

The loader's response was monosyllabic: "Shit!"

A different voice – a hollower-sounding one – came from inside the turret. "Would you just clear the hell out of here, Juraj? Don't piss me off. Move!" This was the gunner, Sergeant Žloudek.

"Why don't you take a flying eff?" retorted the loader. A hollow crunching sound came from inside the turret, like the sound of iron striking a tin pot.

"Ow! Let me go! Keep your fucking hands to yourself, cunt!"

"Dumb rookie," said the voice inside the turret. "Are you going to camouflage the fucker or not?"

"All right, all right."

Bamza quickly jumped down from the turret.

"Okay, boys," said the tank commander. "Go get some

grass and a couple of branches. Just toss some on the turret and scatter a bit on the breastwork up front."

Holený looked around and the loader followed him, muttering to himself. Střevlíček climbed onto the motor casing, spread his coat out, lay down, and wrapped the coat around him. A pleasant warmth rose through the louvers. The driver farted and promptly fell asleep.

Tank Commander Danny Smiřický began his tour of inspection. He was a timid and therefore conscientious man, and standing orders made him answerable for the tank and its crew. Yet the driver and the gunner, who should have been carrying out a technical inspection of the tank, were asleep, and the tank wasn't even camouflaged yet. If one of the brass – a captain or a political officer – found out that they hadn't actually dug the pit themselves, but had simply driven the tank into an old one hidden with brush, there'd be an awful fuss – and they'd have to dig a new one, with the officers looking on. True, Střevlíček insisted that all the officers had long since turned in and were sound asleep. But the tank commander was one of those people who believe that wherever there's ointment, there's a fly.

He walked a short way off to look for branches. In a nearby thicket he broke off two large limbs, and hauled them back. Juraj Bamza was already standing on the turret, scattering handfuls of grass around him. Holený was sticking delicate little sprigs behind the handgrips on the side of the turret, and into the louvers. Danny leaned both his branches against the front armour-plating of the turret. He was cold. He looked at his watch. If he bedded down now, he could get about three hours' sleep. Great! But he should post a watch, he knew, and they should all take turns – about half an hour each. He knew, too, that he had no way of compelling Střevlíček and Žloudek, who were both in for the extra months, to do anything so pointless. He decided to hand the duty over to the two new recruits. *I'm their commander,* he thought. *I have a right to rest after the digging-in is complete. It's their duty to obey my orders. So I'll give them an order and go to sleep. If they don't keep a proper watch, if they go to sleep too, that's their problem. If someone catches them at it, I'm off the hook.*

"Hey, Juraj," he said. "You and Holený here are going to take turns."

"Take turns at what?"

"Sentry duty. An hour and a half each."

"Screw you."

"Don't be an asshole. I'm out of here in a couple of months, and in the meantime I don't plan to get in any shit," said the tank commander severely. He climbed onto the turret and slipped inside through the driver's hatch. *I gave them the order,* he said to himself. *I handled the situation precisely according to regulations, in a military fashion, following the example set by the battalion commander.*

He lowered himself carefully through the hatchway and sat down on the driver's seat. Behind him, on the ammunition boxes, Sergeant Žloudek was sound asleep and snoring. Danny felt for the safety lock on the hatch, disengaged it, then closed the hatch in battle position. But he opened the observation slits so that he could see anyone coming. He took Střevlíček's padded helmet from the seat next to him and put it on his head as a substitute pillow, and snuggled up against the hand-grenade holders and the ventilation tubes.

A star shone brightly through an observation slit and the tank smelled of diesel fuel and oil. Outside he could hear the faint blows of pickaxes; the other crews were still at work. He put his hands under his armpits to warm them and peered out at the star. As he began to doze off, it crossed his mind that he should have his picture taken soon in Okrouhlice. Perhaps

Lizetka would like a photo of him wearing his leather tank helmet. She'd probably think it was a hoot. But he'd have to hurry because — he heard the loader's voice coming from the turret: "That's enough, dickhead!" and then he heard the man's ironshod boots clanging over the armour-plating. The engine louvers rattled. *They're settling down to sleep now*, thought Danny, half asleep himself. *But I've given them their orders.* He felt an unpleasant lump in the small of his back, where his pistol had slipped. He pulled it around to his stomach. If there was a war they'd get no sleep at all, they'd be too busy shitting their pants. Military statisticians had allotted tank crews a life expectancy of four minutes in battle. He had no trouble imagining that kind of fear. But perhaps there wouldn't be a war.

Then again there probably would, he thought, but as he drifted into sleep he was thinking about how he would soon be returning to civilian life, and about what it would be like. Would the maddening Lizetka continue to spurn his advances? He'd been in love with her, or rather yearned terribly to fuck her, for close to three years. But either she was serious about her Catholic prejudices against marital infidelity, or she was made of ice-cream. The latter was much more probably the case than the former. But a man never knew the extent of female bitchiness. Maybe Lizetka wasn't made of ice-cream at all, but simply had the mind of a police torturer. Maybe she was a sadist, as most women were — at least, most of the ones he knew. Maybe the devil knew....

It was one o'clock when the tank commander fell asleep. By that time, Captain Matka, stretched out on his comfortable bunk in his staff vehicle, had long since surrendered to slumber. According to operational orders, he should now be inspecting the dug-in tanks. The educational officer for the Seventh Tank Battalion, Lieutenant Hospodin, was also asleep in the cab of the Tatra ("Provide political instruction to the tank crews on the role of proper camouflage in the struggle for peace"). After a heavy supper, the politruk, First Lieutenant Růžička, was tossing and turning on his bunk in the staff vehicle, dreaming heavy dreams ("Inspect the quality of political awareness among the tanks' crews"), and First Lieutenant Pinkas, the chief of the battalion's staff ("Ensure that the crew commanders have familiarized themselves with the battle situation and that the crews have been properly briefed on firing instructions") was trying to calm his nerves with doses of sleeping pills while driving thoughts of his wife, Janinka, out of his mind; she was asleep alone in their flat, but what if she was neither alone nor asleep?

Beneath a stretched-out tarpaulin in another Tatra, three squadron commanders were just as soundly asleep ("Check on the activities of all ten tank crews"). Only the fourth officer, Lieutenant Hezký of the First Tank Squadron, was diligently carrying out the duties assigned to him. Moreover – to the dismay of the privates under him – he was helping Sergeant Vytáhlý's crew dig a miserable excuse for a tank pit, since the crew consisted of only two men. (The rest were in the guardhouse.) Captain Matka was always taking advantage of the lieutenant's eagerness to please, but at the moment the only high-ranking officer to observe his good work was the Lord Himself – whose existence the army command officially denied.

Towards two o'clock in the morning, the last blows of the pickaxes and shovels fell silent. Weariness had overcome even Lieutenant Hezký's zeal. One by one the tank motors burst briefly into life, and the tanks crawled forward into the shallow depressions that were meant to be pits, and settled in like broody hens.

A great and allegedly just silence settled over the lower reaches of Old Roundtop. In that silence the moon, filtered

through night mist, looked down upon the metal tanks. Inside them slept the crack soldiers of the Seventh Battalion of the Eighth Tank Division, dreaming of the free and sunny realms that would be their world in a couple of months.

★ ★ ★

Thus, when the jeep bearing the number of the division's staff emerged from the pre-dawn fog, the eyes of Major Borovička – called the Pygmy Devil – encountered a tranquil and realistic picture: a landscape with tanks. There they lay like squat, overfed boars in their shallow trenches, a light early-morning breeze flirting with the tufts of grass and sparse branches stuck into them here and there. The heart of the tiny major fluttered with joy at this opportunity to assert his rank. He ordered his driver to stop. Nimbly he jumped out of the jeep and hurried up to the battalion's highly visible staff vehicle, his legs in their brightly polished boots scissoring briskly back and forth in military fashion.

The foot of Old Roundtop lay wrapped in a pleasant silence uninterrupted even by birdsong, since most birds lacked the discipline to wait for the Seventh Tank Battalion's term of service to end and had irresponsibly flown south. Major Borovička walked through the dew-covered grass to the staff vehicle and, with some effort, climbed up onto the running-board of the driver's cab. When he peered inside, a satisfied smile spread across his face. In the driver's seat he saw Lieutenant Hospodin wrapped in an army blanket, with only his nose and a stubble-covered chin showing. The tiny major balanced on the high running-board a moment, then snorted contentedly and looked around. He wanted to jump down, but when he saw the drop – almost a metre – yawning beneath him, he lost his nerve. Gripping the door-handle firmly with his small hand, he bent his right knee until his trousers strained ominously, and felt around with his left foot for the ground. But his right foot slipped and he fell, striking his crotch on the step. He groaned weakly. For a long, painful moment he remained motionless, and then, with great effort, he pulled himself back up on the step, carefully edging around to stand with his back to the door. After considering his position, he slid his back slowly down the door until his behind met his feet. He perched there for a while, staring into the abyss, and then jumped and landed on all fours, with his hat down over his eyes. He bounded to his feet at once, regained his bearing, and, with a victorious, bloodthirsty grin, walked towards the staff door at the rear of the vehicle.

The air inside was warm and fetid, rank with the odour of wet sheepskin, cigarette smoke, and stale beer. Captain Matka lay on a field cot, breathing the funk in deeply. He had obviously made himself at home; at one end of the bed two filthy socks peered out from under the sheepskin, and at the other end the captain's face, weathered to a ruddy brown by the wind and sun, glowed faintly in the dark. One boot lay on the floor, the other on a map on the table under the blacked-out window.

For a few moments the little major just stood there, savouring this heaven-sent scene. Then he drew himself up to his full height, his chest thrust forward and his buttocks sharply outlined in his tight breeches, and opened his mouth. The smiling general who was about to pin the Order of Kutuzov on Colonel Matka's chest opened his mouth too, but instead of a eulogy, out poured a piercing voice: "Atten*tion!*" Ignoring the smoke billowing out of the shattered American tanks, Captain Matka swung his legs out of the bed and came to attention as quickly as he could manage, gaping at the general. The general's face dissolved itself into the familiar countenance of the Pygmy Devil.

"Comrade Captain," said the tiny major, with diabolical menace in his voice. "The time is now oh four hundred and forty hours. Your orders are?"

The captain swallowed. He was barely awake, and bits of his dream were still mixed with raw reality. He almost reported a stunning victory over the American armoured units, but then he remembered the written orders. Automatically he reached into the side pocket of his trousers, then realized that he should know them all by heart. Abruptly his mind cleared. It was always the same; every set of orders to come into his hands seemed like a strange, primordial variation on a basic theme: "The tank battalion will attack the hastily constructed enemy defence system." So he replied briskly, "A state of battle readiness. I am to inspect...." He stopped, realizing that he hadn't inspected anything whatever. Before he could resume, the major spoke up.

"When do we say that a tank battalion is in a state of readiness?"

The captain gasped for air, realizing the full implications of his position: the man-eating Major Borovička had come upon him in the act of sleeping. He felt like a rabbit caught in the jaws of a hyena. Mechanically he began to recite the standing orders, as though they were the Lord's Prayer.

"The tank battalion is in a state of complete battle-readiness when all the vehicles and their crews are in a state of battle-readiness, that is, when all the crews are complete, and in good health, when each vehicle is supplied with the prescribed amount of ammunition, fuel, lubricants, and rations, when the gunsights are properly rectified, and...."

"*What about boots?*" shrieked the major.

"Boots?"

"Boots," the little man insisted.

"What do you mean, Comrade Major?"

"Boots. Ordinary military boots," said the Pygmy Devil sarcastically. Matka looked down, saw his feet shod only in socks, and felt hot shame wash over him.

"Comrade Major," he began, but the major interrupted him with a tirade, firing bolts of malice from his eyes.

"*What could you possibly have been thinking?*" he shrieked in his castrato voice. "What is this supposed to mean? Is this how you carry out military manoeuvres? Don't you realize that such manoeuvres are a peacetime task for the defence of your homeland? And here you are, sleeping! You will report to the division commander, is that understood?"

"Comrade Major – " Matka began, plucking up his courage.

"*Silence!* You will speak when spoken to. You're to set an example to your men in carrying out your duties. Can you be surprised when they fail to carry out theirs? You ought to be ashamed!"

Captain Matka was standing at rigid attention, with rage in his heart.

In an abrupt, energetic motion, the major raised his left arm into the air and pulled off his long-shanked leather glove, revealing a large Swiss wristwatch. "It is now oh four hundred forty-eight hours. I will advance start time by ten minutes. At precisely oh five hundred and ten hours, your battalion will move out on the attack. That will be all."

"Yes, sir!" Matka attempted an about-turn, then realized that, since he was incompletely dressed, the move would look ridiculous. He glanced around, guiltily removed one boot from the map and the other from the floor, and began tugging them on. The Pygmy Devil couldn't resist a final, vindictive remark:

"If this happened in wartime, Comrade Captain, you'd be court-martialled."

"Yes, Comrade Major," Matka said firmly. He thumped out of the vehicle and roared, "Private Holený, on the double!" But his bull-roar voice was swallowed up in the idyllic silence of an early Indian-summer morning.

Major Borovička stood in the door of the staff vehicle, speaking with an icy calm.

"Your driver isn't here, Comrade Captain," he cackled. It sounded like a knife scraping the bottom of a tin pot. "Obviously he's deserted to the enemy."

Matka blushed, then headed in a clumsy trot towards the staff vehicle parked about fifty metres away. On the way, he thought quick, practical thoughts mixed with bursts of helpless rage aimed at the Pygmy Devil, at his own staff, and, as always, at himself – for being such an ass and giving up his soft job in the state insurance agency.

He entered the staff vehicle like a cannonball. First Lieutenant Pinkas and First Lieutenant Růžička were bundled together under a fur coat like an odd couple. "Atten – SHUN!" shouted the captain, and before the two lieutenants could properly respond, he began to carry out Major Borovička's orders. "Do you call this a state of battle-readiness? Where are the squadron commanders? Where's the artillery preparation? It's now oh four hundred and fifty hours. It's time to begin."

Both officers peered at him in dismay through sleep-filled eyes.

"You haven't heard the last of this. You will report to me after exercises. I'm advancing start time to oh five hundred and ten hours. I want to see our forces move out on the attack on the dot. Comrade First Lieutenant, summon the squadron commanders at once. And you, find me Private Holený. That will be all."

The officers jumped out of the staff car. The captain followed them with a rocking gait, and as he glanced towards his own vehicle he saw Lieutenant Hospodin standing at attention, being dressed down by the Pygmy Devil, who was still fuming. But he had no time to indulge his sense of mild satisfaction. He flung open the cab door, shook the driver completely awake, and dispatched him at a loping (and cursing) run towards the nearest pit, with a secret order to wake up all the tank crews at once.

★ ★ ★

Tank Commander Smiřický's crew received the courier's tidings with mistrust.

"What about chow?" was Sergeant Žloudek's salutation to the day of battle. He looked at his watch and added, "Jesus Christ, it's five already. We were supposed to be on the fucking move by now!"

From the driver's seat where he had slept, Smiřický wormed his way past Žloudek. He sat down by the radio and pulled on his helmet. Žloudek followed him with the air of faint contempt worthy of a third-year man.

"I'll never get this piece of crap tuned in properly," sighed the tank commander, desperately twirling the dial of the radio.

"Fuck it," said Žloudek. "You won't get a connection worth dogshit anyway."

But Danny went on twirling the dial. *We got some sleep and we got away with it,* he thought. *Even though Juraj had orders to wake me up and he didn't. But now I've got to establish radio contact or there'll be hell to pay.*

"What did I tell you, my friends?" Andělín Střevlíček said. He got to his feet on the motor casing and peered curiously through the dark towards the staff vehicles. "I'll bet old Matka was sawing wood, and Růžička too."

Smiřický gave up trying to get the radio to work and pulled himself into the commander's turret. The area around the staff vehicle was swarming with officers, and runners were rushing about in confusion. The little major was just approaching this whirlwind.

"Lord above, Borovička's here!"

"Old Pygmy Devil himself?" asked Střevlíček in genuine delight. "Jesus, he'll have the brass's ass in a fuckin' sling."

"Andělín, get inside," said the tank commander. "I don't want some asshole saying — you know what."

"Don't worry, Danny," said Andělín. "They can all kiss old Střevlíček's butt." Still, he walked slowly around the tank, then prudently crawled into the driver's hatch. The tank commander noticed Juraj Bamza still asleep on the cool motor.

"Juraj, damn it, get up and get inside!"

"Fucking lay off, will you?"

"Jesus, this is no time to screw around. Borovička's here."

"Who gives a shit?" said Bamza, but he stood up, stretched, and yawned. Below Smiřický, inside the tank, Žloudek had again made himself comfortable on the ammunition boxes. The tank commander looked outside. In the commander's turret of the neighbouring tank, about fifteen metres to his left, he could see, from the waist up, the figure of Sergeant Soudek.

"Josef!" Danny called. "Did you manage to get radio contact?"

"Are you kidding?" replied Sergeant-Major Soudek defiantly, in a strong Hana accent. "My radio's buggered. To hell with it, I say."

Just then a runner came up. "If you haven't got radio contact, watch the battalion commander and do what he does. The gunners are supposed to really work the guns. The Pygmy Devil's big on artillery. We attack on red, the enemy attacks on yellow, and a green flare means the exercise is over. And

fix up the camouflage, the Pygmy Devil's coming to inspect
it personally."

"Ours is okay," said Bamza, and he sat down in the loader's hatch. But he had to move aside for Žloudek's head, which
appeared underneath him.

"What are they doing?"

"Consulting," said Danny.

"The hell they are. Old Pygmy's making them eat shit,"
said the sergeant.

★   ★   ★

And so he was. To all the officers of the battalion, Borovička
was reeling off a list of the blunders they had made during
this final round of training. It was a long list. As he improvised
this lecture, the Pygmy Devil was privately astonished at himself, at how systematic he was and how much he had actually
learned about the art of tank warfare. Talking to the officers
made him feel like a hardened front-line soldier. He was having the time of his life. He knew they all hated him, but he
also saw how helpless they were to do anything about it; he
was secure inside the armour of discipline and rank. There had
never been anything in the world more perfect than this.

The delight he took in browbeating the lesser officers was
of an even higher order than the thrill he had felt long ago, before the Second World War, when, as Corporal Borovička, he
had castigated layabouts in the quartermaster's store. Start time
had long since come and gone, and the soundest sleepers had
by now crawled into their positions and were watching inquisitively while the small circle of officers stood there, being
dressed down by the strutting, sputtering little cock. Even the
signholders on the upper slopes of Old Roundtop, and those

who represented enemy tanks concealed in the terrain farther away, were now awake and wondering why the attack hadn't begun yet. Had they slept too soundly and missed it?

The major kept berating the officers until it seemed he might go on until he dropped dead. One by one they were all given what for. The zealous Lieutenant Hezký felt his world collapsing. (The things he had left undone! The things he had forgotten to do!) The timid cadet officer, Sergeant-Major Sliva, was trembling with fear. The impertinent cadet officer, Dvořák, could hardly keep from laughing out loud. The apathetic Lieutenant Grünlich thought, with some distaste, about the unsatisfactory state of his growling stomach, and the unobtrusive Lieutenant Šlajs worried about the inadequate pits his squadron had made. The boorish technical officer, Lieutenant Kamen, was thinking, *You can kiss my ass, you jerk*, and Lieutenant Tylš, the mess officer, prayed silently that the major wouldn't remember that his men were supposed to have brought up breakfast at oh four-thirty. He had no idea where the breakfast was.

At last Major Borovička was through, and he invited his audience to follow him. Start time was put off until some uncertain future, and would now probably take place in broad daylight, which meant that every error and lapse as yet to be committed by the men of the Seventh Tank Battalion would be perfectly visible. The small group of officers gathered behind the little major and set off with him into the field, and a ragged salvo of metallic clangs came through the grey morning light as the hatch covers slammed shut, isolating the tank crews from the world in which, for the moment, the Pygmy Devil was giving vent to his rage.

★   ★   ★

The inspection party reached the first tank. It stood in a small depression with a low embankment of rocky soil around it, like the dams children build with mud to hold water back after a rain. Here and there, tufts of grass were scattered over the armour-plating.

"Whose machine is this?" brayed the major.

One of the squadron commanders, the unobtrusive Lieutenant Šlajs, brought his heels smartly together, thrust his chest forward, and sang out, "Mine, sir! First squadron, Seventh Battalion. Squadron Commander Lieutenant Šlajs, sir."

The major fixed him with a piercing look. "Have you inspected the pit yourself?"

"Yes, Comrade Major."

Not a muscle moved in the Pygmy Devil's face. "Have you checked on the adequacy of the camouflage?"

"Yes, Comrade Major." There was a note of sadness in the lieutenant's voice.

The major cast his eyes over the tank, and the whole group followed suit. Lieutenant Šlajs was obviously a man of modest standards.

Captain Matka tried to reassert his authority. "Comrade Lieutenant," he barked, "do you call this a – "

But the Pygmy Devil interrupted him. "Silence, Comrade Captain. I have not given you permission to speak." He turned to the unhappy Šlajs. "And have you ascertained whether the crews in your squadron have familiarized themselves with the situation, the battle orders, and their targets?"

Lieutenant Šlajs tried to fudge. "I've done spot inspections, sir."

"Have you, for instance, inspected the crew of this particular tank?"

"No, Comrade Major," Šlajs replied, still hoping to be let off the hook.

"But you did give the required orders to the squadron commanders?"

"Yes, Comrade Major."

"And you are satisfied that the squadron commanders have passed these orders on accurately to their tank commanders?"

There was no escaping the iron logic of the military mind. In a tone of weary resignation, Šlajs replied, "Yes, Comrade Major."

"Then please test the commander of this tank."

Having played his ultimate trump, the Pygmy Devil slid his hands into his pockets and waited.

"Yes, sir," said Lieutenant Šlajs, and, as if trying to stall for time, he stepped up to the tank. All its hatches were closed, in battle position. That was the only thing right about it, though. Not a sound came from inside the tank. It was as if no one were there, as if the machine had been abandoned.

"Sergeant-Major Soudek!" called Lieutenant Šlajs.

"Sir!" The voice inside the tank sounded hollow.

"Dismount!"

"Yes, sir!" The commander's hatch lifted and, with a grand flourish, a large boiler-maker's hand secured it in position. After the hand, a helmet emerged, framing the ruddy face of a powerfully built country lad. Tank Commander Soudek slowly emerged from the hatch, sat on one edge of it, and then slid to the ground in an experienced move. He assumed the non-chalant, slightly arrogant stance of a third-year soldier confronting a superior officer.

"*As you were!*" shrieked the major. "Comrade Tank Commander, is that any way to dismount? Do it again, and do it right this time."

The tank commander from Haná shot a contemptuous glance at the major, but said nothing. He turned around and climbed back up on the turret.

"What is this, a slow-motion film?" shouted the major. "I think next Sunday we'll be practising our mounting and dismounting techniques, won't we? And don't think that just because your time in the army is almost up, you're no longer subject to discipline."

Soudek sat on the edge of the turret and looked at the major with expressionless eyes.

"Inside! And close the hatch! And when you hear the order to dismount, you will open the hatch and jump down from the turret. Do you understand? *Jump* down, don't climb down!"

"The ground's rocky," grumbled Soudek. "I'd rather not break a leg just before I get out of here."

The major turned red. "That is the limit! Don't you know what an order is? Orders are not there to be discussed. If you break a leg, that's just too bad. Now – obey the order!"

Soudek turned around and backed into the opening. For a moment he had trouble closing the hatch, and this nettled the Pygmy Devil. "You heard me – *quickly!*"

"The latch is buggered."

"You watch your language!" squealed the major, but the hatch crashed shut over his words. Borovička turned to Šlajs, who had meanwhile slunk into the background and was as quiet as a mouse.

"Discipline, Comrade Lieutenant, discipline," said the major, shaking his head in a schoolmasterly fashion. "Give him – no, give the whole crew the order to dismount."

"Yes, sir!" said Lieutenant Šlajs firmly. He set a grave expression on his face and approached the tank. "Crew – dis – MOUNT!"

Nothing happened at first. Then suddenly all the hatches opened. Soudek's face shone in the commander's hatch, ruddier than usual from the effort. He propelled himself out of the turret with such force that his body flew through the air directly at the major, like the shadow of an avenging angel. The major barely managed to jump out of the way, and as he did so he stumbled over a pile of dirt. Captain Matka gallantly caught him before he fell.

"Look where you're jumping! Are you *blind?*" squawked the major. He was slow to regain his composure, and so failed to notice the lackadaisical way the driver, Desider Kobliha, crawled out of the tank in defiance of all regulations.

The crew then lined up in front of the tank in the proper order: first the commander, and next to him the driver, the backup driver, the loader, and the gunner. With a sinister wrinkling of his brow, the major gave Lieutenant Šlajs the order to test the loader, Private Mengele, on his knowledge of their disposition and the disposition of the enemy. He deliberately chose the loader because he assumed he would be the least informed crew member, an assumption that was all too correct.

In truth, even Lieutenant Šlajs had only a very imprecise notion of where the enemy was, and he knew little more about where he himself was. He only knew that his situation, at the moment, was pretty hopeless. He assumed the regulation stance and issued a bland order to Private Mengele. The private's face radiated contempt for everything around him. From his posture, you would never have known that he had just come through almost thirty months of military service.

"Comrade Private, where are the enemy forces?"

The contempt in Mengele's face deepened. Lazily, he waved his arm in the general direction of the hillside. "The enemy forces are – over there."

"Can you be less vague?" Lieutenant Šlajs coaxed.

"On Old Roundtop."

"That's correct," declared the lieutenant. "And where are we?"

"We're at the bottom of Old Roundtop," said Mengele. So

far, he was turning out to be highly informed.

"And what is our strength?"

"Our strength is about one tank battalion."

"What do you mean, 'about'?" shouted the Pygmy Devil. "What exactly do you mean, 'about', Comrade Private? Don't you know the unit you belong to?"

Unfazed, Mengele replied that he knew.

"Then what do you mean by 'about'?"

"'Cause we don't know how many we lost yesterday," Mengele replied coolly.

The private's logic stumped the major, who'd been sure he'd scored a point. He opened his little mouth to protest, but only a short puff of air came out. For a moment, no one said a word. Lieutenant Šlajs tried to look unperturbed, and the major gained enough self-control to say, "Go on, Comrade Lieutenant."

Lieutenant Šlajs turned back to Mengele, who looked at him affably. He was sincerely trying to help his commanding officer out, but he really knew nothing at all. The lieutenant thought hard about how to phrase the next question to draw out a clear answer, but only managed to determine that he knew little more about it all than the loader. He decided to begin with a broad query. "Comrade Private, what is the enemy's strength?"

Mengele scowled. "The enemy's strength is one infantry regiment."

Šlajs glanced sideways at the major, but the major's expression remained inscrutable. Either that was the right answer, or the major himself didn't know. The latter possibility was the more likely, the lieutenant thought. He was just about to ask the next question when a bolt of lightning struck from an unexpected quarter.

"Correct him, Comrade Sergeant." It was Captain Matka's

voice. Matka had just managed to sneak a look at the battle plan, and now he was trying to re-establish some of his lost credibility. His punishment was swift and immediate. "You – " and then he stopped in horror, for he'd forgotten the sergeant's name. For the commander of the battalion, this was inexcusable. "You – with the whiskers!"

A sergeant who looked dandyish even in uniform clicked his heels together. "Sergeant Vejvoda," he announced, but that was all he could say. Once again, Lieutenant Šlajs tried to look unconcerned.

"Well?" Captain Matka said to the sergeant. He felt more confident because the major hadn't tried to stop him. "What is the enemy's strength?"

The elegant sergeant hesitated. "The enemy's strength –" Then he made up his mind and declared with complete certainty, "The enemy's strength is two infantry regiments."

With granite-like impassivity – his face was too plump to convey a true impression of granite – Matka turned to another member of the crew. "Comrade Private?"

The man questioned – the backup driver – clicked his heels together and bellowed, "Lance-Corporal Lakatoš!" and then fell silent.

"Well?" Matka encouraged.

"The enemy's strength is...," Lakatoš made no effort to dampen the intensity of his voice, but roared out again, "STRENGTH IS – IS – " There was a long pause.

"Three – " prompted the captain, maliciously.

"Oh, yeah – three – "

"Special – "

"Spatial – "

"No, not spacial – *special.*"

"Special."

"Automotive – "

"Automotive – "

"Chemical – "

Lakatoš was now silent.

"What? Chemical what?" asked the captain.

An apologetic smile spread over the Slovak's face. Then he said in a voice that was almost conversational, as though he didn't care any more (and he didn't), "Comrade Captain, I'm afraid I don't know the answer."

What followed was a classic military response: "How is it possible that you don't know the answer?"

"I forget," said Lakatoš, almost happily.

But the corporal's love of truth found no favour with the captain. "'Forget?'" he roared, and turned to face the rest of the crew. "Which of you knows the enemy's strength?"

The crew stared back at him with blank but serene expressions. The captain felt a hot flash of panic pass through him. In his attempt to look good in front of the major, he had forgotten the crucial bits of information he'd managed to glimpse in the battle plan. He glanced at Lieutenant Šlajs, who was staring neutrally at his crew. He looked at the little major, who displayed nothing more than his usual expression of anger and petulant malice. The captain tried desperately to think of a question that would conceal the fact that the enemy's strength was an unknown quantity in the units under his command, and at the same time avoid the catastrophe that would certainly ensue if he was asked to come up with the answer himself. He looked around at his fellow officers, who were trying to be invisible. He noticed that the arm of the eager Lieutenant Hezký was twitching, and was just about to ask him, but then thought better of it. He could not, after all, test his own officers in front of the enlisted men.

He was saved by the nervous Cadet Officer Slíva, who asked to speak. "The enemy's strength is about two infantry battalions," he said smoothly, "reinforced by a squadron of tanks and two artillery batteries. They are drawn up in a battle line in the Jablko Woods." As he spoke, he indicated the directions by waving his hand. "The triangulation point on the horizon, elevation point two hundred and fifteen, the Bumbal Woods – "

"That's enough," the Pygmy Devil interrupted. "Carry on, Comrade Sergeant-Major."

Sergeant-Major Barák gave a start, but then picked up where the cadet officer had left off. "The Bumbal Woods," he said resolutely, "the Bumbal Woods," and his eyes scanned the top of Old Roundtop as though the answer lay somewhere up among the pines, "the Zadni Woods, the – the – "

"That will do," said Borovička calmly. "You, Comrade Tank Commander," and he stabbed Soudek with his eyes. "What is the enemy's firepower, according to recce?"

"Recce has determined that the enemy has the following firepower." Soudek cleared his throat carefully and tried to remember what he had learned the evening before, on the recce mission. To be honest, he had learned several intimate details about Corporal Střevlíček's last leave – details concerning the corporal's girlfriend. Because they had all sat there in the trench ignoring the anxious voice of Cadet Officer Slíva, who was informing them of the results of the reconnoitring operation, the tank commander had absolutely no idea what the enemy's firepower was. His only problem now was how much he could say and get away with.

"Two anti-tank cannon," he said, after a moment's thought, "four heavy machine-guns, and one tank, hull down" – and he looked inquisitively up at Old Roundtop – "to the left of that isolated patch of shrubbery two fingers to the right of orientation point two."

"And where, Comrade Sergeant," said the major, breaking

into Soudek's ad lib and turning to Desider Kobliha, "is orientation point two?"

An incredulous smile played around the corners of the driver's mouth, and he turned towards Old Roundtop, where a small figure carrying a sign over its shoulder had just appeared. Kobliha's arm described an uncertain arc, and his voice sounded like a voice crying out in the wildness. "Over there," he said.

"Where exactly is 'over there'?" snapped the major.

"Over there — two fingers to the...left...of the isolated shrubbery...." He kept his arm out as though he were blessing both the historical battlefield and the lone pilgrim walking down the hillside with the sign. "Over there...."

"Over there, over there!" howled the major. "Is that all you can say? Where is 'over there'? I want the exact coordinates."

Kobliha looked vaguely into the distance somewhere beyond the hilltop, and the major feigned calm.

"Give me a topographical reference," he ordered.

Holy shit, Kobliha thought, *I've never bothered to figure out where north is. And I can't see the sun....* He raised his arm once more and said, "Before us is — north." He paused, waiting to see what the major's response would be. There was none. "Behind us is south," he said, with more certainty. "To the right of us — west; to the left — east."

The major was by now standing on his tiptoes, his pale cheeks flushed red. "What kind of blathering nonsense are you talking? Since when is west to your right if south is behind you? You call yourself a sergeant? And a tank driver? Would you mind telling me how you can take your tank across the battlefield if you don't even know where north is?"

A good-natured smile spread over Kobliha's good-natured face. "It's that way, Comrade Major," and he raised his arm again, but this time the gesture was energetic and confident.

"Right over there, where that big hollow is, I go round and to the right because there's this muddy patch on the left I got stuck in last spring, then I take her up to that fir tree and go into first because I have to jink left around that shell-hole from the last time we used live ammo, but you can't see it from here, Comrade Major, I'd couldn't do her in second because last time Střevlíček tried it she stalled on him. We always stop for five seconds on the other side of that shell-hole to finish off an enemy ATC, then I take her right to the top, right between the triangulation point and those little bushes, then I goose it to the wayside chapel on the other side of the hill, go into third, swan down to the road, cross over, and go steady on. Oh, right, and I have to haul up by the road because there's always an enemy recoilless cannon in that little stand of trees that lets us have it, and then I head straight for that meadow near Okrouhlice, and then I stop and wait for the evaluation."

The Pygmy Devil wanted to object but, given the way things were done on this oft-conquered battlefield, he hardly knew what to object to. He was saved the intellectual effort because the figure carrying the sign had by now reached the group and was looking around for the highest-ranking officer. When he saw the tiny major, he approached him briskly, rested his sign on the ground, and steadied it with his left hand while he saluted with his right. The eyes of all those present read the ominous device:

THREE SHERMAN TANKS

"Comrade Major," sang the enemy, "request permission to ask a question."

"Permission granted."

"Comrade Major," said the private, "Comrade Lieutenant Hořánek would like to enquire if the attack is about to begin and if the enemy should commence to open fire."

"Not yet!" roared Matka. "He shouldn't even think of opening fire. We're not ready yet."

"Yes sir," called the private.

"Don't the enemy have their orders?" Major Borovička couldn't resist being sarcastic, nor could he let a mere captain have the last word. "Don't the enemy know that the red flare applies to them as well?"

"Yes sir," repeated the private, less sure of himself now. "Comrade Major, request permission to return to my position."

The major granted him permission. The private executed a not entirely successful about-turn on the loose earth and began marching back towards enemy lines. As he walked away, they could see the back of his sign. There was another device painted on it, in the same red letters:

ONE TROOP OF CROMWELL TANKS

"Follow me!" commanded the major, and he set off in search of further victims.

★   ★   ★

Tank Commander Smiřický's crew eyed the approaching peril through their periscopes. They could see the little major and his suite stopping at every tank in the line, where the same dumb show would take place, framed in the periscope's smudged field of vision. The Pygmy Devil would shout something, the officers' faces would turn towards the turret, the hatch would open, and the tank commander would jump out after a fashion and then, in full battledress, with his leather helmet on his head and his revolver nestled in a holster against the small of his back, he would stand at attention. The major would ask him a question, then chew him out.

Sweeping the scene with his periscope, Danny found some comfort. *In the end, he thought, my tank's not in the worst shape, and the major's chewing everybody out, so the law of diminishing returns should apply.* He began to feel almost safe, and let his mind wander back to the girls in the political economy course he'd taught in Hronov before being called up. They'd given him a bottle of French cognac when he left to do his military service, and he'd given them all excellent marks — especially the pretty ones. Like Vixi, in those balmy civilian days in the woods behind the lookout tower, with the cherry trees in blossom....

As the procession drew nearer, the tank commander's mind came back to reality. The Pygmy Devil, his hands clasped behind his back, displayed all the signs of apoplectic outrage. Two paces behind him, Captain Matka walked energetically, the wattles of his double chin shaking. Behind him was the suite of officers. Danny's heart began to pound. The officers took up positions around his tank and the major ran his eyes over it. Safe inside his iron turret, Danny could look him straight in the face through the periscope. The Pygmy Devil's voice sounded faint through the armour-plating.

"Now, this is approximately what an entrenched tank should look like," he was saying. "Roughly like this. It might have been more carefully camouflaged, but this is the first vehicle, Comrade Captain," and he turned to face Matka, "that is properly dug in. Who's in command?"

He said this with a malicious glint in his eye. The captain puffed out his cheeks and emitted a throaty sound intended to convey an effort to remember. In his state of mind he'd completely forgotten the tank commander's name. He repeated his performance several times. Lieutenant Hezký, over-zealous as always, hesitatingly raised his hand. The major made a face and coolly turned to him: "Did you wish to say something, Comrade Lieutenant?"

Lieutenant Hezký expanded his scrawny chest and said in his nasal voice: "Comrade Major, permission to speak."

"Permission granted."

"This is the second vehicle of the first troop of the first squadron of the Seventh Tank Battalion. Its identification number is T34/8697 and its crew is as follows: tank commander: Sergeant-Major Smiřický; gunner: Sergeant Žloudek; driver: Corporal Střevlíček; loader: Private Bamza. The backup driver – Private First Class Hlad – is to be found at the present time in the base infirmary, room number – "

"Summon the tank commander," the major interrupted.

"Tank Commander Smiřický," Hezký honked obediently.

On the other side of the armour-plating, Smiřický moved like lightning. In his haste he almost broke some bones, but within the regulation three seconds he was ready to utter the regulation formula:

"Comrade Lieutenant, Tank Commander Smiřický."

"Comrade Tank Commander," said the Pygmy Devil ominously. The tank commander made the regulation quarter-turn to the right. "Comrade Tank Commander," the major continued, in the darkest and gloomiest voice his short vocal chords could muster, as though he were about to pronounce a death sentence. "I compliment you on a well-executed pit. This pit can stand as an example to the other pits – as you were – to the other comrades."

"I serve the people," the astonished tank commander managed to bark. The first thing that flashed through his mind was that such official praise went into the record book of rewards and punishments; he'd soon be looking for a job, so his personnel record was starting to become important. He'd have to remind the battalion registrar to enter it. The major then ordered him back to his tank, and as he slammed the hatch shut behind him in combat position, he heard Andelín say, "Now ain't that a good fucking joke!"

"You can say that again," said the tank commander.

*   *   *

The fog had lifted and the yellow early-morning autumn sun touched the crowns of the oak forest on the slopes opposite Old Roundtop. The grass on the hillsides glistened with dew and the grey combat vehicles looked like a herd of elephants at rest. *My stint is coming to an end*, thought Tank Commander Smiřický, and all at once it felt good to be in the army, and with the tanks. When things come to an end, they suddenly seem good. Life, as he often said to himself, was all a matter of the past.

In a few weeks, this do-nothing existence would be over and he'd have to make a living. In Hronov he'd supported himself for not quite two years — or, more precisely, he had been supported by the dear, sweet daughters of the local farmers, who longed to graduate successfully (which they did) and to marry early (which they didn't, at least not with him). He'd been the only unmarried teacher at the school and, had he stayed on, it wouldn't have lasted. But he wasn't ready yet to stumble into marriage, and that was why he didn't want to go back to teaching. He also wanted to stay away from the country and small towns, where life was so easy and so aimless. He wanted to go to Prague, to that tease Lizetka. He didn't want to marry her — not that he could, with Sergeant Robert Neumann on the scene. He only wanted to get her into bed.

A light breeze rippled through the rusty chestnut trees on

Old Roundtop. The hillside dazzled in the glow of the morning sun, and there was a dusky, intimate light inside the tank. His clunky, ill-fitting army boots made him feel calm and sure of himself. Yet, he reflected, the time was fast approaching when he too would find a girl and get married. A girl from a good family — cultivated, pure, silk and nylon, and with a slowly expanding midriff from too many pastries. The kind of girl he used to dance with at soirées put on by the American Institute before the Communists took over. They smelled of perfume and imported linen and, unlike Lizetka, their heads were usually vacuous. Given what he wanted from her, Lizetka's wits were only an impediment.

He heard footsteps on the motor casing. Through the observation slit, he could see a pair of officer's breeches and riding boots. Then there was a banging on the hatch. He reached behind his head and flipped it open with a practised move. Silhouetted black against the sky was First Lieutenant Bobby Kohn.

"Leave your hatch open. I'll navigate," said the officer.

"Yes, sir," said the tank commander politely.

First Lieutenant Kohn, who seemed to gain in dignity when his superior officers were safely absent, was in a communicative mood. "Some trick," he said sarcastically. He had been with the political division in Martin and it was wise to be wary around him. He had the reputation of being a real rat. But his hopes of advancement had been dashed by his own exceptional laziness, and his wife's exceptional interest in his fellow officers and, recently, even draftees.

"Some trick!" he repeated. "You don't seem to realize that you're just playing games. Wait till there's a real war. Then you'll wish you'd learned how to dig a real pit!"

The tank commander made a face behind the armour-plating. He always felt strangely moved by the thought of a soldier about to die in a real war and regretting, now that it was too late, some inattention to a crucial part of his training. Their officers saw war as a test of maturity, a final exam to be passed successfully only by those who hadn't weaseled out of morning exercises, who had dutifully studied recoil mechanisms in the evening. In this worldview, only the lazy lost their lives; the diligent learned the arts of dodging incoming shells and bullets, gas, and atomic radiation.

The tank commander's crew, being intellectually simpler, didn't content themselves with sarcastic thoughts.

"There was nothing wrong with our pit," came Žloudek's voice from inside the tank.

"That's because the major had both eyes closed," said Bobby Kohn. "You'd all be shot for a pit like that at the front."

"You'd shit your pants first," Střevlíček howled into the intercom. Danny looked anxiously up at Kohn, but the officer clearly hadn't heard. He stood indifferently on the turret, his hands on his hips, his sharp eyes surveying the terrain.

"Are you on the air?" he asked.

"The radio's on the fritz," said Danny.

"On the fritz? Why can't you just admit you don't know how to operate it."

"Really, it's on the fritz."

"Don't talk rubbish!" shouted the officer. "You may think you're going home in a few weeks; but just be careful we don't slip you another year so you can learn how to operate a radio."

He stopped, savouring the moment. His black eyes scanned Old Roundtop, where a sign saying BAZOOKA had just been raised into battle position. Through the morning silence a thin, small voice came wafting across the valley.... "You'll live to regret this!" Someone over in the enemy lines was getting chewed out. They never heard what the unfortunate soldier would live to regret, because just then a flare whistled out of the trees and into the lightening sky. It was deep red, almost purple, and it looked beautiful.

"Driver — advance when ready!" roared the tank commander, pushing his contact mike closer to his throat. The electric starter growled, Střevlíček pumped the accelerator several times, and the engine caught. It sounded like the roar of a rhinoceros about to trample a bothersome tourist to death. The driver put the tank into reverse and it rose slowly out of the pit, backwards.

Through the rear observation window, Tank Commander Smiřický could still see riding breeches: Lieutenant Kohn was standing on the tank with his legs apart. While Střevlíček shifted gears, the tank commander ran his periscope over the side of Old Roundtop. To their right, another tank shot out of the bushes and roared up the hill.

"Driver, advance! Full speed!" said the tank commander into the intercom, but it was too late. The astute Bobby had quickly spotted his opportunity.

"Get a move on, man!" he yelled. "Look where you're going! Get into line! I'll have your hides if you don't smarten up!"

Střevlíček shifted into second and they bolted forward with the engine roaring, as if shot from a cannon. Danny lifted his head out of the open hatch, looked up towards Kohn's ominous face suspended above him, and roared his excuse: "The rest of them had shallow pits, they drove straight out."

"Cut the backtalk. Guide your driver!" Bobby yelled. *Kiss my ass*, the tank commander thought. He grabbed the handgrip on the ceiling with his right hand and held tight to the periscope with his left, bracing his padded forehead against the padding on the periscope. Střevlíček accelerated like a madman. Like all the drivers in the unit, he had so often conquered this peak that was now lifting its bare crown to the cold sun that he knew the route by heart. Into the intercom, the tank commander sang, *We walked into the catacombs, along the line of yawning graves, amid the coffin's icy draught, she took my hand, and then....* From where Kohn was standing, it looked as though Danny were directing the driver. There was no risk of being overheard: the motor was roaring, and the ammo boxes and tools scattered around the compartment were all clanking like a load of scrap iron. They drove out of the bushes and onto the bare hill. On either side Danny could see other tanks, some too far out in front, others still emerging from the bushes. Seen through the observation slits, they seemed to be standing still, and it was only by their flashing tracks that he knew they were in motion. It felt like being in a movie; it made him feel manly, and a pleasant sensation of safe adventure – an officer's feeling – washed over him.

Bobby's high-pitched voice pierced the confusion of noises and the whistling wind: "Hold the line, damn it!" Danny could also hear the clear and cocky voice of Andělín Střevlíček over the crackling intercom: "Hang on, my friends, I'm going to dump the sonofabitch."

They were approaching the first line of trenches. The tank commander looked around at the loader, who wasn't wearing a radio helmet and therefore hadn't heard Střevlíček's warning. But in this familiar combat situation no instructions were necessary. The loader stood braced against the cupola, holding onto the grips with both hands. Danny turned back, tensing all his muscles, gritting his teeth, and pressing his padded helmet tight against the periscope.

"Boom!" said Střevlíček, and the tank pitched forward, then backwards, and then, with a deafening crash that rattled everything inside, lurched forward again. The tank commander looked up and straight into the livid face of Bobby Kohn. The manoeuvre hadn't worked.

"That swine of a driver!" Bobby shouted above the din.

"He'll spend Sunday on the obstacle course. And *you'll* be learning how to navigate!"

"I *am* navigating," the tank commander shouted.

"The hell you are," Kohn roared back. He looked around and yelled, "Give orders to destroy enemy anti-tank cannon at trig point two."

There was a stiff, pleasant breeze blowing into the open hatch. The tank commander tried to remember what trig point two was, but couldn't.

"Did he fall off?" asked Střevlíček.

"No!" Danny shouted, and then haphazardly bellowed the only version of the order they had ever used: "Enemy ATC at five hundred; driver stop, gunner fire when ready." The crew was supposed to respond immediately. It didn't.

"Driver, stop!" Danny shouted into the intercom. But Střevlíček still didn't stop. He was trying to make up for lost time.

"Are we going to bloody shoot or not?" yelled Kohn from above.

"Damn it, Andělín, stop!" shouted the tank commander. In his earphones came the calm reply: "He can shove it."

"Why isn't the gunner traversing his gun?" Bobby went on. "What kind of jerk is he, anyway?"

"Karel, move the goddamn cannon," Danny implored, and Žloudek played around with the aiming handle. That silenced Bobby for a while.

The tank commander looked through the periscope again. A tank was roaring along about twenty metres to the right, about even with them. Slightly behind him but close together and to the left there were two more. An ideal target, Danny thought. Ahead of him he could see the horizon line approaching, and against it rose a small figure holding a sign that said THREE SHERMAN TANKS. Quickly, and with

obvious delight, the soldier fired off three flares in rapid succession at the approaching tanks.

"Answer his fire!" said Bobby, who'd recovered his wits.
"Can't you see the enemy's opened fire? Christ almighty, I'll
make you eat this one!"

The tank commander let go with his left hand, tapped
Bamza to catch his attention, and gestured him to load the
cannon. Bamza made an inaudible remark, no doubt vulgar,
but he got up, braced himself against the recoil buffer, and
rammed a blank shell into the breech. Just then, Andělín
braked sharply and the whole crew lurched forward. There was
a loud, harsh explosion and the compartment filled with acrid
smoke. As Danny crashed into Žloudek from behind, he heard
someone say over the intercom: "Andělín, you fucking cunt!"

"Why in hell's name did you fire?" asked the tank commander as he scrambled back up on his seat.

"I didn't fire, man," said Žloudek. "I caught hold of the
bloody lever and the fucking thing blew up."

At this point Kohn chipped in: "What the hell was that
supposed to be? Firing while you stop? You can't hit shit that
way. Who gave you the order?"

Danny succumbed to the temptation to pass the buck.
"Not me!" he shouted. He felt ashamed right away, but before
he could make up for his lapse, he was treated to another of
Bobby Kohn's strident sermons.

"Not you, eh? Your crew is so democratic they fire when-
ever they feel like it? And what's that dumb cluck of a driver
doing just sitting there? In real combat you'd all be in the bag
ten times over."

"Andělín, advance! Go like hell!" the tank commander
yelled into the intercom. He looked around. The whole hillside behind him was crawling with tanks. Some were just
emerging from the brush, others were already climbing the

hill. One of them was nose down in a ditch with its rear sticking helplessly in the air; the commander was just crawling out of the hatch.

Another sudden lurch and their tank leaped forward again, throwing everything in it, living and inanimate, to the rear. They came over the crest of Old Roundtop. Before them lay a gentle sloping plain with clusters of trees and churned-up ruts across it and, in the distance, the white houses of Okrouhlice. They swanned down the side of the hill at full speed, passing tanks to the left and right. They were going too fast.

"Slow down, Andělín!" the tank commander yelled over the intercom.

"Keep in line!" Bobby Kohn shouted, like an echo. "And tell the gunner to bloody well keep his cannon moving or I'll have his balls."

"Karel, move that thing about. Make the poor bastard happy," Danny said.

"Let the stupid fucker eat shit," said Žloudek, but he began moving the controls back and forth.

"Orders!" yelled Bobby.

"ATC dead ahead," roared the tank commander, no longer caring what was outside. Žloudek yelled something back. From his right, Bamza piped up with a remark about shit, but he said it like a loader responding to a gunner's order. The tank clanked and rattled and crashed and roared, Bobby was shouting, the intercom was crackling, and everything was being tossed back and forth; it took all their strength to hang on. Danny abandoned the periscope for fear of breaking his nose. Suddenly the tank tipped forward precariously, something inside it snapped, and they were again roaring downhill. They ran over a large obstruction, something broke loose inside the turret and fell to the floor, and then, just as suddenly, they were moving forward smoothly again. They had driven over the Okrouhlice Road into the ditch and then back off into the countryside. In doing so, they had broken through enemy lines, and they were approaching the rallying point.

"*Gott in Himmel*, that driver's a pig!" said a shaken Bobby Kohn through his teeth as he clung to the turret. "I'll have him locked up. And is that any way to command a tank? The gunner could have rammed the cannon into the ground. Hasn't he ever heard of elevation? In a real battle, you'd have — "

At that moment, Střevlíček jammed on the brakes.

"What now?" asked the tank commander.

Andělín's voice came back: "A green flare, my friend. They're going to fry our balls."

Through the observation slit, Danny saw a jeep, and standing up in it was the little major. The driver was using semaphore flags to signal all subordinate commanders to rally on the jeep.

"You all stay where you are!" shouted Bobby, and jumped down. Danny pulled himself out of the turret and sat in the open hatch. Bobby walked around the tank to the driver's hatch.

"What circus did you learn to drive in?" he hissed at Střevlíček.

"It won't go into second, Comrade Lieutenant," replied Andělín calmly. "And the clutch is slipping."

"Slipping, my foot. You don't know how to drive."

"But the clutch is slipping." Danny could tell by the driver's tone that Bobby's reprimand had irked him.

"Don't blame it on the bloody machine. A good driver can drive anything, even a wheelbarrow."

"But not a piece of junk like this."

"Do you realize what you're saying? These machines have been through several Soviet offensives."

"It sure as hell shows."

Bobby Kohn's mouth was open and his black eyebrows were twitching. But before he could come up with a politically correct riposte, a new flare swished up from the jeep, flew like a gob of green spittle into the now golden sky, and burned out over a stand of birches by a pond. Kohn looked around and discovered some officers converging on the jeep, so he merely said in a sinister voice, "I'll settle this with you in the presence of the commander." And then, on legs that were spindly and slightly knock-kneed, he trotted off to join the dispirited group of officers – the most prominent of whom was Captain Matka, his tired face a glowing red.

"That chickenshit little Jew!" Střevlíček's voice echoed through the quiet tank. "Thinks he can tell us how to do things when he doesn't know ratshit about tanks."

"And these are the motherfuckers we support when we work," said Žloudek philosophically.

"Let him go to hell," said the tank commander.

"He's permanently pissed off 'cause somebody's having it off with his old lady," explained Bamza.

"You're kidding. Who?"

"A sergeant from the 106th," said Střevlíček. "A few days back, Kohn drove her out into the street naked."

"Jesus!" said Bamza. "But she's real cute."

"Yeah, but she's a whore."

"What woman isn't?" said Bamza philosophically.

"Well, Kohn's wife is, for sure," said Corporal Střevlíček. "You can tell just by looking at her."

They all watched the officer as he headed towards the jeep.

"Boys, on New Year's Eve she was all over me. Got me stiff as a fencepost," said Střevlíček wistfully.

★   ★   ★

The conclusion of the exercise — the conquest of another hill called Kužel Peak — was deplorable, and the major's heart soared. From the brow of the hill, where he had positioned his jeep, he had a splendid view of the sunlit north-east slope of Old Roundtop. From the foot of Kužel Peak to the horizon, the landscape was swarming with armour. The first tanks, in mild disarray, were grinding up the slope. They should have been advancing in a line, but they weren't. The lead tank was only about fifty metres from the Pygmy Devil — so close that he could see the sun reflecting off the glass in the gunner's sights in the turret, and the ruddy face of the driver, who had left his hatch open to get a better view. (This was improper in a battle situation, and strictly against orders. The major happily made a mental note to remember it.) Just below the summit stood a tank that had shed a track. Near it was a small armoured car hung up on an unexpected lump in the terrain, like a turtle belly down on a slat with its feet flailing in the air. This was Captain Matka's command vehicle. He stood beside it, belabouring the unhappy driver, who was trying, with the inadequate strength of his own muscles, to free it. The captain had forgotten about the tanks of his own squadron; they were swarming over the sunlit green grass, growing smaller as they receded. At least three of them were squatting motionless in the landscape, tiny figures in leather helmets scurrying busily around them, while flares arced above the field and squibs of imitation shrapnel burst everywhere. The enemy (carrying signs) fired enthusiastically and the tanks returned their fire. This part of the exercise was coming off perfectly.

Then the Pygmy Devil's attention was drawn to a tank rapidly swanning down a hillside to the foot of Kužel Peak, firing great cannon-bursts of backfire from its exhaust pipe. Behind the turret stood an officer, and as the tank drew nearer, accelerating and decelerating jerkily, the officer could barely hang on. The tank reached the embankment above the road that led around the foot of the hill. The major raised his binoculars to look. The driver had his hatch open, of course. Now he would decelerate and – but instead the driver gunned his vehicle and the tank slid quickly forward and dropped onto the road with a metallic clang. The officer on the turret disappeared. When the tank had advanced a few metres, he reappeared in the major's binoculars. He was now on the ground, trying to regain his footing, but he fell back, and from the way he moved his mouth the major concluded that he was yelling.

By this time the first tanks were beginning to rally on the major's jeep, and the officers were jumping down and running towards him. Other tanks arrived, and in ten minutes the whole formation had assembled. The last to pull up were three wheezing self-propelled guns, their crews gathered casually behind the armour-plating like tourists in an open sightseeing car. Captain Matka loped up on foot, drenched in sweat. Behind him stood a group of markers with flare pistols in their belts, engaged in loud conversation. A group of medics brought up the helpless Bobby Kohn on a stretcher of camouflage canvas. He was groaning and at intervals he aimed vile curses at someone whose name they couldn't catch. They set him down on the ground and a medic leaned over and took him by the leg. Kohn let out a roar of excruciating pain. After several more painful probes and pokes, the medic declared that the lieutenant had broken a leg. The news spread rapidly. "Serves the sonofabitch right!" said Střevlíček. "Pity he didn't jam his tailbone up his ass while he was at it."

★   ★   ★

They lined up the tanks and brought all the cannon to the same elevation. "We shall critique the exercise later, Comrade Captain," said the Pygmy Devil coldly, "when we return to camp. For the moment, I merely want to point out a few short-comings to the crews. Have them fall in."

Captain Matka was furious — especially at fate, which had seduced him with visions of unlimited power while blinding him to the fact that this power was unlimited only in a down-ward direction. Upward, the power structure was like the feu-dal system he'd learned of in his political schooling. He stood at attention in front of the row of tanks and roared like an alcoholic bull:

"Battalion crews in order of troops — fall in!" Instead of a frenzy of bodies falling rapidly into order, as called for by the regulations, there was a slow, confused stirring of smudged and dirty figures. After two minutes of pushing and shoving, a ragged and incomplete column of men, four deep, had formed beneath the row of raised cannon.

"You look like you're lining up for a bloody funeral," Matka declared, so he couldn't be reprimanded later for tolerating slackness.

"And no talking during falling-in," First Lieutenant Růžička added. Matka executed an about-turn, raised his hand to his cap, and set off across the uneven terrain that separated him from the Pygmy Devil. His fat legs moved smartly back and forth in an attempt to represent a proper marching step, but he spoiled the effect by stumbling on a lump of dirt, making visible all the comic possibilities of this strange clown show. Matka approached the major, halted, clicked his heels together, and announced that the Seventh Tank Battalion had fallen in as ordered.

He was instructed to stand at ease, and did so with the chilling awareness that he would face a post-mortem when they got back to base. He fell in behind the major, whose eyes were flashing with sarcastic delight. The Pygmy Devil maintained a long, rhetorical silence, and then began to address the troops.

"Comrades!"

"This should be more fun than a kick in the crotch," whispered Bamza, who was standing behind Danny.

"The purpose of today's exercise," the major continued, "was to test our capacity to mount an armoured assault on a hastily constructed defence system put in place by the enemy. It was an utter farce! A parody! It was chaos piled on confusion!"

"He has a nice, clear way of putting it," said Sergeant Vytáhlý, a science graduate, under his breath.

"And he even uses big words properly," remarked Sergeant Krajta, who was standing to Danny's left. "Where would we be without our highly qualified officer corps?"

"What you may be tempted to call an attack by this battalion on a hastily constructed enemy defence system, comrades," the major went on, "looked more like a rabbit hunt. You were going every which way, you ended up in every possible hole. One daredevil started his turn on a slope so steep I was expecting him to roll right over at any moment. Comrades – you have put the lives of your comrades-in-arms in danger, and you have shown that, in all your time in the army, you have learned nothing at all. Where was the line? Where was the regulation fifty metres between vehicles? Obviously two years of training is not enough. We will have to think seriously, comrades, about extending the training period to three years. And another thing: there are comrades among you who have already been with us for two and a half years. One would have thought longer training would mean better training. But this exercise has shown that even these comrades are only capable of Švejking about. They do not take the battle plan seriously. They do not take drill seriously. They do not take digging-in seriously. But remember what the great Soviet commander Kutuzov once said: 'More sweat – ' "

" ' – on the training field, less blood on the battlefield,' " a quiet chorale of sarcastic voices echoed.

Now the Pygmy Devil got angry. "Yes, comrades," he shot back. "When war comes, many of you are going to regret it. Many of you, comrades – except for that tiny handful of conscientious soldiers among you." The Pygmy Devil pointed a finger towards heaven. "I wouldn't normally say this because of a few slackers. But these slackers are a danger not only to themselves, but to all their comrades. They are a danger to your wives and your mothers. They have abused the confidence that the working people have placed in our army. But never fear, comrades, we know how to deal with them. They needn't think we don't know who they are. They needn't think our working people will let them undermine what they have built with their own hands. No, comrades – "

His voice echoed over the leather-helmeted heads of those slackers, ninety-two percent of whom – according to the card index of class origin put together by First Lieutenant Růžička and often vaunted in reports sent to high command – were from working-class or peasant backgrounds. He was all but drowned out by a rising breeze that began to flap the soldiers' overall legs, making a sound like the snapping of many flags in the wind. They learned nothing new about the errors and imperfections they had perfected from exercise to exercise, but they did hear these darker threats, in which the working class became a strange, paranoid, bloodthirsty beast with its sharp eyes pinned on the army, and the army became seething with sedition and treachery spawned by that very same working class. The Pygmy Devil described the proclivities of this beast as though he were speaking for a neutral third party.

Who knows, thought the tank commander, *maybe he is*.

The sun hid itself in the clouds and the four ranks of men in oil-stained coveralls and leather helmets stood silently in front of the dark tanks. Above them the wind gave wild chase to grey autumn clouds, and carried away the angry voice of the tiny officer auguring a relentless series of sinister acts that this unprepossessing monster – the people – might yet perpetrate.

When he gave up, defeated by an eddy of wind that swept an enormous column of dust from the roads and pushed it over the hill into civilian territory, Corporal Andělín Střevlíček said out loud: "He's so full of shit, it's running down his chin."

2

THE FUČÍK BADGE TESTS

One of Tank Commander Smiřický's few pleasures in life was polishing his boots. He would sit on his box near his bunk and, with lightning strokes of his brush, polish the black leather to a mirrorlike sheen. Among all the things lying about the dormitory floor of Number One Squadron of the Seventh Tank Battalion — shirts with circles of sweat under the arms, coveralls reeking of oil, greasy paper from parcels of pastries sent from home, dirty towels spattered with blood drawn by the cheap razor blades sold in the camp store — his boots were something beautiful, something aesthetic he could cling to in a world otherwise dominated by military orders and the grey prospects they offered. Compared to the other things permitted during the mass cultural activity period (a stroll through the evening boredom of base camp, writing the thousandth letter to Lizetka, or sleeping through a Soviet movie in the base cinema), boot-polishing came closest to what a master of yoga does when he stills his mind by contemplating his own navel.

Danny's attitude was not typical of the Seventh Tank Battalion. Most of the men in the first squadron, now lounging about on their trunks and their beds, thought of boot-polishing as something for greenhorns. Their boots lay strewn under their beds and in the aisles, caked with mud and dust from the manoeuvres of that morning.

The squadron had spent the afternoon cleaning and re-
pairing the tanks. Now they were resting in a room crammed,
like a submarine, with twenty-five sets of bunk beds with sag-
ging, straw-filled mattresses, trying to kill time. The driver,
Střevlíček, was over by the doorway, arguing with Sergeant
Očko about the superiority of the German-built BMW motor-
cycle over the Czechoslovakian Jawa. Over in the Third Tank
Battalion, four privates had been court-martialled for praising
enemy technology and thus undermining combat readiness.
But the last informer in the ranks of the Seventh Battalion,
or at least the last one known to its members — a certain
Otakar Hrouda — had long ago been rendered harmless by
constant badgering, and in the end had jumped out of a second-
storey window. Dr. Sadař, a physician in basic training, had
said Hrouda was suffering from serious mental imbalance, and
he had been sent away to a military hospital in Prague. A few
beds over, Private Bamza was reading a greasy, well-thumbed
paperback, and on Sergeant Žloudek's bunk, soldiers were
showing each other snapshots of girls, some in states of par-
tial undress. Several of the men were asleep on their bunks.
The only one in the whole battalion doing anything that could
be remotely construed as mass cultural activity was Private
Mengele, who was strumming on a three-stringed mandolin,
surrounded by a silent group of musicaily inclined soldiers.
His sentimental voice carried through the room as he sang:

> *Last night, I had a fit of masturbation –*
> *I did it twice, it's very nice....*

The political officer of the squadron, Sergeant Mácha, was
sitting on a trunk with his back to the musical circle, biting
his tongue and composing a letter to his wife, Majka. It was a

quarter after seven, and the plan for mass cultural activity that evening (the sergeant had drawn it up himself and was personally responsible for its execution) said: *1900 – 2100: Singing circle rehearsal, chess tourn., FB circle prepare for FB test.*

Meanwhile Sergeant Mácha wrote:... *I'm clipping the last fifty centimetres of my tape measure. I'll be home before you know it, with you and Marenka, and all I'll have left of the army will be beautiful memories.* Then he crossed out the word "beautiful". His memories could not bear writing about in detail, because they included the raven-haired daughter of the manager of the Jan Žižka Inn, located in the nearby village of Okrouhlice.

A cry of "Gin!" came from somewhere in the rear of the room, followed by a dry slap. This was a tournament, all right, but it was hardly chess. The voice of Private Mengele rose above it all in a lyrical expression of protest:

First, you do the long stroke; up and down, up and down,
Next you try the short stroke; tickle the crown, tickle the
crown....

Sitting on the last bunk in the corner, Sergeant Krajta was working on the third chapter of a book to be called *Czechoslovak Army Folklore.* He had conceived the work in terms of orthodox Jungian psychology, and it was not intended for publication.

★　★　★

At eight-fifteen, the door of the dormitory opened and in walked Sergeant Feurbach. He was wearing a pistol on his hip and a red armband around his sleeve, indicating that he was on duty. He bent forward so that he could see under the top bunk, and nodded to Tank Commander Smiřický. "Hey, man, Růžička wants to see you."

"What the hell's he want?"

"No idea. He just said get there on the double."

"Tell him not to shit himself," said the tank commander, setting his brush down and pulling his boots on. He tugged the cuffs of his trousers carefully over the tops of his boots, took his jacket from the bedpost and put it on, did up his belt, set his cap on his head, and took a last look at his boots. They were gleaming. Satisfied, he walked out of the room, followed by Private Mengele's operatic plaint, with the whole singing circle singing along:

> Bang it, whang it, smash it on the floor,
> Squeeze it, tease it, stick it in the door....

The profound loneliness implied by those lines moved him as it always did. For two years he'd been unable to forget the terrible, ebony-black despair that had filled him one November day, ages ago, when he'd sat staring at the cubicle wall where a cynical soul had carved the words *730 to go*, and he had listened to another chorus of soldiers singing the same song with deep feeling.

A true soul of the people — unlike a purely intellectual spirit — doesn't give in to sentimentality, because such a soul holds the world and its torments at bay with a vengeance.

When the tank commander had closed the door behind him, the voices of the singing circle remained almost as loud, for they were raised in a rousing finale:

> But for personal perfection I prefer the human hand!

*   *   *

The tank commander walked out of the barracks, and the night air, heavy with the smell of ripening chestnuts, enveloped him. He walked past the illuminated windows of the staff office to the door that led to battalion headquarters. A sentry was sitting beside it with his nose in the only extant copy of a trashy nineteenth-century novel called *A Bloody Encounter, or, The Smugglers of Dark Glen.* It had somehow survived from the days of the Austro-Hungarian Empire, when the army base had been built. So absorbed was the sentry that he didn't notice the tank commander, nor did his assistant, who was standing behind the wicket in the bright foyer and leaning on the counter, engrossed in reading a sheaf of dog-eared papers that couldn't possibly have come from the military press; however, the sheaf was cleverly concealed inside an open copy of *Rules and Regulations Governing the Comportment of Guards and Duty Officers.*

Danny walked through the office of the technical chief, where several soldiers under the command of the foul-mouthed First Lieutenant Kámen were deep in a conversation about extra-military matters, and went into the typing room. Private First Class Dr. Mlejnek was there, angrily pounding a typewriter. He seemed out of sorts. A quarter of an hour ago, he had been summoned there on orders from Captain Matka, and now, instead of reading the manuscript of Sergeant Krajta's book on the folklore of the Czechoslovak soldier, he had to assemble a work of fiction called *The Commander's Report on the Field Exercise in Which a Tank Battalion Mounts an Attack on a Hastily Constructed Enemy Defence System,* although as staff typist he hadn't taken part in the event. He looked as disgusted as Sergeant Kanec, who was sitting at the next table drawing the phases of the battalion's attack on a map for Captain Matka's personal use the day after next, during staff exercises. An experienced glance told the tank commander that these two over-qualified soldiers had enough work to last them at least four hours past lights-out.

"Danny, come and give us a hand," Dr. Mlejnek implored.

"I can't. Růžička wants to see me about something."

He grabbed the latch and opened the door of the political department, stepped in, clicked his heels together, and recited the formula: "Comrade First Lieutenant, Tank Commander Sergeant-Major Smiřický reporting at your request, sir."

The two battalion political officers appeared to be deeply engrossed in their work. Hospodin was typing something with two fingers. Looking over his shoulder, the tank commander could read the title of the work – REPOTR ON PSIVTIVE VETTINH – and below that, in small letters, *on Sorg. Amt. Paveza.*

Hospodin didn't look up from the keyboard, but peered sideways at a piece of paper covered with corrections, from which he was trying to type a clean copy of his vetting report. Růžička stared at the tank commander with his handsome eyes and stubbed a cigarette out in the ashtray. He looked intelligent, but this was a beautiful illusion. He picked up a freshly sharpened pencil (he wore an enormous ring on one of his fingers) and began to tap it against a mimeographed sheet he had in front of him.

"Smiřický," he said with playful sarcasm, "you're the cultural worker in the battalion's branch of the Czechoslovak Union of Youth, are you not?"

"Yes, Comrade First Lieutenant."

"Then let me read you what's just come down from division headquarters." The lieutenant began reading from the mimeographed sheet: " 'Unit groups and their cultprop reps will ensure full co-operation in fulfilling the pledges made on May Day 1951, on Army Day, to gain their Fučík Merit Badges by taking part in and passing the necessary tests in the Fučík Merit Badge examinations. The FMB tests will take place in all units at the same time, in the week between 9 and 16 September.' "

At this point Lieutenant Růžička stopped, raised his eyes, and looked at the tank commander; the week in question was already ending. Then he went on reading: " 'Unit groups of the Czechoslovak Union of Youth and the cultprop officers, along with Party organizers, agitators, and political workers, will provide....' " But Danny wasn't listening any more, for he was secretly glancing at a far more interesting text, the slowly emerging positive vetting report that Hospodin was preparing on Sergeant Antonín Paveza. Over the lieutenant's shoulder, he read:

Comrad Pacez is of worjing class orejin and pollicicaly on averrage level. He is contientious and loyil to the poeples demogadic systim. He is goodnatred and well liked by his colectiv. He caries out miltery and union duties well. He can be arogant and mouthy even thow he is not a comm –

That was as far as Hospodin had got for the time being. But because Růžička was still reciting his letter with almost religious intensity, the tank commander kept his eyes on the typewriter keys set hesitantly in motion by Hospodin's fingers. First an "i" followed the "comm", then in rapid succession "s-h-u-n-d", and then, after a long pause, an "o", an "f", and a cluster of letters: "i-s-e-r".

" 'And the cultural workers are personally responsible for the event'," said Lieutenant Růžička firmly, and the tank commander had just enough time to look him in the eye and nod attentively. The first lieutenant then went back to reading the orders, while Danny covertly observed Hospodin's stumbling progress. After further exhausting effort, Hospodin leaned back in his chair and with some satisfaction read what he had just written: *even thow he is not a commishund ofiser, he gives advise to others.* Danny wasn't sure whether this was meant as a positive or negative characteristic.

But he had no time to give it any more thought. Lieutenant Růžička had raised his voice and was glaring at him. " 'A report'," he read, " 'shall be submitted by the cultprop officers not later than 17 September' – that's tomorrow – 'to the commander of the higher units. Signed: Commanding Officer of the Cultural Club, Major Kudrnac.' "

He looked up craftily at his subaltern. "You have to have the test planned by tomorrow, Smiřický," he said. "How's the Fučík Badge thing going, anyway? Things proceeding according to plan?"

The tank commander shrugged his shoulders. "There are no books, Comrade First Lieutenant. The comrades are keen to participate, but we haven't got a fraction of the Fučík Badge books in our unit library."

"Yes," Růžička admitted, "there are difficulties, but that's no excuse. You'll just have to find a way around it, as the comrades in the Komsomol did. Not only did they not have books," he pointed out, a tragic tone creeping into his voice, "but often they didn't have enough to eat. Yet *they* fulfilled *their* pledges. How many of the comrades are prepared to take the Fučík test?"

"Let me see," said Danny. "About ten." He based this guess on the number of men in his squadron who either were ready for anything, or couldn't care less.

"But that's not enough, Smiřický," objected Růžička. "You pledged thirty percent. That's a minimum of fifteen men.

You're aware, of course, that the onus is on you?"

Why was this idiot bringing personal onus into it, Danny wondered. It was Růžička who had prepared the pledge, and he had merely handed it over to the tank commander to sign "on behalf of the group". Anyway, what was he worried about? The examination would take place before a commission consisting of those who already had the Fučík Merit Badge – that is, the cultural worker (Danny himself), Private First Class Dr. Mlejnek, and Sergeant Kanec. *The pledge will be 120 percent fulfilled, as everything always is – perhaps even 130 percent, if Matka's scrounging for special praise. This is all obvious to both of us.* Danny swore to himself. Out loud he said, "I know, Comrade First Lieutenant. But I've pointed out to you several times that we have no books, and neither the comrades nor myself have the time to go looking for them. You promised me you'd get them."

"I know. But more important fundamentals got in my way. And the Komsomols, I remind you again, Comrade Tank Commander, didn't have books either, yet they passed their Fučík Badge – I mean, they did what was asked of them. Now, have you involved the politruks in the FMB circles? Are the unit and squadron groups working well? Are they helping? What about the examination committee, how many of them have their Fučík Badges? You know, don't you, that they're all supposed to get them?"

Růžička's voice rose censoriously at the end of every question. And of course he was right. He was washing his hands of the matter. He knew well enough that the examination committee hadn't even met yet. Why would it have?

"That's my worry, Comrade First Lieutenant," Danny assured him. "Everyone here will get the badge."

"But you're not going about it the right way, Smiřický." Růžička's tone was still censorious, but more affable, in response to Danny's confident manner. "Cramming at the last minute is a bad way to catch up." As his misgivings subsided, his itch to preach increased. He began feeling that he'd done all he could, and that the responsibility now belonged solely to the tank commander. "Is that the proper way to understand the mission and purpose of the Fučík Badge? What do you think?"

The tank commander adopted a tone of comradely confidentiality. "You know how it is, Comrade First Lieutenant. How much can you expect out of guys who are doing an extra six months?"

"That's not true, Comrade Tank Commander," said the officer, shaking his head. "Just look at how those very same comrades did in the machine-gun competition, shooting from a moving tank at a fixed target. Think how well they fulfilled their pledges there. Why can't they do the same with the Fučík Badge?"

Danny knew that the real reason for those legendary results was the skill of the target-master, Sergeant Kobliha, who had simply punched better results into the target with a poker. But he offered a different explanation: "That's not quite the same thing, Comrade Lieutenant. The reward for doing well in target practice was a five-day leave of absence."

"And that's precisely your job as cultural worker — you have to motivate the comrades, show them that leaves of absence are not the real reason for trying hard." He spoke firmly, underlining with a professional flourish a line on the mimeographed sheets that said: *fulfilling the pledge by passing the test*. Tapping each of the underlined words with his pencil, he added, "It's wrong to try to pass these tests by cramming at the last minute. Plan to do them in the noon break tomorrow. In the evening, you'll have to test the officers and their wives."

Danny was astonished. "For the Fučík Badge?"

"Yes," said Růžička. "Here's a list." He rummaged around in a drawer. Over Lieutenant Hospodin's shoulder, Danny caught sight of the final sentence of the positive vetting report: *Comrad Pacex is a compatent comrad. He is calpable of holding ofıce in the Uouth Ynion in his local district.*

"Here it is. You'll carry out the tests tomorrow, at two o'clock. Here."

He handed the tank commander a list. Glancing at it, Danny saw among the familiar names one with a feminine ending: Jana Pinkasová. That was enough to raise his spirits.

"Yes, comrade," he said, and with a lilt of delight in his voice he declared, "Comrade First Lieutenant, request permission to leave."

Permission was granted with no further objections.

★   ★   ★

Darkness had fallen outside. A quiet breeze rustled the leaves of the chestnut trees in the park across from the political department, the distant clatter of tanks leaving for night manoeuvres drifted in, and a radio in the officers' mess across the park was playing brass-band music. The night air was full of warmth and, though it was already September, it radiated the extraordinary summer beauty of life. The sentry had laid aside his novel of blood and thunder and was sitting on the steps with his hands in his pockets, staring at the moon with absent eyes. The moon was drifting through the treetops, and little winking red and green lights were moving through the clouds. Somewhere up there, the roar of a jet engine drowned out, for a moment, the murmuring silence of the dark. The daughter of Colonel Vrána walked along the path among the trees, her white summer dress swaying seductively in the night breeze;

the tank commander followed her for a long time with hungry eyes. Even the assistant in the foyer looked up from the trashy reading concealed in the rules and regs and smacked his lips loudly. The colonel's daughter was used to this kind of attention and didn't even look around. Her white skirt vanished into the darkness, the hum of the jet faded, and the trees resumed their murmuring. In the face of such beauty, everything else seemed unimportant.

*   *   *

But the master of fate, bored by the uneventful progress of life in the Seventh Tank Battalion, had prepared an unpleasant surprise for the following day. This took the form of six new lieutenants freshly graduated from the armoured division school. They reported for duty to the commanding officer, ablaze with as yet undimmed enthusiasm, as bright as the sparkling pips on their epaulettes. By now their predecessors were walking about like bodies without souls, their boots unpolished, their golden pips tarnished, between the camp store and the officers' mess, languishing for Bobby Kohn's fun-loving wife, who sunbathed nude in the woods within range of the binoculars trained on her from the observation tower of the shooting range. Instead of being mindful of their duties, they were dreaming up ways to get off the base on Sunday. But the six new musketeers promptly asked for work to do. Five of them received immediate satisfaction, so much so that for the next twelve hours – that is, until well after lights-out – they were bent over tactical maps, carefully sketching in battle situations. The sixth and last officer looked about in vain for a map of his own to work on, and during his search he unfortunately happened to come across Tank Commander Smiřický's notice on an otherwise empty bulletin board:

The test for candidates for the Fučík Merit Badge will take place in the Political Department today at 1:30.

Flashing his own brand-new Fučík Badge, the officer immediately offered his services to Lieutenant Růžička. The delighted former waiter welcomed the offer and, exercising his authority (if not his foresight), appointed the lad chairman of the examination committee, a post that not a single officer of the Seventh Tank Battalion could qualify for.

Thus Tank Commander Smiřický was relieved of his post. The demotion didn't bother him, but the new appointee did fill him with misgivings. He felt that he himself would have had greater success in enticing the more reluctant recruits to try out for the silver badge (which looked very much like a decoration for valour). After all, the makeup of the original examination committee had been a guarantee of absolute fraud. Private First Class Dr. Mlejnek was known as a last resort for those who had unsuccessfully requested passes, because he had access to the necessary stamps and could imitate the signatures of all the commanding officers. Then there was Sergeant Kanec, a bookkeeper in the canteen who provided luxury items from the stores for private Saturday-night parties held by those who weren't able to attain even Dr. Mlejnek's counterfeit passes. And it went without saying that Danny would stand behind the fraud. But after lunch, when word got round that a certain Lieutenant Prouza, a greenhorn from the armoured training school, had just been parachuted into the chairmanship of the examination committee, a group of soldiers that Danny had almost persuaded to take part in the ritual crowded around him, protesting angrily.

"They can go eat shit as far as I'm concerned."

"Are they all out of their fucking minds? Nobody here's read bugger-all."

"They can stuff their Fučík Badge right up their ass."

And so, of all the candidates who were supposed to fall in at thirteen hundred hours to march over to the political department under the leadership of Tank Commander Smiřický, only one first-year private showed up. His name was Pravomil Poslušný, and he was trembling with anticipation because, although he had read all the other books on the list, he had missed *Lenin, Stalin, and Kalinin Speak to Young People*, and he felt badly prepared. The rest of the potential candidates stayed behind in the barracks in protest, getting ready for their afternoon rest break.

Danny ordered Poslušný to review the material silently, and went over to the political department. First Lieutenant Růžička was livid. "How is this possible? Is this what you call fulfilling your pledge? Why won't they volunteer?"

"They're afraid Comrade Lieutenant Prouza here will be too strict with them," said the tank commander, tilting his head towards the spit-and-polish officer and hoping Růžička would catch his drift.

But before the politruk could say anything, Lieutenant Prouza intervened. He spoke in the warm, comradely tone that some of the cadet officers, at least the more naïve ones, had learned at the training school. "Afraid?" he said in astonished tones. "You can tell the comrades, Comrade Tank Commander, that this will be a comradely discussion. That ultimately the purpose is to satisfy ourselves not, in the end, as to whether the comrades have actually read everything, but as to whether they have somehow managed to absorb, as it were – to take into themselves – what those books are all about – something that will stand them in good stead throughout their future work." As the tank commander listened to him, the last hope of avoiding catastrophe died within him.

"I told them all that," he said, "but they're still afraid."

"But they gave their pledges," said Růžička, "and now they have to realize that this is simply their duty as members of the Union of Youth."

"Just go tell the comrades what I told you, Comrade Tank Commander," said Lieutenant Prouza. "Here, the point is simply for us to explain and clarify problems to each other in the form of a comradely discussion. If something isn't clear to one of us, then we explain it to him, and ultimately he may be able to explain certain problems for us in return. This is how we do things in the People's Army, and ultimately it will help us all eliminate barriers to our further work."

Danny looked at the lieutenant as though he were a creature from another world. "That's what I told them," he said darkly. "But it didn't do any good."

The tank commander was unaware that, at this very moment, the voice of the instructor in moral and political readiness at the school, Major Kondráč, was speaking in the young lieutenant's mind. *We have good people*, said the voice, *but we don't know how to persuade them of the truth. We have not discovered a way to stimulate their interest.* Electrified by this great thought, the lieutenant jumped up energetically, straightened his uniform in front and back, smoothed out the wrinkles on his hips, and said, "In that case, Comrade Tank Commander, I'll go with you."

"Please do, Comrade Lieutenant," said Růžička, and he turned to face the tank commander. "You see, Smiřický, you and the committee may have made a pledge, but you haven't been able to turn it into a concrete reality. When that happens, your work becomes alienated from the comrades. You may well be fulfilling *your* pledge, and carrying out *your* duty, but what good is that pledge and that duty if you can't carry them down among the people?"

Danny said nothing. Meanwhile Lieutenant Prouza had finished primping his uniform, and with perverse delight he brought himself to attention and said, "Comrade First Lieutenant, request permission to leave."

And the waiter awoke in Lieutenant Růžička, and he opened the door for them and mumbled distractedly, "Right this way, please."

★   ★   ★

But Lieutenant Prouza, fired up by the great mission before him, scarcely heard. Woodenly, but in full accordance with regulations, he made a half-turn and strode out of the room, with the tank commander following along behind him. He marched enthusiastically under the chestnut trees, responding to all the salutes, no matter how slovenly, offered by the second-year soldiers lounging in the sun outside their barracks; his arm bounced up and down as though it were spring-mounted. At the Seventh Tank Battalion's barracks, he turned the door handle energetically and pushed the door open so abruptly that it hit the nose of a myopic sergeant who was intently studying the daily cleaning schedule pinned to the inside.

"Asshole, can't you watch where the fuck you're going?" shouted the sergeant, but when he looked up and saw an unfamiliar lieutenant standing in the doorway, he resolved the situation by scurrying down between the bunk beds and climbing out an open window. The lieutenant took several steps into the room. Four or five faces looked up to see who it was, then quickly turned away, pretending not to have noticed him. Nobody wanted to be the one to call the room to attention.

The lieutenant knew that he was required to display patience and understanding for the common soldier; he was not just a commanding officer, but an adviser, so he was tempted to overlook this dereliction of duty. Then again, he also recalled the words of Major Kondráč: *Discipline begins with a missing button. You have to be tough and consistent in demanding that soldiers fulfil even the most minor duties. This, comrade, is precisely what will make the soldiers begin to respect you.*

What the wretched lieutenant didn't know was that the major's advice had been based solely on reading brochures which, in turn, were based on wishful thinking. His response, therefore, was guided not by common sense but by a non-empirical military pedagogical science. He walked slowly down the narrow aisle between the two rows of bunks, to the other end of the room, in complete silence. *From your every gesture*, he heard the major's voice intone, *from your every action, the soldiers must recognize that you are both their comrade and their commander.* Then he turned around and walked back in the deep silence, starting to realize that it would not be easy to combine these two functions. He began to perspire. He looked at the tank commander, who was doing nothing to help him. *A non-commissioned officer is the closest assistant to the commanding officer*, said Major Kondráč. Why wasn't the tank commander supporting him? The lieutenant walked back to the door, feeling awkward and embarrassed, and stopped in front of a soldier who was sitting on a trunk pretending to be utterly absorbed in mending a hole in his tunic. The tunic bore corporal's stripes. The lieutenant decided to act.

"You there, Comrade Corporal — " he said. His voice sounded confused and uncertain. The soldier looked up, his face ruddy. He put down the tunic and slowly got to his feet. The tempo of these actions did not comply with regulations.

In something that sounded like a Polish accent, he said, "Corporal Střevlíček."

"Comrade Corporal," said Prouza, with as much severity as he could muster. "Don't you know what the duty of a private or NCO is when an officer enters the room?"

The brick-faced corporal smiled strangely, almost insolently. "Sure I do."

"Then why haven't you done so? How is this possible?"

"I didn't see you," said the corporal matter-of-factly.

The silence in the room was now tangible. "How is this possible?" the lieutenant repeated mechanically. Wasn't his tone commanding and comradely enough?

"Because I was sewing on a button," said the corporal.

"Don't you lie to me!" Prouza exploded, but he caught himself. This was hardly a comradely tone. "Don't try to tell me,..." he began, and stopped again. "How should you stand when you talk to me?" This definitely didn't sound comradely enough.

The corporal looked down at his dirty boots, appeared to examine each one separately, and asked, "At attention, right?"

"And you call this at attention?"

"I got bow legs, Comrade Lieutenant," said the corporal.

To salvage what he could from the débâcle, the lieutenant — this time with no effort to speak like a commanding officer who was also a comrade — said, "What is a soldier's responsibility when an officer steps into the room?"

"He has to call everyone to attention."

"Then do it!" This seemed like a brilliant way out of the impasse, and the lieutenant was about to breathe a private sigh of relief when, from somewhere in the back of the room, a hoarse voice said, "It's our afternoon rest period."

Prouza's first instinct was to determine the speaker's identity. It was, after all, a breach of regulations to speak in the presence of an officer without permission. But he couldn't muster the courage, so he merely glanced at his watch, blushed, and lied loudly in the direction of the voice: "The time is now five to one. The rest period doesn't begin till one."

Then he turned to the corporal, who was still standing there in his shirtsleeves, and said energetically, "Carry out the order, Comrade Corporal."

If that's what he wants, I'll give it to him, Střevlíček told himself, and, in emulation of the famous good soldier, he carried out the order with exaggerated zeal. In the voice of a wounded lion, and with grotesquely deformed pronunciation, he roared: "All those pre – SENT – HA – TEYUN – *SHEN!*"

Throughout the room, figures in shirtsleeves rose raggedly to their feet. Some were in boxer shorts and one, Corporal Vomakal, a recruit from somewhere deep in the forests of the Sumava in south Bohemia, was wearing a filthy set of long underwear. The unhappy lieutenant felt a healthy desire to give all these unwashed idlers a proper tongue-lashing, to drag the bow-legged corporal on the carpet before the CO, and to cancel all leave. But the pedagogical delusion that had formed him led him astray once again.

"Comrades," he said, "don't think I want to make you jump through hoops, or 'chew you out', as you sometimes say among yourselves." *The occasional use of military slang will have a positive impact on the men; it will remind them that you all live together in the same collective, as it were.* "But discipline must be maintained and duties must be performed. I too must do my duty, and if you do yours, we'll get along. Isn't that so, Comrade Sergeant?" and he pointed to Sergeant Kostelník, for Major Kondráč had said that, as often as possible, one should address detailed questions to individual comrades, because in doing so one communicated more effectively with the collective.

"Right," mumbled the sergeant.

This unsoldierly response gave the lieutenant pause, but he continued in a fatherly tone: "And why, you might ask, have I come here among you, comrades?" He paused and looked around. "I have come to ask you how the preparations for the Fučík Merit Badge exams are proceeding in your squadron. What would your response be — Comrade Corporal?"

This time he directed his question to Frištenský, a driver who had earned the nickname Bullrider because he had twice managed to break the gearshift stick and one of his steering levers in his T-34. He responded by barking: "Corporal Frištenský!"

"Comrade Corporal, is your troop fulfilling its Fučík Badge pledges?"

"Well — yeah, we are."

"You are?"

"Yeah, we are."

"Then why is it no one wants to come and try the test?"

Frištenský merely laughed awkwardly and shrugged his shoulders, and even the lieutenant could see that he would get no answer from him. "What would you say, Comrade Sergeant-Major?" he asked, turning to Soudek.

The regulation answer came back: "Sergeant-Major Soudek!"

"Have you read all the required books?"

"Not all of them, no."

"Which ones have you not read?"

"Well, I — like the one about — " and his brow furrowed. The list of books he hadn't read was long, but he didn't even know the list. "About the — that — oh God, what was it called — *It's a Long Way to Moscow City* — "

"*Far from Moscow?*"

"Yeah, that's the one."

"And otherwise you've read them all, is that correct?"

Soudek swallowed and nodded.

"There now, you see, Comrade Sergeant-Major? That's not even a compulsory book. It's optional. So surely your fear of taking the examination is exaggerated." He looked out over the sphinx-like faces in the room. "Now, what do you say, comrades? Can you do it?"

Not a muscle moved in any of the faces, and with a sinking feeling Lieutenant Prouza turned to a private whose face seemed less hardened than the rest. This time he was fortunate; he happened to choose the diligent, eager-to-please Pravomil Poslušný, the one who had read everything on the list except *Lenin, Stalin, and Kalinin Talk to Young People*.

"What about you, Comrade Private, can you do it?"

"I can, Comrade Lieutenant," Private Poslušný replied. His voice was full of respect, which Prouza mistook for a sign of budding good will.

"So what about the exam? Will you come, comrades?" he said to the whole group.

There was no reply. "Come, comrades! Come," he intoned hypnotically, "and you will see for yourselves that you can do it. As Suvorov used to say, comrades – " and he stopped, because he suddenly remembered that Suvorov had said nothing at all about the Fučík Badge. But Major Kondráč kept him steady and he went on: " – as I repeat to you – it's just a matter of showing how you've learned from the experience of the great Julius Fučík. And you can do it. I believe you can. I know you can. Comrade Tank Commander," and he turned to Danny, "in ten minutes you will have the candidates form up and you will march them over to the political department, is that understood?"

"Yes, Comrade Lieutenant," said the tank commander, without the slightest faith in his ability to carry out the order.

"Then I will see you, comrades, in a quarter of an hour."
Turning his back on the assembly of fifty blank stares, the lieutenant walked out the door with a spring in his step.

★   ★   ★

Ten minutes later, the only soldier standing in the aisle fully
dressed was Private Poslušný, and he was trembling in fear.
The tank commander again ordered him to review the material in his mind and, muttering, "That snot-nosed little prick,"
he left for battalion headquarters. He wasn't entirely indifferent to the outcome; he was afraid that if he failed to round
up candidates, he'd be dropped from the examining committee to test the officers' wives that evening.

Rounding the corner, he ran into one of the career non-
coms, Sergeant Semančák, known to most people as "Cash".
As his nickname suggested, Cash had an insatiable appetite
for money, free time, fun, indolence, and therefore all the honorary badges and decorations that made free time, fun, and
indolence more accessible. Without really knowing why (perhaps it was out of skepticism or a sense of gallows humour),
Danny called out to him, "Hey, Comrade Sergeant! Come and
take the Fučík Badge exam with us!"

"Yeah? Uh, when?" asked Cash cheerfully.

"Right now. In the political department in fifteen minutes."

"But, uh, I haven't read a bloody thing," said Cash glee-
fully. He spoke Slovak, but a long time in the company of
men who spoke mostly Czech had transformed his mother
tongue into a living exemplar of that officially unrecognized
language – Czechoslovakian.

"No sweat. I'm on the exam committee."

"Oh well, in that case,..." said the NCO. "But you'll have

to, uh, tell me what I'm supposed to say."

"Don't worry. So you'll come?"

"Sure thing. But don't forget to help me out. Ain't nothin' in *my* head." And he walked off towards the kitchen.

Just let them try to say I've done nothing about all these commitments, Danny said to himself. *I've even roped a professional non-com into a consciousness-raising session. But it won't do me much good – it's going to be a disaster.*

He walked into battalion headquarters and knocked on the door of the political department. On the other side he heard a sharp "Enter!", and he did. Inside the room, Růžička and Hospodin were standing at attention before Matka, who was in the middle of dressing them down. Lieutenant Prouza, also at attention, was standing to one side, and though Matka was obviously not upbraiding him, Danny thought the grave expression on Prouza's face suggested someone whose cherished illusions were beginning to crumble.

"Tank Commander Smiřický!" Danny announced himself.

Matka turned around to face him. He had obviously worked himself up into the state of histrionic rage that so becomes officers.

"What do you want?" he roared.

"Comrade Captain, permission to speak with Comrade First Lieutenant."

"What about?"

"I've come to report to him on the Fučík Badge candidates, Comrade Captain."

Under any other circumstances, the captain would probably have thrown him out and ordered him to wait outside. But because Matka was always on the lookout for things he could push down his underlings' throats, the tank commander's arrival piqued his interest. He quickly concluded that this report on the Fučík Badge tests might come in handy.

"Give him your report, then," he said, and stuck his hands in his pockets.

Danny, who had guessed what was going on and took malicious delight in making his officers' lives difficult, turned to Růžička. "Comrade First Lieutenant, I have to report that only two men have come forward as candidates for the Fučík Merit Badge."

"How is this possible?" Růžička replied hoarsely, trying vainly to maintain his authority before the tank commander — no easy task given that he was on the carpet himself.

"I tried to win the comrades over," Danny assured him, "and the lieutenant here did as well" — he turned his head towards Prouza — "but they still don't want to take part."

"Is that so? Well — then — " Růžička fumbled for something to say. "You'll be responsible for this upstairs, you know that?"

"It's a problem, Comrade First Lieu — " Danny began defensively, but Matka abruptly intervened: "How many men did you say came forward?"

"Two, Comrade Captain."

"Well, isn't that wonderful," said the captain slowly, his tone suggesting that his confidence in his men had been bitterly misplaced. He turned to Růžička. "Is this what you call political work? Is this what you call political agitation? A battalion of two hundred and fifty men, and only two come forward? What a wonderful comment on your work, Comrade First Lieutenant."

Růžička took a deep breath, but let it slowly out again. As for Prouza, he experienced the demise of yet another ideal. Here was one officer berating another in the presence of a non-com inductee, when standing orders were so clear: verbal reprimands to officers must be given *only* when there were no soldiers of lower rank present. There must be a lot that still wasn't perfect in the lower units, the young officer thought bitterly.

"Isn't this grand," the commanding officer went on. "During a spotcheck I discovered that not a single man — *not a single man*, Comrade First Lieutenant — knows the names of any government ministers. I discovered that not a single man knows what the capital of Bulgaria is, comrade, nor do they know when the October Revolution was. The *Great* October Revolution. And the report on mass political activity for August isn't ready yet and it's the end of September already. The political agitators are not given regular time for indoctrination. The ten-minute poli-pep talks in the morning are mere formalities, and the political billboards are gapingly empty. And now only two men — two men! — show up for the Fučík Badge test."

"Comrade Captain — " Růžička tried to interrupt him.

"Two men, Comrade Lieutenant!" Matka continued harshly. "What do you intend to do about it? Well? What do you intend to do?"

"Comrade Captain — I'll go down to the barracks and — because I know I can't depend on the non-coms, I'll carry out — Lieutenant Hospodin and I will try to initiate a personal campaign to — "

"Isn't it a bit early? Isn't it a bit early to start a personal campaign, Comrade First Lieutenant?" said the captain bitterly. Růžička's attempt to shift at least part of the blame to the tank commander obviously hadn't worked. "A month ago, two months ago, half a year ago, is when you should have started this campaign. Well, there's no time now to use persuasion on these men, so we'll get things going army fashion." He turned and strode energetically out of the political department, followed by the three officers and the tank commander. Typists and officers on the way out got quickly to their feet; the sentry at the main door gave a regulation salute as they passed. Danny was last in line as they entered the corridor of the dorm, and could already hear the inhuman voice of the man on duty roaring: "Ten – SHUN!" and then the sharp click of heels as the soldiers fell in, and finally the report, shouted out with a drill sergeant's proficiency by an old hand:

"Comrade Captain, beg to report that while on duty with the Seventh Tank Battalion, nothing of note occurred. The company is preparing for the afternoon rest period. Sergeant Feurbach reporting."

"At ease, comrades," said the captain, and then burst into the dorm of the first squadron. "Attention!" he roared, without waiting for anyone else to do it. There was a flurry of activity among the beds and in a moment two ragged rows of soldiers stood in the narrow aisle. Some were in their shirts and undershorts, but most of them had their trousers on, and some were still wearing boots.

"Those in undershorts, once pace forward," commanded the captain. About ten men stepped out of the lines. "Get into bed right now and stay there until the rest period is over. The rest of you pay attention. In three minutes the duty officer will ask the candidates for the Fučík Merit Badge to assemble in front of the building. All of you who are so unfamiliar with the standing orders that you spend your afternoon rest period fully dressed will report for the exam. If you don't, I'll have your balls in a vice. When Comrade Tank Commander Smiřický gives the order, you will march to the political department. As your political agitator, Sergeant Mácha will see to it that all you deadbeats who don't know the standing orders report for this test."

Matka turned about smartly and marched out of the room, followed by his suite. Danny stayed behind. The soldiers condemned to try for the badge that army brochures referred to as "every man's pride" began to curse heartily.

*   *   *

Fifteen minutes later, a group of about thirty soldiers were crammed together at the back of the room in the political department, as far as they could get from the table at the front where the examination committee sat. They were bunched up, body to body, their backs tight against a row of cupboards that divided the room in two. In the centre of the cupboards was a narrow opening that led to a gloomy area full of dust-covered piles of ancient reports and fetid tin cans that had once held food. In front of the soldiers, rows of unoccupied chairs filled the otherwise empty space, and at the very front, alone, Private Poslušný sat hunched over, right under the noses of the committee, cramming from a crib card hidden in his boot. The committee, chaired by Lieutenant Prouza, sat behind a long table beneath official portraits of statesmen, while Růžička and Hospodin, in their role as observers, had placed themselves modestly behind a writing table at the window.

Lieutenant Prouza stared silently at the men's strange expression of shyness, while his daemon whispered in his ear: *You must overcome the mistrust the comrades sometimes feel towards you. Often soldiers are ashamed to admit an interest in literature because they fear ridicule from others. You must gain their confidence through the appropriate behaviour.* He stood up. "I'd like you to move forward, comrades," he said cheerfully. "There's plenty of room, and I won't eat you."

But the soldiers refused to budge, and the gap between officers and men — an abyss, really — remained as large as ever, while the absurd, lonely figure of Private Poslušný, a model soldier with a Youth Union button on his tunic, cowered in front.

"Please move forward, comrades. Don't all jam into the

corner." Prouza wanted to say something encouraging, something human, so he told them, "As the great Stalin said: 'With our new forms of work, you know, we are more or less rebuilding the old system of education on, as it were, the basis of comradely co-operation between the teacher and the pupil.' None of us here is driven by the desire to give any of you a hard time, as they say. All we'd like to do is have a friendly discussion about books that everyone in the Union of Youth should know to help him develop and grow further."

The stony mass of silence at the back of the room remained unmoved. Danny, who was sitting beside the lieutenant, came to his assistance.

"Come on, boys, move your butts a little closer. There's no point jamming yourselves into a corner. It won't do you any good anyway. So come off it."

But the lieutenant felt that this approach was inappropriate. To erase any negative impression the tank commander's appeal might have made, he added quickly, "How would it be, comrades, if some of us up here were to come down there and sit with you, so you wouldn't feel as though you're at an examination? We'll come and sit with you and just discuss things with you, because in the end that's the real meaning of the Fučík Merit Badge."

Again there was no response. The lieutenant had almost lost heart when suddenly the door flew open and in came Sergeant Semančák, out of breath and carrying his own chair. He looked about the room to determine who the highest-ranking officer was, put the chair down on the floor, and sang out: "Comrade First Lieutenant, request permission to join the group."

"By all means," said Růžička, from behind him.

"Are you coming to try out for the Fučík Badge, Comrade Sergeant-Major?" Lieutenant Prouza asked pleasantly.

"I sure am," said Cash, and the trusting enthusiasm that radiated from his voice renewed the lieutenant's hopes. Semančák
put the useless chair in the corner, sat down beside Private
Poslušný, and looked expectantly at the committee.

"There, you see, comrades?" said Prouza. "Comrade Sergeant-Major came right up here to the front and took a seat.
Now, all of you move in closer, so we can begin."

Cash turned around and addressed the crowd: "Come on,
comrades," he sang. "There's nothing to fear. Plenty of room
up here. Come on now, up you come."

The glowering cluster of soldiers began to move at last.
The first to unstick himself from the cupboard at the back was
the political agitator, Mácha. Perhaps some ancient awareness
of his responsibilities moved him to do it. He was followed by
Mengele, Kobliha, Bamza, and several others. Poslušný and
the little sergeant-major remained alone in the front row, but
the abyss that had threatened Lieutenant Prouza's fondest
hopes began to fill up quickly. Despite their dirty boots, their
oil-stained uniforms, and their unshaven faces, the men didn't
look as formidable as when they'd been crammed into the corner. They were just young people, and their officers simply
hadn't been able to get close enough to them. Prouza was
filled with a pleasant, visionary feeling: this could well be a
watershed in the life of the Seventh Tank Battalion. He took a
deep breath, expanded his chest, looked around at the assembly with fire in his eye, and initiated this historic turnaround:

"Comrades! We have come together here, as it were, to
take stock of how we have managed to carry out the pledges
we have all made to attain the proud title of bearers of the
Julius Fučík Badge of Merit, a man who over and over again,
as it were, exhorts us, as Comrade Lenin ultimately put
it, to study, study — " He paused and then, remembering
something, added, "Study!" That was well put, he thought,

but there was still something missing:

"We have to study, and study hard. As Fučík said, we have to catch up to and surpass, in every way, the capitalist power-mongers, so that we may break through and crush the enemies of our country and our people's democratic system, so that we can, as it were, learn to do and know what we can be taught by the people and their great leader and teacher Generalissimo Joseph Vissarionovich Stalin – and Comrade Malenkov" – he quickly added the name of the deceased immortal's successor – "and so that we will, in the end, fulfil the tasks of our combat and political training as we enter the year nineteen hundred and fifty-three. So, comrades!" he said, taking a breath. "And now, to start, to get the discussion flowing, as it were, let's take something from the reading list. Are we in agreement, comrades?" He turned to the committee with the vague feeling that his introductory remarks had not come off as well as they should have. The committee nodded.

"Let's begin with a book you've all read, and perhaps even seen at the movies – *Far from Moscow*. Which of you has *not* read it, comrades?"

He had deliberately begun with a trick from the pedagogical arsenal of the unforgettable Major Kondráč. *We know from experience*, this exemplary teacher would say, *that if we ask soldiers which of them knows, has seen, read, or heard of something, they will all remain silent, and that if we ask them which of them does* not *know, or has* not *seen, read, or heard of etc. etc., they will often remain silent as well, but in the latter case we have at least constructed a natural springboard to further questions. For instance, we can come back and say, "Well, in that case, how would it be if you, comrade," and point to a specific comrade....*

"Well, in that case," Lieutenant Prouza said into the dark silence that filled the room, "how about telling us something about the book — " and he looked around, giving the soldiers a moment to think about an answer. "Just use your own words, as you remember the book. How about — " and he searched the faces in front of him, some of which were dumb and frowning, others screwed up into what was meant to look like an attempt to remember, and still others staring intently at the ceiling. Three or four of the candidates were suddenly overcome by an urgent need to blow their noses loudly and thoroughly. The lieutenant's eyes came to rest on the contented career sergeant in the first row. *Should I try him?* Cash was smiling with trusting eyes, apparently delighted at the prospect of another easy medal, but the lieutenant interpreted his optimistic look differently. Here is a career non-com, he thought. He must have prepared properly for this test. His example will encourage the others.

"Well then, Sergeant-Major, why don't you tell us what you remember about the book."

Semančák's response was not what the young officer had expected. Obviously terrified at being singled out, he turned pale and began to stutter incoherently. "*Far from Moscow* is — well, like they say, it's — uh, the thing about it is, I mean — it's a book, right? — where the guy — the writer, I mean — he writes about, the thing he tells us is all about the stuff — uh, the stuff that goes on over there, you know, far from Moscow, I mean a long way from Moscow, which is the capital city of the — uh, the Union of Soviet Socialist Republics...."

Danny, who was trying desperately but unsuccessfully to remember what *Far from Moscow* was all about, was at this point lost in the memory of a rather dirty and totally unprepared urchin he had been examining in zoology once, during his brief pre-army career as an elementary-school teacher. He'd challenged the boy to tell the class what he knew about the Indian elephant. The grubby pupil had started hesitantly,

"The Indian elephant...is an...animal that...lives in India...."
Here he had left a long pause, before suddenly launching into
a fluent explanation: "India is a country where capitalists still
exploit workers. Exploitation means – " and he had droned
off a perfect Marxist definition of exploitation, which was all
Danny had learned that day about Indian elephants.

He shook his head and returned to the present, where Cash
went on droning, "and he wrote about how it was over there,
back then, I mean when they were – well, they were working,
right? – I mean not very well, because like I said, they were a
long way from Moscow, right? But these people, they worked
there a long time, but not all of them were too good at – uh –
at what they were doing, except for these guys – I mean, they –
well, anyway, they figured out that they had to do everything,
like for themselves – work, I mean – everybody who was –
uh – and there weren't no more capitalists to – uh, exploit
the peasants any more – and so they had to, well, do even better at, you know what I mean, reaching the whaddayacallums –
the norms I guess is what they say, because everything belongs
to the people, right? And so from then on they came up with
a lot of good ideas on how to – uh, how to make things better and stuff like that, so they made all these socialist pledges,
because in those parts it wasn't just that the people knew –
but like the priest told them they'd rot in hell if they worked –
so I mean even the kulaks and even the guys doing sabotage,
I mean they all went – went to – to those parts that were –
well – a long way from Moscow, the capital city of the Union
of Soviet Socialist Republics – " Danny suddenly realized that
Cash had given them the gist of the universal story which was
repeated, with minor variations, in novel after novel, and in
that sense his answer could be classified as correct.

But Prouza, instead of accepting Cash's digest, headed dog-
gedly towards disaster. He hadn't expected such inarticulacy,

or such ignorance of the book. After all, there was nothing in it about priests. Or was there? He was suddenly unsure of himself, realizing that he too had forgotten exactly what the book was about.

"Can anyone be more specific?" he said, looking around at the scattered assembly.

No one volunteered.

"No one?" he asked, disappointed, and rested his eyes on Sergeant Mácha. Mácha had been blowing his nose when the questioning began, and he had stopped when Cash started to speak, but when it was clear that he would soon run out of breath, Mácha had pulled out his handkerchief again and begun using it for as long as seemed prudent. Now, just as he was putting it back in his pocket, he became the committee chairman's next victim.

"What about you, Comrade Sergeant? Wouldn't you like to help the comrade sergeant-major out?"

"Sure," said Mácha sadly. "The novel takes place in — in — " and he thought hard, then made up his mind — "far from Moscow, in the Kyzl Kum desert."

"I think you're mixing it up with — "

"I know! I kind of overshot. It takes place in — in — "

"Would it be Siberia?"

"That's it, Siberia. And the Party secretary, he — he organizes the work details there. According to new methods." Mácha was sure of himself now. "The workers there work by the old methods, but the Party secretary persuades them it's better to work by the new methods. A few of the workers are, are politically clueless, and they don't like the new methods because they think it makes them work harder, but this guy, the secretary, he shows them that if they set things up properly, they won't have to work their butts off. And that's how they manage to meet the plan and — and — "

"Good!" said Prouza. "So they erect the building in less time. Do you remember how they do that?" He was hoping the well-read sergeant would remember now, because he suddenly realized that he couldn't even remember – and this was terrible – what it was they were supposed to be building. The sergeant did not disappoint him.

"They erected it in less time because using the old methods they would have finished it a lot later the way they had it planned, but with the new methods, and using the shock-worker movement, giving prizes for extra work, they built it in less time because they could start production a lot sooner than they planned it according to the old methods they made the plan by, which would have been a lot later – "

"That's right! And can you tell us what importance this had for the Soviet Union, that they were able to build things faster? Perhaps you could answer that, Comrade Private?"

Private Mengele got to his feet. After a long pause, he answered, "Well, it had great importance."

"Of course. But what did it allow them to do?"

"It allowed them to" – Private Mengele hesitated, then went on – "to increase productivity – "

"Yes, that's exactly right! They could ultimately increase the productivity of work and increase the norms as they fulfilled the plans. There, you see, comrades? It's not that difficult! You mustn't be afraid of literature."

Encouraged by the success of his dialectical method, Prouza next asked the assembled students about a book he presumed would be more familiar to them than the Russian novel. After all, the badge they were going to earn that day was named after its author. But when he enquired about *Report from the Gallows*, only one man raised his hand – Sergeant Mácha. It came out that he'd only read an article on Julius Fučík in the current issue of the magazine *The Czechoslovak*

Soldier. Challenged to reproduce its content, Mácha proved that his knowledge of even the brief article was hazy. "It was called," he said, " 'Julius Fučík – Soldier'. Fučík" – he thought hard – "Fučík served in the army during the first pre-Munich bourgeois capitalist republic and he took part in illegal political agitation among the comrades."

Prouza nodded and the sergeant felt encouraged. "He can be an example to us political workers about how to work with other comrades."

He looked questioningly at Prouza, who nodded and said, "That's right."

"In fact," the political agitator continued, more confidently now, "he was one of the first political agitators."

"Excellent, Comrade Sergeant," said the lieutenant. "Julius was, in fact, in a manner of speaking, one of our first political agitators, right inside the capitalist army of the pre-Munich republic. And now, Comrade Sergeant, what should we take from his work as a model for our own?"

The sergeant, now utterly sure of himself, answered firmly, "This Fučík told the comrades how to make army life easier. He told them that, like, when an officer gave them an order to sing, they should do what he said, but only so they didn't get forced to do pushups, because they had to save their strength for the real struggle once they went back to civilian life. He always stood up for the soldiers against the officers and the ball-busting – as the soldiers in the capitalist bourgeois army used to call it back then, and – and – "

The lieutenant quailed. Mácha's interpretation of the article was materially correct, but somehow his verve gave it a meaning that lost sight of the correct point of view. He knew his facts but he hadn't grasped them from a class perspective, whereas Lieutenant Prouza was able to give a class perspective even to problems he knew nothing about. Like many of his colleagues, the lieutenant could find the politically correct point of view in a situation without knowing any details whatsoever, and knowing that gave him a calm self-assurance. "Back then, that was certainly the right approach," he said. "But in what way can we use Julius's work as a direct model, in a sense, for our own work today? Do you see what I'm trying to say, Comrade Sergeant?"

Mácha looked less than entirely sure. "Well, in – like, in the way he always defended ordinary soldiers against officers – I mean – "

Suddenly the figure of Lieutenant Růžička rose behind Prouza. So far Růžička had remained silent, but now he had decided to rescue the hapless fledgeling officer.

"Wait a minute, Mácha," he said, and turned to the young lieutenant. "Comrade Sergeant has the right idea, you just have to get him to be more precise. Mácha, what do we say the first republic was?"

Faced by his immediate superior, the agitator's eloquence and loquacity faded. "A bourgeois democracy," he said curtly.

"And what else?"

"Capitalist."

"And what do we say the ruling class was?"

"Capitalist."

"And who served in the army?"

"The people."

"And who were the officers?"

"The capitalists."

"And today?"

A light finally went on in the sergeant's head. "Today we say," he replied quickly, "that officers are sons of the working class."

"And the people *what*?"

"Rule."

"And therefore there is no *what* between the officers and the men?"

"Gulf," sighed the sergeant with relief.

"That's right," said Růžička. "And therefore, was Fučík correct or incorrect to urge the comrades to carry out orders only formally?"

"Correct."

"Whereas today is it still correct to urge the comrades not to carry out their duties, to avoid responsibilities, not to take part in exercises, to neglect their political growth?"

Růžička's tone of voice left no doubt as to what the proper answer was and Mácha responded with utter certainty: "No, it isn't."

"So Julius Fučík, who was really our first political agitator, provided what example?"

"His example was," said the sergeant — beginning bravely, but then lapsing into some confusion — "his example was — he encouraged the comrades to carry out their duties — to be politically aware — to take part in exercises and be ready for combat — "

"Yes, comrades," concluded Růžička, who was no longer listening to Mácha, but was preparing a few grand, ceremonial phrases to wrap things up. "Julius Fučík was able to fire up the comrades with enthusiasm for socialism and for the struggle of the working class. As the great Stalin himself said, 'Those who wish to fire others up must burn themselves.' And Julius Fučík burned, comrades, and he fired up the weaker comrades. And we too must burn, comrades, and inspire the weaker comrades to carry out their duties, to follow orders, to be politically and physically prepared for combat, to be disciplined, to exercise with all our might, because, as Kutuzov has said, the more sweat on the training field, the less blood on the battlefield."

"Amen," said Private First Class Dr. Mlejnek. As a member of the committee, he had spent all this time scribbling notes under the table on the most interesting statements made by the men and the officers, so that he could offer them to Sergeant Krajta for his *Czechoslovak Army Folklore* in exchange for an old issue of *Amazing Stories*.

"And that, Comrade Lieutenant, is how you must guide the comrades to the correct answer." With those words, Růžička swept triumphantly out of the room with the air of someone who had done his duty well, leaving Prouza to face thirty soldiers alone. Prouza felt humbled by Růžička's masterful performance. There was so much more he had to absorb, to make truly his own. There was so much he didn't yet know how to do. He looked around the assembly, and suddenly he lost the will to continue in the role of chief inquisitor. He resorted to a trick used by all pedagogues who have run out of inspiration or forgotten their facts. He turned to the committee, which up until then had maintained a non-committal silence, and asked: "Do you have any questions, comrades?"

This jolted the committee out of its lethargy. The first to come to his senses was Dr. Mlejnek, who singled out Private Bamza and said, "Have you, Comrade Private, read anything by Jiří Wolker?"

It was not an idle question. Dr. Mlejnek knew that several evenings ago, in the barracks, a whole crowd of these men had read Wolker's poem "The Ballad of the Unborn Child", although not, of course, in preparation for the test. He knew, too, that Bamza had read a certain passage from it out loud to the others.

"You mean, have I read anything by Wolker?"

"That's what I said."

"Yeah, well, I read that — what d'you call it — that ballad about the aborted kid, right?"

"The unborn child."

"Right, the unborn child."

"And how did you like it?"

"I liked it okay."

"Anyone else read it?" Dr. Mlejnek turned to the group. It mumbled in affirmation.

"And who can tell us what it was about?" asked Dr. Mlejnek, raising a more complex question.

The hand of the ill-fated Private Bamza flew into the air. Lieutenant Prouza half rose out of his chair, intending to stop him from speaking, but then thought better of it and sat down again. Dr. Mlejnek nodded to the private.

"It's all about these two dough-heads who fall in love," declared Bamza, "and he knocks her up but they're both poor, right? So she has to, you know, get rid of it."

"Good. Has anyone read anything else by Wolker?" asked Mlejnek quickly, hoping to shift the discussion to a safer theme. But Lieutenant Prouza's daemon seized him once more, against his will. *It can't be left at that*, he thought. *A poem that raises the issue of how capitalist society destroys everything pure, including love, should be fully exploited for its pedagogical benefits.* The lieutenant raised his hand and interrupted Dr. Mlejnek.

"Excuse me, Comrade Private. Comrade Private, you described the subject matter of the poem correctly, as it were, but what do you think the poem tells us about the present, about today?"

Bamza looked at the lieutenant with sullen eyes.

"D'you see what I'm getting at?" Prouza pressed. "What was the poet, as it were, trying to criticize?"

Bamza stared at him without a flicker of comprehension.

"What I mean is," the lieutenant continued, groping for ways to rephrase the question, "can such things happen even today, in our People's Democracy?"

A dark cloud filled Bamza's eyes. "You mean, do guys still knock up unmarried women?" he said warily.

"Well no, not that – of course, I mean that too, I mean yes, such unfortunate practices still survive here and there, but what I meant – "

"Oh, I get you. You mean, do women still have to get rid of it, right?"

"Something like that. What I was really thinking of was whether young people still have to resort to such extreme measures, do you see? Are such things still necessary in our People's Democracy?"

By this time Bamza's scowl was intense. "Well, yeah, sometimes, yeah."

"But for health reasons, of course. Is that what you mean?"

"Well, yeah, sure, there's that too," said Bamza. "Or like when a woman's pregnant and a guy walks out on her and she don't want to live with the scandal – "

"But try to understand me, Comrade Private. Do people still have abortions today because they can't, as it were, afford to keep the baby?"

"Yeah, sure they do," said Bamza without hesitation. "Where I come from in Žižkov there was this guy who had eleven kids, all boys, and this spring his wife got rid of the next one because he said, like, who's going to feed the little bugger, and besides, he'd named all his kids after the twelve apostles and the only name left was Judas and that's a hell of a name to hang on anyone, and anyways the priest would never of christened it that, and he couldn't give it any other name because it would of screwed everything up and he was all nervous about having an unchristened kid because he was a devout Catholic and so – "

"Comrade Private!" said Prouza, interrupting the tide of

words. "That's possible, of course, but it's not typical, as it were. And the poet wasn't writing about cases like that, because literature has to represent what is typical and positive. Do young people today who love each other and want to start a family – do they have to resort to such methods?"

After a short, gloomy pause, Bamza admitted that they didn't.

"There, you see?" said the lieutenant. "And why did young people in the past have to resort to abortion?"

"Because they were poor."

"Right. You see, all you have to do is think about the poem a little. Now, why were they poor?"

"Because there was a depression," replied Bamza.

"Right again. And can there be a depression today?"

"No."

To Prouza's great relief, Sergeant Mácha stepped in. "There can't be a depression today," he said, with the assurance of an expert, "because today the people own the relations of production. There used to be depressions before, because the relations of production belonged to the capitalists."

There was something that didn't seem quite right about his reply, but Lieutenant Prouza let it pass. "But in the end, concretely, as it were," he said, "to whom do these, ah, relations of production belong?"

"To the people," replied Sergeant Mácha resolutely.

"Whereas before? Someone else answer now – Comrade Sergeant?" and Prouza pointed to Kobliha.

With equal resoluteness, Kobliha replied, "Before, they belonged to the capitalists."

"Yes, comrades," Prouza concluded. His tone was tragic. "Now do you see what meaning this poem has, ultimately? It directly demonstrates how, during the capitalist republic, even love, as it were, was joyless and wretched, and how, ultimately, young people got married for reasons quite different than today. Now, can anyone explain to us the motive force under capitalism, when two young people wanted to get married?"

"Money," Sergeant-Major Semančák piped up.

Someone at the back snickered, but the lieutenant nodded. "Correct, Comrade Sergeant-Major. And today?"

The present-day reasons for getting married seemed quite beyond the comprehension of the tiny Semančák, and Sergeant-Major Soudek had to answer: "They have to be fond of each other, right?"

"Yes, comrades. Under capitalism, the woman was not much more than a burden, as it were, to the man. Her only duty was to bring him a dowry. We say that the bourgeoisie desocialized the wife's role. Today, under our people's socialist system, the relationship between men and women has changed from the foundations up, as it were. Nowadays, men look for something quite different in women. Take you, Comrade Private," he said, addressing Bamza. "Suppose you wanted to get married. What would you most value about your girl, ultimately?"

Bamza looked dreamily at the lieutenant and seemed to be hesitating.

"Well?" said the lieutenant encouragingly. "What about... this, as it were?" and with the fingers of both hands he tapped the centre of his chest. It was a gesture intended to indicate purity of heart, but it was hardly Marxist; it harked back to a distant period in his life when he had been as enthusiastic about the catechism and serving as an altar boy as he now was about military pedagogy. "What about *this*?" he repeated, questioningly.

"Tits?" replied Bamza, warily.

The reply threw Prouza off balance, but it brought new life to the wilted assembly. A hum went round the benches

and a trumpeting sound came from the table where the examination committee was sitting. This was Dr. Mlejnek using
his handkerchief.

"No, no, legs are the most important," Střevlíček suggested. It was the first time he had spoken.

"What's so important about legs?" retorted Soudek dis-
dainfully. "You can't see their legs in the dark."

"You can't see their tits either," objected Střevlíček.

"But you can feel them," countered Soudek.

"You're not going to spend all your time in bloody bed with
her," said Mácha, making a political point. "You'll be going on
walks with her, right?"

"If walking's all you want to do, then wooden legs would
be good enough," Soudek shot back.

"And a dowry's important too," Semančák added. "An
eiderdown, bed linen, even a little money in the bank wouldn't
hurt."

"The hell with that," said Bamza, by now an experienced
literary critic. "They bring in currency reform and your bank
account's worth dick. A house is more like it, right?"

"Listen to this smartass," called out Mácha, as though
Bamza had struck a nerve. "Put money into a house? Today?"

"But you got equity in a house."

"They'll nationalize your equity when they nationalize
your house," said Kobliha.

"They haven't yet."

"Don't worry, they will."

As Lieutenant Prouza followed the discussion, he felt more
and more like Alice in Wonderland. His brochures had not
anticipated such a situation. A weak groan escaped his mouth,
unnoticed by the candidates for the Fučík Badge. As though
all restraint had left them, they expanded on the theme, going
deeper and deeper into it until Lieutenant Hospodin inter-

vened. Hospodin had remained silent for a long time, not because he was bewildered by the turn the discussion had taken, but because he too was deeply interested in the problem. At last, however, he remembered his responsibilities, stood up, and called out, "Just a moment, comrades."

The animated faces of the debaters turned towards him, and hardened once again into expressionless masks. "What the comrade lieutenant was getting at was, what is a woman today supposed to be like from the point of view of socialist morality?"

The room was silent.

"Well?" asked Hospodin. "What kind of spiritual qualities would you look for in a woman? Soudek?"

The sergeant-major hesitated. "I – I'm not sure what you mean."

"I mean from the psychiatric point of view," explained Hospodin, who was a self-taught baker in civilian life.

"I – " Soudek shrugged his shoulders.

"Her character, if you like," added the lieutenant, trying to be more down to earth.

"Oh, I see," said Soudek. "Well, she should be wholesome."

"That's important," allowed Hospodin, "but it's hardly the most important thing. What are the principles of socialist morality that every girl must live up to? Just remember, now, we studied it in a brochure called 'Towards a Higher Socialist Morality'."

"I know!" cried Sergeant Mácha. "She has to be faithful to the people and – " He gave a sidelong glance at Hospodin, who nodded encouragement.

"She has to be faithful to the people and the people's democratic system, she has to help her husband, she has to…to…."

"What kind of relationship must exist between husband and wife?" asked the lieutenant.

Mácha tried to recall the correct answer but couldn't. It was Private Bamza, frowning like a thundercloud, who put his hand up.

"Yes?" said the education officer brightly.

"It has to be legitimate," Bamza declared gravely and gloomily. He obviously meant it, but Hospodin took the answer as an impertinence and lashed out at him.

"This is a serious discussion, Bamza. Keep your jokes to yourself." And thus, without being aware of it, he planted in the reactionary soul of this proletarian from Žižkov the unshakable conviction that Communism, in its depravity, was against the institution of marriage.

★   ★   ★

At that moment, relief, like a *deus ex machina*, came in the form of Captain Matka, who flung the door open and stepped briskly into the room in his overstuffed riding-pants. Glad to be distracted from a discussion that was going nowhere, Hospodin yelled, "Attention!" at the top of his voice, took two loud steps towards the captain, who casually raised his hand to his cap, and announced: "Comrade Captain, the candidates for the Fučík Merit Badge are carrying out their tests. Number present: thirty-five. Education Officer Lieutenant Hospodin."

"At ease, Comrade Lieutenant," said Matka. He sat down informally on the edge of the committee table and asked, almost affably, "Well, boys, how's it going?"

The candidates said nothing. Some of them, with weaker nerves, grinned vacuously.

"It's going well, Comrade Captain," Mácha reassured him.

"Well then, I'll just listen in," said the captain in a jovial tone. He was in an exceptionally good mood that seemed imbued with an almost democratic spirit. "I'll listen in, and maybe I can learn something. We're going to be under fire here ourselves tonight."

All the anxiety created by the commander's arrival melted away, and Lieutenant Hospodin grinned. The captain addressed him in a friendly tone: "Please continue, Comrade Lieutenant."

"Yes, Comrade Captain." The former baker turned to the men and said, "Now we've done Jiří Wolker from the point of view of his poems." Then he had a bright idea, based on the age-old tendency of officers to exploit the abilities of their underlings for their own glory. He turned to the committee and said, "Do you have any other questions about Comrade Wolker, comrades?"

The committee had none.

"Now then, Comrade Tank Commander, would you mind carrying on?"

And so Danny was shaken out of the generally pleasant role of amused onlooker, and took the matter into his experienced impostor's hands. To bring the tests to a successful conclusion, he used a method he had perfected in the school in Hronov, whereby information can be elicited from utterly ignorant people.

"And now, comrades, let's analyse the book by Alexander Fadyeyev called *The Young Guard*," he said. "As you recall, it's a famous book about the underground resistance of young Soviets against the German occupiers. Now, bearing in mind the title, who led this underground resistance? Sergeant Mácha?"

Mácha stood up and said that Soviet youth had led the resistance. Was Soviet youth satisfied with merely passive resistance, or did they struggle actively as well? Tank Commander Hykal replied that their resistance was active as well.

Then Danny asked what active resistance was, as opposed to passive resistance, which meant that no acts of sabotage were committed and no guerrilla warfare was waged, and Sergeant Kobliha correctly defined it as resistance in which acts of sabotage were committed; he even added, without being prodded, that the guerrillas also blew up bridges. In this way the committee disposed of *The Young Guard.*

Employing the same simple technique, the committee went on, during the next hour, to dispose of most of the books on the reading list. Even the captain joined in the discussions, and the impression left was that the candidates were, on the whole, well prepared.

At the end of it, Danny asked Lieutenant Prouza, who had been sitting on his chair like a body without a soul, if he had any further questions. Prouza had none. The tank commander turned to the captain with the same question, and he, flattered that the discussion had given him the chance to show off his experience in combat training, began to talk about a book called *The Story of an Ordinary Man*, about a heroic Soviet fighter pilot who returned to duty after both his legs had to be amputated, and continued to shoot down German Messerschmitts like so many clay pigeons. Matka compared the heroism of this hero to the heroism of Sergeant Blahý from the Tenth Tank Battalion, who, despite a high fever, had driven the squadron commander's tank during manoeuvres so that his squadron wouldn't lose marks in the final evaluation. Unfortunately, the men in the captain's battalion already knew the story from personal acquaintance with the heroic sergeant, who made no secret of the fact that the real motive behind his heroism was the promised dropping of charges of stealing boxes of sugarcubes from the battalion's kitchen and selling them to black-marketeers.

In any case, after the unexpectedly positive evaluation, by

the division commander himself, of the recent disastrous manoeuvres, the captain was in a genuinely good mood, the glow of which enveloped even the Fučík Badge candidates and their foggy knowledge. Pressing them (in his mind) to his valiantly plump breast, he granted them absolution. The test ended in general satisfaction with the exception of Lieutenant Prouza, and he'd wormed his way into this situation at his own risk. The captain rose – Lieutenant Hospodin quickly took advantage of his good mood and asked for two days' leave for family reasons – and the candidates rushed noisily out of the room, their heads dancing with pleasant visions of thin metal stars on their tunics to dazzle the girls back home. The committee walked along the alley of yellowing chestnut trees over to sick bay, where they sat around the hot stove with tin cups of cooling tea in their fingers and amused themselves with gossip about the officers. The seance was headed by the gynecologist Lieutenant Dr. Sadař, who had started studying black magic and was preparing, during the next officers' training session, to serve a black mass for the death of First Lieutenant Pinkas, for he lusted excessively after Pinkas's pretty wife.

*　*　*

But Dr. Sadař, that vessel of longing, was not a member of the Fučík committee that evening, so he wasn't in the political department when the sun went down and the first cool autumn breeze wafted through the treetops in the dusky park. It was his loss, because Mrs. Pinkasová was there in all her rather remarkable beauty; like a precious stone, she adorned the shabby company of Captain Matka, First Lieutenant Kámen, Lieutenant Hezký, and several other lieutenants. The only one missing was Lieutenant Prouza, who had excused himself to attend to some mysterious business in Prague. (Sergeant Kanec concluded that he had gone to get drunk.) She was sitting there with melancholy eyes, with bright lipstick on her lips, wearing a tight-fitting yellow sweater. Rumour had it that her overworked husband was unable to satisfy her sexually. Frequently, Captain Matka would ask the poker-faced first lieutenant to stand in for him during staff exercises that could last for days at a time, and this conscientious self-made man would then spend many nights in the secret map room (instead of in his flat in the married officers' quarters on Zephyr Hill, which commanded a scenic view of the tank shooting range), poring over maps, orders, and battle plans with working-class diligence. Despite his dedication, he had never been promoted. Years before, as a young boiler-maker's apprentice, he had escaped from the German-occupied Protectorate of Bohemia and Moravia and had a series of unwanted adventures in western Europe which no one (except for a few foolish young people) now envied him. After France fell to the Nazis, he hid for a while in Vichy France and then managed to escape in a motor launch; a storm came up and they capsized, but a Portuguese merchant ship rescued him and set him ashore on the east coast of the United States. Suspected of being a spy, he was interned, but when the Japanese attacked Pearl Harbor he found himself in an American uniform, caught in enemy crossfire on the beach at Okinawa. Wounded and decorated with several imperialist medals, he finally made it back to the Czechoslovak units in England and spent the end of the war on the Western Front as the driver of a Cromwell tank, which, because you could only get out of it when the turret was in a certain position, was a fiendishly efficient crematorium for anyone unlucky enough to be caught inside when it was hit.

These colourful adventures had caused the first lieuten-

ant's curly hairline to recede considerably, and further years
of service in the People's Democratic Army had changed its
natural brown to a neutral grey, and turned his face into a
mask of iron. Dr. Mlejnek might make fun of him, but Danny
sometimes wondered if this mask, unlike the masks worn by
other officers, was not in fact a genuine mirror of Lieutenant
Pinkas's soul.

No one, however, knew anything about the real nature
of the sexual service he rendered to his wife, and naturally
that beautiful young lady never talked about it. In fact, Mrs.
Pinkasová was unusually silent, and only her black eyes spoke
as she waited in her yellow sweater, evening after evening,
under the chestnut trees just outside the battalion perimeter,
holding the lieutenant's first offspring by the hand. She would
ask the sentry to enquire as to whether her husband was coming home that evening. The sentries always complied with
unusual alacrity and precision. Usually, however, they had
regretfully to inform her that Comrade First Lieutenant Pinkas
was tied up and that she wasn't to wait up for him. In a sad
little voice the lovely lady would thank the sentry and walk off
down the alley of chestnut trees, watched by the wide-eyed
soldiers, who would crowd around the windows until the yellow sweater had vanished among the shadows cast by the
spreading treetops. Unlike the rumours surrounding the wife
of Bobby Kohn, and other wives who were objects of untram-
melled erotic mythology, the rumours about the melancholy
Mrs. Pinkasová didn't say whether she had ever acted upon
her alleged dissatisfaction – at least in the manner longed for
by Dr. Sadař, who was resorting to demonology in his shyness,
rather than exploiting his charms as a gynecologist.

*   *   *

Since Tank Commander Smiřický was often entrusted with important duties in battalion headquarters, he was frequently called upon to supply the first lieutenant's wife with that depressing information about her husband's workload. In the course of doing so, he also had the opportunity to look into the black depths of her melancholy eyes — and they *were* black, so black that it was scarcely possible to read anything in them about the woman and the life she led in the flat above the shooting range. Still, the tank commander was convinced that behind that amorous anthracite lay smouldering sparks that needed only the warmth of human breath to fan them into flames.

Imagine his joyous hope, then, when he saw that gentle flower brightening the half-circle of glum officers. Her black eyes met his, and it seemed to him that they paused slightly longer than propriety would dictate before turning to look into the unimpeachable middle distance in front of her.

The committee was chaired by the tank commander and First Lieutenant Růžička himself; the other two, Dr. Mlejnek and Sergeant Kanec, were merely extras. Because they all knew each other, they began without the usual inspirational speeches, and as they proceeded it became clear that the officers were almost as well read as their men had been. Their answers, on the other hand, were far bolder and more inventive. Captain Matka set the tone right away when, asked about Alois Jirásek's *Hussites, Victors over the Crusaders*, he declared that it was a novel about Jan Hus, who had struggled against the Jesuits because they burned Czech books and allowed German settlers to move into the border areas of Bohemia. The chairman pointed out that the burning of books by Jesuits took place "somewhat later", but the captain waved his hand dismissively and said, "It all began back then, anyway."

The others, discipline aside, appeared to be trying to outdo their commander in a fair fight. First Lieutenant Kámen thought that Julius Fučík had written his *Report from the Gallows* for the Communist Party daily *Rude Právo* and had been sent to prison for it under the Nazi occupation; he was surprised to hear that it had been the other way around, but concluded that he had only got the chronological order mixed up. Then the eager-to-please Lieutenant Hczký informed the committee that, before the war, Fučík had also taken up musical composition – a fact the brochures about him unfairly omitted – and had composed "The Skater's Waltz". He seemed unfazed by the information that the composer was a different Fučík, maintaining that, all the same, their names were identical and they were both interested in art. The fact that Lieutenant Šlajs thought *Spring on the Oder*, a novel about the Soviet offensive during the Second World War, was a novel about Polish raftsmen, or that Mrs. Pinkasová mixed up the political novelist Ostrovsky with the bourgeois playwright of years earlier, seemed petty beside such sterling achievements.

In any case, Mrs. Pinkasová added considerable lustre to the proceedings. For a long time Lieutenant Růžička was too shy to ask her anything, but he finally overcame his hesitation and asked her to comment on a novel called *The Wind Shall Not Return*. When she replied, her melodic mezzo-soprano seemed to fill the empty clichés with new life. Danny was intoxicated by her charm, her muted voice with a tone colour like that of the cor anglais, her soft perfume, sweet, artificial, as artificial as those garnet lips and the pearly sheen of her teeth and the pitch-black arches of her eyebrows and the hair undulating in waves around her entrancing neck. He was struck dumb. He loved artificial things. They were created with effort, maintained with effort, and in the end they succumbed to natural decay like everything else. He was exploding with an ardour that reached out towards her, an utterly material longing that must have touched her, grasped her by the heart, for she wasn't made of wax, after all, she was only artificial on the surface. But if his feelings touched her, the lady gave no evidence of it. She replied to the question, but the committee members were so mesmerized by her voice that no one knew what she was saying. Then the first lieutenant turned to the committee and asked if anyone had anything to add. Danny mastered himself, stood up and again looked straight into the candidate's eyes, and asked her what she could tell the committee – a committee frozen in erotic catalepsy – about Jiří Wolker. The black eyes disappeared for an instant behind her tender eyelids and her entire face seemed to darken slightly. When she began to speak, in that quiet, oboe-like voice, the committee sighed involuntarily and the tank commander felt the gentle tickle of an electric force-field between them. He lost himself in her eyes and she no longer glanced away, nor dropped her gaze; her black, unfathomable eyes revealed only that it was here, within their depths, that he must seek the answer to the question his sudden, sharp longing had expressed.

Jiří Wolker, she said, was a poor boy from a proletarian family who even in childhood had to do hard physical labour, and often suffered from hunger. But diligence and energy got him to university, where, at the age of twenty-four, he succumbed to the ravages of poverty and undernourishment and died of tuberculosis. The first bourgeois capitalist republic tried to suppress his poems in all kinds of ways; no publisher would publish them, and so they circulated only among circles of enthusiastic young people who loved Wolker and mimeographed his poetry and circulated it illegally. Today, however, Wolker was the poet of all young people, and his work helped us to create a new, better, and happier life for ourselves....

The radical proletarization of the politically correct but

rather well-to-do classical poet was received by the assembly
in charmed silence. And when the melancholy woman – at
Danny's request – recited something by Wolker that she knew
by heart (it was a poem about a mailbox on a street corner)
and her face grew darker still, the words became one with the
sighing of the wind in the chestnut trees, and the Kobylec
army base was wiped off the map of the world. When she finished, the assembly burst into thunderous applause, abruptly
and ceremonially bringing the Fučík Badge exams of the Seventh Battalion, under the successful leadership of Captain
Matka, to a close.

*　*　*

But Danny wasn't nearly as satisfied as the captain and his
political officer, who, amid the clicking of heels, formed an
escort for the pretty new holder of the honorary badge. Just
that afternoon, her husband (representing the captain) had
left for a five-day preparation for divisional manoeuvres. She
had a long walk ahead of her through the dark army base to
her home on Zephyr Hill, which rose in silhouette against
the starry sky, and she needed protection. The officers gallantly gathered around her, opened the door, and let her walk
through first, not noticing that her black eyes flashed a brief
message towards Danny's deadpan face. Then she left, and
walked among the black boots and epaulettes through the
alley of chestnut trees into a realm beyond recall, leaving
Danny alone in the office with his longing. Because his desire
for her was enormous (and he despised masturbation), he tried
desperately and in vain to find forgetfulness in work, a measure, we are told, that cures everything. He started writing an
outline for the political schooling of non-coms on the theme

"Lysenko and Michurin's Agro-biology: A Powerful Tool in the Hands of Czechoslovak Agriculture".

Lieutenant Hezký had to speak on this theme the following day, but because he was a former grocer's apprentice who had enrolled in the training school for tank officers to escape being sent to the mines, he was unprepared for such intellectual feats. So he had made a secret deal with Danny – a bloodsucking arrangement, at that – by which, in exchange for three such outlines, he would grant the tank commander a single, one-day leave.

Danny started work without the benefit of any textbooks. He knew nothing whatever about Lysenko and Michurin's biology, but it was a science totally unfamiliar to the whole tank division, and no one expected the non-coms to learn anything about it anyway. All they were required to take away from the lectures was the conviction that Lysenko and Michurin's agrobiology was a powerful weapon in the hands of Czechoslovak agriculture because it exploited the advantages of Soviet science, whereas, before, the kulaks had made all the decisions themselves and consequently the poverty of the small farmers had grown year by year.

The tank commander worked hard. He was driven by frustrated desire and therefore he wrote with a passion. By the time he was finishing the last paragraph, the clock showed eleven, the time for lights-out. There was absolutely no connection between what he had written and the theme of the lecture, but the ideological content was just the kind of thing Růžička would like. *And that time*, he wrote, pouring into the text all the energy behind an unexploded charge that could hardly go off that night, *is gradually coming to fruition. Despite the thousands of obstacles placed in our path by the class enemy, the enemy who sits on the boards of directors of American monopolies, the enemy who hides behind the slogans of our own party, the enemy who waits for his chance to act here among us, and who, using weapons of doubt and irrational thought, tendencies of thinking that our eyes and ears put into his hands, and the dark movement of holdovers from the ancient past, destroys and suppresses within our hearts the flame of revolutionary zeal. But no matter how violently he may rage against it, that flame is unquenchable. It burns in our nervous systems, in our hearts, it consumes our brains, its red glow veils the globe. And the time is ripening. Perhaps even tomorrow, the great conflagration shall sweep around the world, the great world-wide revolution that will consume all the filth in the world, in us and outside of us, and with an exclamation point of fire and blood will mark the true beginning of the history of mankind.*

His passion silenced and appeased, he lounged comfortably for a while in the commanding officer's chair, gazing out at the night sky intermittently visible through the chestnut trees. Outside the gossamer night sighed and the face of the first lieutenant's wife appeared before him and he could hear once more the duet the rustling leaves had sung with her voice. Thus it was only with a subconscious ear that he heard the voice of the sentry and the clicking of heels, that strangely atavistic sound of gallantry. What happened next therefore came with the abruptness of a shrapnel explosion.

The door opened and in it appeared the real first lieutenant's wife, with her wonderful mouth, her black eyes, and her sweater. She smiled at the tank commander. "Excuse me, but I think I left a basket of plums here."

Danny shot out of his chair as though he'd been caught doing something illicit. "Certainly – of course – please – "

The first lieutenant's wife walked slowly to the coat rack and, sure enough, there was a large wicker basket full of plums. When she lifted it up, it was obviously too heavy for her. But she smiled again, said good-night, and started to leave.

By this time, Danny had almost recovered his wits. He moved to take the basket. "Wait, Mrs. Pinkasová, let me help you with that."

"Oh no, that's all right, I can carry it," she said, but she let him take it anyway. The basket was heavy but at that moment the tank commander could have carried a recoilless cannon. A mere smile from her had moved him to such a flurry of activity that he had lost his tongue.

They walked in silence through the foyer, where the sentry nimbly saluted and gave the tank commander a knowing grin, and suddenly they were outside under the stars. Her footsteps clicked on the pavement as they walked among the barracks, where only the sentries still sat on the steps of the illuminated entranceways, staring at the damp stars and mechanically turning their heads to follow the yellow sweater as it passed. The tank commander battled against a complete mental vacuum; he had turned into a tongue-tied idiot, incapable of uttering a word. The whole thing was clear. She would have to be supernaturally absent-minded to forget the basket; it weighed fifteen kilos, at least. And it was past eleven. She must have remembered it just as Matka and Růžička said good-night to her outside the married officers' quarters on Zephyr Hill and marched off through the night to join their own wives; they would bring those ladies pleasure tonight, at least. The situation was clear, his brain was working brilliantly, logically. Unfortunately, he couldn't think of any good openings. And so it was she who, at the crossroads by the heavy machine shops, said, "It weighs a lot, doesn't it?"

"No, not at all."

"I can take it from here. It's just a short way now."

She put her hand on the handle of the basket. A kittenish

touching of fingers. "And you have to get back to your unit," she said quietly.

A warm finger continued to stroke the back of his hand.

"Go now," she said.

"No, I won't," said the tank commander. "I won't go back."

"You'll get into trouble."

"No I won't. And even if I did – getting in trouble for you would be worth it."

"Would it? And what if they put you in the guardhouse for getting back late?"

"I'd be delighted to spend the night in prison for your sake."

She smiled mysteriously. It was not her normal smile, the one she used with enlisted men and officers alike. But then she turned her profile to him, melancholy, tender, inscrutable. "It's a beautiful night," she said. "But it will soon be autumn."

"Yes," said Danny. "And we'll be going back to civilian life."

"You must be looking forward to that."

"You know how it is – we've been here for two years – "

"I've been here for four," she said. Bitterly, he thought.

"I guess it's not much fun here, is it?"

"You can see that for yourself."

"I can," he said, and was silent again. It was probably better not to talk at all. She belonged in a silent film. With separate musical accompaniment. Her eyes, her mouth, the duet with the chestnut trees, that voice. The wonderful shadows of her thighs....

"Couldn't the Comrade First Lieutenant arrange to be transferred to where life is more interesting?"

"Where? All tank bases are just like this one."

"Sometimes they're located in cities."

Her brow furrowed and she spoke so bitterly it took him aback. "My husband has to stay here."

"Why?"

"He has to, that's all," she said, and again fell silent. Then she said, "If he ever wants them to promote him again, he has to stay here. You must know why, Comrade Tank Commander. You weren't born yesterday."

"Yes, I know why." He knew a lot of things. The kind of things they talked about at the secret sessions of the black-magic circle run by Dr. Sadař, on endlessly boring Sundays which were supposed to be devoted to the joys of the new pulsating life of this super-just, self-satisfied society. There were those, it seemed, who didn't know these things, and it was certainly grave knowledge to have to carry around. But, he told himself, she's certainly not one of those who don't know. There was always a strong bond of rapport between those who knew. At that moment, it merely reinforced the other, more interesting rapport between them.

But the overture heightens the pleasure of the first act. As they walked up Zephyr Hill, towards the tank shooting range and the new housing for officers, they could hear the roar of motors and the dry thud of the cannon, but so far the sound was muted, since it came from the other side of the hill. The Thirtieth had night firing-practice.

The first lieutenant's wife broke the silence again. "You're a student, aren't you?"

"I was. Unfortunately not any longer."

"What did you study?"

"Philosophy."

"So you have a doctorate, right?"

Danny hesitated. The age when people flaunted their academic titles was over. But she belonged to the magic circle.

"Well, yes, I do."

She sighed audibly. "Ah, you're so lucky to have made it. I wanted to go to university too. I wanted to finish high school with a private instructor, but – "

"Why didn't you?"

She shrugged her shoulders. "I got married."

"Did that make it impossible?"

"You're familiar with my husband, aren't you?" Then she added quickly, "Everything is difficult here in Kobylec. Besides, I don't have the head for it, and I had a child soon afterwards – " She tossed her head back. *My rose of Sharon*, said the tank commander to himself, *what do you need to know anything for?*

"It's not something to be concerned about," he said.

"What do you mean by that?"

"Just what I said. Do you think knowing things can bring happiness?"

"I don't know. But it must be nice to know a lot."

"There are nicer things," he assured her.

"I don't think there are," she said. "What you know, no one can take away from you."

"There are other things that can't be taken away from you."

"No there aren't. Everything else can. You can lose everything."

They walked to the top of the hill and to their left, below them, the shooting range sloped away, dark in the greyblackness of the night. Across it moved clusters of little lights and the big black shadows of the tanks. On the slope above the valley, the targets were blinking. The motors roared and phosphorescent tracer shells poured out of the cannon and machine-guns and flew in rapid arcs – which seemed slow, for all that – across the valley and towards the targets.

They stopped, and Danny put the basket of plums on the ground. The shots were cracking and echoing below them, and black figures moved back and forth around the lights. *Lizetka would turn her nose up at her*, he thought, *this igno-*

rant woman with her age beginning to show, tied down with a kid and God knows what desires lurking in her little brain. But Lizetka wouldn't be entirely right. Lizetka, you little bitch from Radlice. You may have a university education, but she'll give me what you won't. You can go to the devil, my dear; I don't understand you anyway.

A new salvo rose from the range below them and Danny looked into her black eyes. Tiny images of the floating tracer bullets swam across their moist, convex surfaces. *You I can understand*, he said to himself. *You I understand, my rose, though that's nothing special, everyone understands you. And the rumour about you is probably the straight goods.*

"My dear Comrade Tank Commander," said the first lieutenant's wife, as though to confirm the rumour, "what are we waiting for?"

So he waited no longer.

"Take me home, Jana," he said. "I want to go home with you."

She took his head in her hands and kissed him. "I bet you do. You don't have to tell me. This little soldier's been here two whole years. Two whole years he's been bored to death. And now he can kiss the wife of First Lieutenant Pinkas."

"Who is sweet and beautiful."

"Beautiful." She frowned. No matter what she did, she looked good. "So beautiful that all the soldiers turn to look at her, and none of them believes she's faithful to her first lieutenant."

Danny laughed.

"Not even the tank commander, does he?"

He shrugged. "He hopes," he said, "that if she is, she'll make an exception in his case."

"She won't. Because she's not a faithful wife. Not in the least."

He embraced her and she began to kiss him hungrily in the middle of the road. The night wind sighed, the motors roared from the shooting range, the tank tracks rattled, orders were shouted. Then she pulled away from him and said, "Come."

She walked quickly down the road in the moonlight, and he picked up the basket and strode breathlessly behind her. They turned off at a group of new apartments. She walked around one of the buildings and stopped at the door. A red flare arced into the sky. She unlocked the door and they went inside. When she'd locked the door behind them, he embraced her again. She kissed him hard and hungrily and said, "It won't be long now."

Jana, said the tank commander to himself. *An ordinary, frustrated, neglected officer's wife – but what a woman! She's sad. She's sad, as most people are. Why not make her happy? Why not make myself happy?* He was filled by the moment, the intoxicating night, the tanks, the end of his two years in the army. Everything filled him to overflowing. He put it all out of his mind and followed her upstairs. On the third floor she unlocked a door and let him in.

"Be quiet," she whispered. "Little Honza's asleep."

She led him to her marriage bed, which smelled of cleanness and fresh air. There were delicate white curtains on the window. When he was lying naked beside her under the covers, he said, "Janička, I – " but she put a hand over his mouth and said, "Don't say anything. Just be quiet. And hold me tight. Don't talk at all, just be here with me, my bad darling, you shouldn't be doing this, oh no, because they'll lock you up for it, and I'll tell them you made me do it, because I'm a faithful wife and not a slut, but can I help it if everything is so – so – just wait, Daniel in the lion's den, oh, how you're going to regret this! But now be happy with me, be happy with me," she babbled on and held him tightly to herself.

This has to happen at the end of my hitch – at the bloody end. What a stupid, cruel joke! I've only got a month left. I could have been rolling about with her for two years, just as others must have, and instead I burned for Lizetka, that bitch from Radlice, that hypnotic piece of ice. Janinka. You don't know what you have until you begin to lose it. When it's almost over. That stupid law of life. Everything comes too late. Too late.

He lay beside her, he lay with her, and outside the window the golden tracers arched through the sky and struck the burning targets, which were visible from the bed because they were on the opposite slope. And so they made love against the background of a fireworks display, while the tanks roared and snorted and clattered across the terrain with their heavy tracks chewing up the sod and Jana kissed him and ran her eager hands over his body. And all at once she gave an angry laugh and said, "Tanks! Tanks! You sweet, impudent foolish boy! Those stupid, idiotic tanks!"

3

A NIGHT IN

THE GUARDHOUSE

Private Bamza walked down the corridor of the guard-house jangling a cluster of keys, banging on each of the cell doors and calling out as he went, "Piss parade, gentlemen. Piss parade."

Of all his duties as an assistant prisoner escort, he carried this one out most diligently. There was, however, a reason for his diligence. Thanks to the brilliant architectural design provided by the Austro-Hungarian builder, the part of the prison meant for the involuntary accommodation of detainees was separated by an enormous iron grille from the area containing facilities for the prison warden and guards. Regulations said (and they were strictly observed because of frequent spot-checks) that the grille was to remain locked day and night, and at night the individual cell doors were to be locked as well. The problem was that the detainees' toilets were located on the guards' side of the grille. One of the assistant escort's duties, regardless of the time of day or night, was to unlock first the cell door and then the grille for any detainee who wished to relieve himself, so it wasn't surprising that Bamza, otherwise a slacker, was conscientious in making sure that the prisoners used the facilities before retiring. Another reason for his extraordinary conscientiousness was the inscrutability of military fate, in which today's escort might, as easily as not, become tomorrow's prisoner.

A clamorous, happy crowd burst out of the cell doors, holding their trousers up with their hands, their belts having been confiscated. Here and there a member of the mechanized infantry regiment, still shod in lace-up boots but minus the laces, shuffled along the hall, dragging his feet to keep his boots on. This company of detainees, deprived of all means of suicide by hanging, crowded noisily into the little room provided for the exercise of bodily functions. Those who couldn't fit in rushed to the stairwell leading to the main entrance, extracted cigarettes from secret places in their uniforms, and cadged lights from the duty guard. Glad of this momentary relief from two hours of boredom, the guard shifted his automatic rifle from the regulation position against his stomach to the forbidden rest position on his back and, looking carefully over his shoulder, lit up too.

The officer of the guards, a young lieutenant in basic training named Malina, walked up the stairs from the yard. In the moonlight pouring down the low red-brick façade of the building, his fleshy pink cheeks grew darker. Against all regulations, he had shown up without his cap. He walked down the corridor, pulled out a cigarette case, offered it round, and then accepted a light from Sandor Nagy, a soldier of gypsy nationality who was serving the twenty-third detention of his two-year stint in the army.

Nagy struck up a conversation at once. "Well then, Comrade Lieutenant, how much longer you got to go?"

"A couple of weeks," said the lieutenant, and he laughed contentedly.

"You lucky, Comrade Lieutenant," sighed Nagy.

The lieutenant wasn't familiar with Nagy's military career, and he said, "Aren't you getting out in a couple of weeks too?"

Sandor Nagy made a sour, hopeless expression, waved his

hand dismissively, and said, "Yo, Maria, it's a hell of a couple of weeks. Those sons of bitches make me eat extra time."

Several detainees gave surly, sarcastic laughs. "What did you do?" asked Malina.

"Nothing," said Nagy in a hurt, unhappy voice. "Buddy of mine write me a letter, say my wife cheating on me, so I go for a recce."

"Without a pass?"

"All right, without a pass," Nagy admitted. "You know how it is, Comrade Lieutenant. I am so jealous I have to take a look. I can't wait until the Comrade Captain give me special pass."

"Did the recce take long?"

"It sure did, Comrade Lieutenant," said Nagy bitterly. "I come home and the wife, she not there. She go to the Erdessys', my mother say. So I go to the Erdessys' and when I arrive Uncle Kolman sit in the living room and my wife nowhere. I say: Uncle Kolman, where's my wife? How should I know? he say. You should keep better eye on her, Sandor. The radio say you're in the army to protect your wives and children. So protect her, dammit, and don't bother me no more about it. That piss me off, and I'm so mad I punch my uncle in the teeth and he do the same to me. Then Istvan, my cousin, show up and light into me. So I show him some knuckle too and the teeth fly. Then Istvan start screaming and yelling and Lajoš and Ferenc, both my cousins too, they show up and start throwing punches and the four of them rearrange me so neat I end up in the hospital for a week. And that's where the army catch up with me."

"And where was your wife?"

"Don't even ask, Comrade Lieutenant." Sandor waved his hands again. "She with the other Erdessys, the ones who are my father's sister-in-law's cousin's wife's second nephew once removed."

Sandor spat across the small, concrete courtyard right into the centre of a round, mosaic-like portrait of an unrecognizable dignitary. The other prisoners laughed derisively again. Private Bamza emerged from the gloom of the corridor and rattled his keys.

"Attention, gentlemen," he said. "We're in for some fun."

"Fun?" said a bored prisoner skeptically. He had a thick growth of stubble and was lounging on the steps.

"I left Mitzinka's cell door locked," said Bamza. "Just listen and wait a minute."

Everyone fell silent, and in that silence they could hear one of the guards snoring in the service room, and the faint slap of playing-cards on a table. Standing orders were being broken right inside the guardhouse. Otherwise the silence was absolute, with the faintly audible hush of the Indian-summer evening in the background, disturbed by the creaking of a chair and the sound of metal-shod boots on the concrete floor. Tank Commander Danny Smiřický – on duty as a prisoner escort – appeared in the doorway of the command room. His belt was loose and the weight of his service revolver, in its scuffed holster, had pulled it far below his waist. The unusual silence had roused him from the half-sleep he had fallen into as part of his duties.

"What's going on?" he asked when he saw the small circle of men listening closely at the door leading into the prison.

"Quiet!" snapped Bamza. "We're listening for Mitzi."

Danny didn't understand, but he leaned obediently against the doorframe, put his hands in his pockets, and cocked one leg across the other. Suddenly the din of sharp blows on an iron door echoed through the building, as though an alarm had gone off. Bamza grinned knowingly but didn't move. The blows echoed through the prison again and this time, through the dusky corridor, came the sound of a high but not unpleasant woman's voice.

"Hey, you greenhorns! Open up! Let me outa here!"

Bamza's face turned red from the effort of not laughing. Sandor Nagy slapped his thighs. The wailing female voice on the other side of the door kept on: "Open the door, boys! Come on! Open the goddamn door!"

Bamza had to bite on a dirty khaki handkerchief to keep from laughing. The voice now began to threaten. "You sons of bitches! I don't care if you open up or not. But just remember, you'll have to clean up the mess yourselves."

"Open her door," said Lieutenant Malina in a worried voice.

"I'm going to count to twenty, and if the door isn't open by then, get yourselves a bucket and some rags, you turkeys, because you're going to need them."

In response to Malina's order, Bamza slowly got to his feet. Nagy held him back.

"Wait, Comrade Lieutenant," he whispered. "I've got an idea. Boys, come here."

The detainees gathered around him. In a feverish whisper that Danny couldn't hear, he explained his plan. Then Nagy's voice, full of suppressed laughter, rose and the tank commander could pick out the words "and I'll give the order."

The snickering group of detainees crowded into the corridor. Behind the cell door, a voice was already counting. The detainees formed two lines, one on either side of the corridor, then Private Bamza marched down between them, rattling the keys. The voice had already counted to twenty and was beginning to issue another ultimatum when Bamza unlocked the cell door, bowed deeply, and said, "At your service, madame."

A slender young woman appeared in the doorway of the cell. She was wearing a tight green sweatsuit and regulation slippers, and looked like a star basketball player. She tossed back her pretty head and stuck out her tongue at Bamza. At that moment, Sandor Nagy's stentorian voice roared out: "Ah – ten – SHUN!"

The two rows of men snapped to attention, sucked in their stomachs, and saluted with the utmost rigidity. Career Sergeant Marie Babinčáková – known as Mitzi – made a face and stuck out her tongue at Sandor Nagy. Whether it was because of her terrific sex appeal, or because of the sex starvation prevalent in the camp, the crotches of most men bulged conspicuously. Sergeant Babinčáková made another face, pointed to the rigidly saluting hands, and said:

"Use your palms elsewhere, gentlemen."

Then she spun around and vanished into the toilets.

The detainees burst out laughing. "Yo, Maria!" Sandor said. "She got a mouth on her like a shark."

"Now, gentlemen, time to hit the sack." Bamza was hoarsely trying to re-establish his authority. "Lights out!" Chatting cheerfully among themselves, the detainees began to straggle back to their cells. Soon the plank beds could be heard creaking, and the voices gradually fell silent.

The tank commander pushed himself away from the doorway and began his rounds. He walked through the open grille and looked into the first cell on his left. It was a large room with a long wooden bench around the perimeter on which twenty detainees tried to arrange their bodies in the most comfortable positions possible. The bench squeaked and complained and the room was filled with the fusty smell of carrion and human bodies. He walked on. Besides the large cell – which was for those who'd been given night detention – there was a row of cells with two beds each, for those doing hard time. At the end of the corridor were several isolation cells. Meanwhile Bamza was locking the doors on the other side of the corridor. Danny walked back to the grille, waited until Bamza had locked all the cells, and took the keys from him.

"I'm going to cork off," said Bamza. "Don't wake me up before two-fifteen."

"Don't worry," said Danny. Bamza disappeared into the escorts' room and the tank commander leaned against the grille. He sighed, thinking — though it was pointless to do so — about his wretched luck. Now, when his stint was almost up, this other stint, far more pleasant, was just beginning. Even so, he knew that next morning he'd do everything in his power to get to Prague on Sunday to see Lizetka. This was because Jana had announced that First Lieutenant Pinkas would be spending the weekend — his third this year — with his family. I'm a real whore, he thought. These two women are whores too, each in her own way, but whores all the same. We're all whores — a republic of whores, he thought, turning and looking back down the grey, bare corridor at the rectangle of the main entrance into the prison, and the figure of Lieutenant Malina silhouetted against the starry sky and the swaying trees.

Sergeant Mitzi Babinčáková emerged from the latrines and walked down the corridor towards him in her green sweatsuit. He made room for her to pass, then followed her back to her cell. Just outside the door, she turned around.

"Are you going to lock me in, Comrade Tank Commander?"

"It's orders, comrade."

"But I don't like being locked up."

"I don't like having to lock you up, either. But" — he made an apologetic face — "I've only got a couple of weeks to go, you know how it is."

"Sure," and she cast him a look of regret. "So I guess I won't see you, then. Good-night." And she slammed the cell door in his face. He turned and walked back to the command room, where a light was burning. Malina was sitting there already, and stared at the tank commander with his forget-me-not eyes.

"Did you lock everything up?"

"Yeah," said Danny, sitting down at the table. Scattered along its length were three unwashed mess tins with scraps of supper left in them, two tin cups of coffee, half a loaf of rye bread, a chunk of salami that someone had bitten into, and three slices of dirty bacon. Amid this debris were two books —one called *Brave Churgali*, bearing the stamp of the base library, and the other Graham Greene's *Stamboul Train*, a considerably dog-eared volume the tank commander had borrowed specially for night duty from Private First Class Dr. Mlejnek, who was a strait-laced Catholic.

Danny pulled a crumpled letter from a pocket on the leg of his coveralls and smoothed it out on the table in front of him.

"It'll be okay tonight," said Malina absently. "Kámen's on duty rounds, and I figure he'll just fuck the dog as usual."

"That's for sure," the tank commander agreed. "We'll have a quiet night."

"That's what I think," said the lieutenant. He raised a tin cup of coffee, took a drink, set it back on the table, and wiped his mouth with his sleeve. "Well then," he said genially, "I guess I'll – take a walk. Know what I mean?"

"Good," said Danny. The lieutenant's blue eyes looked into his, seeking a sign that he'd understood.

"If – ah – if Kámen does happen to show up," the mild-mannered officer went on, "tell him I've gone to check on the guards, okay? He doesn't give a shit anyway."

"Good," the tank commander said again. "I'll tell him."

"Well." The lieutenant stared blankly at the floor. Then he looked at Danny once more. "So – I'm off, then."

"Fine. Go right ahead."

"Right." The lieutenant got to his feet, stretched, and stood there indecisively, apparently examining the walls. "So, I'm on my way," he said, and he took a step towards the door, then stopped again. *What are you waiting for*, Danny said to himself. *She's been for a piss and she's ready and waiting for you.* Malina coughed, and suddenly Danny realized what the lieutenant's irresolution was all about, and felt ashamed for causing the discreet philanderer embarrassment.

"I'm sorry, Comrade Lieutenant!" He jumped to his feet, rushed out into the corridor, walked quickly to the grille, and unlocked it. He could hear the lieutenant's heavy footsteps behind him. They walked to the cell, and Danny unlocked it and peered in. Nothing moved. The lieutenant slipped inside.

"Right," he said from the darkness. "Lock me in and come for me when it's time to change the guard. If anyone shows up, I've gone out to check on the sentries."

"Good," said Danny. "Enjoy yourselves."

"Thanks, comrade," came a female voice from the darkness.

The tank commander peered into the cell briefly, then locked the door and went back to the command room. He sat down at the table and looked at the letter spread out on it. It was from his cousin Alena, an actress who had made a name for herself not long ago playing a sweet young shock worker in a play called *Goat Droppings*, and later in a film with the same title. She was supposed to be finding Danny a job in Prague.

Dear cousin,

I've arranged everything. You can start work the minute you get out. I'm looking forward to seeing you, and what you look like in uniform. You never once came to visit us in all those years in the army. You didn't even come to the theatre. Maybe our place is too far from Radlice, and a soldier has only so much time, doesn't he? My husband, and Comrade Robert Neumann, send their greetings.

When you come to Prague, show your face at the theatre, at least.

Your cousin,
Alena

The bitch, he thought. *How did she smoke out all that gossip? But I suppose Prague's a village and it's impossible to keep a secret.* He recalled the warm, twinkling stars above Radlice Hill, and then the warm, twinkling stars over the shooting range, and to his inner fancy the sweetly melancholy face of Janinka appeared, and was replaced by the basilisk eyes of the girl called Lizetka. *Just suppose,* he thought, and the very idea sent cold chills through him, *suppose someone smokes this romance out too? Pinkas would shoot me. Or he'd divorce her and I'd have to marry her. Not one of those nice bourgeoise girls, but Janinka.* She'd no longer be forbidden fruit. There'd no longer be the excitement of expecting an angry, battle-seasoned husband with his own service revolver to return at any moment. Perhaps Janinka wouldn't be the same without her avenger in the wings, lurching over well-travelled military roads in an armoured car while the fawning little tank commander and his wife…oh, damn! Who could say? He folded the letter, placed a reassuring hand on the pistol in his holster, and fell into a reverie again.

Outside, in front of the guardhouse, the slow, even steps of the sentry's ironshod boots clacked on the pavement of the courtyard. The prison air was alive with the silent music of human respiration. *Everyone's asleep*, the tank commander reflected, *and they're dreaming of cars, motorcycles, girls, journeys home, journeys into the world. Right about now Lieutenant Malina must be shooting microscopic carriers of pink-faced, blue-eyed little Malinas into a rubber lodged deep inside Sergeant Babinčáková, if he's even that careful. The iron First Lieutenant Pinkas must be preparing to carry out his marital duties for the first time in a long while. Captain Matka's probably expected to do something similar, but he's no doubt asleep by now. Janinka's lying in bed and looking at the stars above the shooting range and thinking of me. At least, I hope she's thinking of me. Lizetka will be lying with one of her lovers, allowing him lascivious touches but no more – and as far as I'm concerned she can go to....* He yawned and stretched. His belt was too tight so he took it off and put it on the table, along with his revolver. His waking thoughts began to mingle with the confused events of dreams. His head nodded. He fended off sleep for a while, forcing his eyes to stay open, but at last he too succumbed, to tedium, exhaustion, and dissatisfaction.

He came awake with a sudden start, thinking he'd heard the sentry outside whistle. The sound seemed to penetrate his body, and he wasn't sure whether he'd actually heard it or was still dreaming. He quickly stood up, reached for his revolver, and tried to buckle it on, but his hands were clumsy from sleep and wouldn't obey him. And so he was standing by the table, his feet slightly apart, his face looking down at his stomach, where he was trying in vain to hook the end of his belt to the buckle with the lion, when the door flew open to reveal the Pygmy Devil.

Danny snapped to attention, his left hand holding the belt against his stomach while his right hand flew to his temple in a salute. Too late, he realized that he had left his cap on the table, so he lowered his arm and looked steadily into the Pygmy Devil's eyes. Like an indignant god, Major Borovička planted his legs, in their tiny riding-pants, apart, put his hands on his hips, and, as always, filled his expression with the most concentrated mix of threat and hatred he could muster.

"Comrade Major," the tank commander chanted, his left hand still holding his belt, "during my watch in the guardhouse there has been nothing special to report. Number of detainees: forty-two. All accounted for, and taking their nightly rest. Prisoner escort, Tank Commander Smiřický reporting."

He finished speaking and stood at attention. The major looked up and drilled him with a penetrating glance, but said nothing. In the silence that followed, Danny could hear Bamza crawling out of his bunk next door.

"Comrade Tank Commander," the Pygmy Devil began, "what are the duties of a prisoner escort?"

Danny couldn't recall what they were — he couldn't recall ever having read about a prisoner escort's duties — so he said only what was obvious. "The prisoner escort is responsible for order in the prison. He opens and locks the cells, he ensures that the prisoners are properly escorted to and from work, he carries out head counts, he ensures that prisoners do not smoke or possess items that might be used to inflict injuries, he ensures that — "

"May a prisoner escort take off his weapon while on duty?" the major interrupted coldly.

"He may not."

"Have you behaved accordingly?"

"I have not," Danny admitted.

"How is that possible?" asked the major.

Danny was silent.

"How is that possible, Comrade Tank Commander?"

There was no answer, because there was no excuse for not observing standing orders. Why try to invent extenuating circumstances when they wouldn't extenuate anything? The hell with it. Into the fire. "I did it out of carelessness and neglect," Danny said firmly.

This confession took some of the wind out of the Pygmy Devil's sails. His cheeks puffed out and a nerve in his temple twitched. "Well then," he said after a long pause. "At least you're admitting it. But this carelessness, this neglect, this ignorance of the orders, does not excuse you. Where is your assistant?"

"He's asleep."

"Wake him up."

Danny turned around, managing to buckle his belt as he did so. He opened the door, revealing Bamza, who was standing by the bed with a dumb look on his face.

"Comrade Private, come here," he ordered. Bamza moved forward, came through the door, stood in front of the major, and said in a crude, obscenely hoarse voice, "Assistant prisoner escort, Private Bamza."

The Pygmy Devil looked him up and down. Then he said nastily, "How many detainees do you have?"

Bamza hesitated, frowned, then blurted, "Forty-five."

"Show me the report," ordered the major. While he was studying the paper, Danny wondered what to do about Malina. He was afraid. After all, this would mean time in the clink — and extra time in the army. Oddly enough, the latter thought suddenly made him less afraid. It would also mean prolonging his affair with Janinka. *That girl is having a good influence on me*, he thought. *She's making me brave. Maybe I'll marry her after all. If Pinkas doesn't shoot me first.* He looked calmly at the Pygmy Devil, who was carefully preparing to fly into a rage.

"According to this report," he said icily, "you have exactly forty-one detainees, Comrade Tank Commander. How is that possible?"

"That's the correct number, Comrade Major."

"Then how is it possible that you said forty-two?"

"I was wrong, Comrade Major."

"How is that possible?"

"I forgot what the exact count was."

"How is that possible?"

The major's circular litany angered the tank commander. "I carelessly neglected to read the report," he shot back. *If he says, "How is that possible?" one more time....*

But the major turned to Bamza instead. "You said forty-five. How is that possible?"

Bamza scowled.

"How is that possible?"

"I thought that's how many there are."

"How is that possible?"

"I have a lousy memory. I can't remember nothing," growled Bamza, and his scowl was almost as intense as the major's. Borovička's universal question didn't apply to this. The orders didn't say that a private was compelled not to be an idiot. This was the final refuge of all soldiers – except for the few unlucky ones with university degrees, who couldn't hide behind stupidity.

The Pygmy Devil snorted, then turned back to the tank commander and asked the question he'd been expecting: "And where is the duty officer?"

Now there was trouble. Danny replied as Malina had instructed him, but there was faint hope the Pygmy Devil would swallow it. "He's out checking on the guards, Comrade Major."

"Very well, then," said Borovička. "Show me the guardhouse."

The tank commander took the ring of keys, stepped out into the corridor, and walked towards the grille. The murky light was on, as regulations required, and the sentry's footsteps in the yard sounded crisper and more watchful than they usually did. *Things are pretty much as they should be,* Danny said to himself. *Except for one cell. Perhaps he'll get tired of the inspection before he gets to that one.* He unlocked the grille, which creaked as he opened it, and the little major trotted into the prison.

"Show me the men with one-night detentions."

The tank commander obediently unlocked the cell door and turned on the light. In the large room, the prisoners lay jammed up together on the benches beside each other. The bright light woke some of the delinquents, and voices were raised saying, "What the fuck!" and "Turn off the fucking light!" but they fell silent again. Then a frightened soldier realized what was going on, jumped to his feet, and yelled, "Atten – SHUN!"

A handful of detainees half-raised themselves on their elbows to see what was going on. The older and more experienced ones pretended to be asleep. Perhaps the Pygmy Devil had originally had no intention of waking them up, but such an obvious lack of respect angered him. He ordered Danny to give the order to fall in and then he carried out a thorough inspection, with disastrous results. Six of the detainees were found possessing cigarettes, five of them had pocket knives, one of them had a crucifix hidden in an eyeglasses case. The Pygmy Devil also confiscated a mickey of rum, several condoms, and four live rounds of pistol ammunition. He ordered a precise record made of everything they found. Danny felt as though he were writing out his own death warrant.

They went into two more large cells, and two cells for prisoners on longer detention. An inspection of these areas revealed further packets of illicit cigarettes, a notebook filled with verse of a rather salacious and anti-military nature, four pulp novels, and a piece of salami weighing about a kilo, all of which would be entered in the record against the prisoner escort. But the greatest disaster was yet to come. Now they stood in front of the isolation cell where the career sergeant was imprisoned.

"Who's in this one?"

"Sergeant Babinčáková. Fifteen days' detention."

"Hmm," said the Pygmy Devil. For a moment it seemed that discretion would triumph over natural curiosity. Unfortunately, Lieutenant Malina was ignorant of what was going on, and suddenly his deep male groans emerged from the cell. The Pygmy Devil flushed a deep red. "Open the door," he hissed.

Danny stepped up to the door and began fumbling noisily through the ring of keys. He took his time.

"Make it snappy!"

The fateful key was found and slipped into the lock. Inside, they could hear the sounds of someone thrashing about, while the cot creaked and groaned. Then there was a suppressed yelp of panic. For a while longer, Danny tried to pretend the lock was stuck, but the Pygmy Devil impatiently pushed him out of the way and unlocked the door himself. He flicked on the light. The naked bulb cast its dim glow over the spartan cell. Standing at attention beside the cot was a red-faced Lieutenant Malina, in an unbuttoned tunic and trousers with the fly open, capless, revolverless, and staring at the Pygmy Devil with horror-struck forget-me-not eyes. Behind him, on the cot, lay Sergeant Babinčáková, covering herself modestly, if incompletely, with a crumpled green sweatshirt.

For a moment it looked like a diorama: the Pygmy Devil, the naked sergeant, and the lieutenant, with the pale tank commander looking on helplessly in the background. Then Malina, obviously addled by fear, pulled himself up to stand at full attention and declared in a sonorous voice, "Comrade Major, during my watch in the guardhouse there has been nothing special to report. Officer of the guards, Lieutenant Malina."

"Bring your pistol and come with me," said the Pygmy Devil icily. "You," he said, addressing the sergeant, who had assumed the position of a reclining Venus, "will remain here." And to Danny: "Lock the cell."

While the other two men walked out of the cell and strode briskly down the corridor towards the command room, Danny winked at the sergeant, who was frowning but still had the presence of mind to stick her tongue out at him. He clasped his hands together in a gesture of begging forgiveness, and locked her in the cell. Looking down the corridor, he saw the

stunned figure of Lieutenant Malina silhouetted against the light, tottering after the major, his service revolver swinging back and forth on its belt. Bamza, who was standing beside Danny, leaned over and whispered hoarsely, "He's going to have to eat a whole pile of shit, man."

"So are we," said the tank commander quietly, and started off after the lieutenant. He heard Bamza behind him wheezing, "But we don't know nothing, do we? As far as we know, he went out to check on the sentries."

"And who locked him in?" Danny shot back as he closed the grille.

"Oh shit, you've got a point there!" said Bamza gloomily. They both stepped into the command room. The Pygmy Devil decided to sit on the table, for effect. He raised his buttocks and felt awkwardly for the edge of the table, but couldn't reach it. He tried standing on his toes and wriggling his behind, but that didn't work either. He was enraged. He turned scarlet and sat down on a chair, hungry for blood. The chubby lieutenant stood stiffly at attention in front of him. He hadn't dared do up his tunic or close his fly, or even buckle on his revolver. His eyes were wide with fear, and greasy beads of sweat appeared on his forehead. Danny remained to one side. The Pygmy Devil looked from one to the other, then said to Danny, "Send your assistant out of the room."

This could mean only one thing. The officer and the noncom would be served, in the absence of ordinary soldiers, what was euphemistically referred to in regulations as "a verbal reprimand". Danny turned to Bamza and said, "Go next door."

"As you were!" shrieked the major.

Danny turned to face him.

"Don't you know how to give an order properly, Comrade Tank Commander?"

"I do, Comrade Major."

"Then why don't you do it properly?"

You swine, thought Danny, but he swallowed his disgust and uttered the only sentence possible in the situation:

"Comrade Major, request permission to give an order to Private Bamza."

"Permission granted."

"Comrade Private," Danny said with theatrical severity, "go to the other room!"

Bamza scowled, then wheezed hoarsely: "Yes, sir!" He clicked his heels together and left the room. The silence grew. The others could hear the sentry making his rounds in the courtyard.

With some effort, the Pygmy Devil crossed his legs, stretching his breeches tightly across his genitals, then just sat there drumming his fingers on the table-top. In his tiny, close-fitting outfit, he looked like a child whose parents have perversely dressed him to look like an adult. His small eyes radiated evil, and the evil focused on the innocent, rosy face of Lieutenant Malina, who stood beside Danny like Lot's wife.

"Comrade Lieutenant," the Pygmy Devil began, "is this your idea of the proper way to carry out guard duties?"

A dramatic pause. The lieutenant opened his mouth wider and emitted a sound somewhere between a belch and a death rattle. Then silence again. Over the silence came the grand, overwhelming question: "How is this possible?"

Danny noticed that Malina had turned almost brown, as though he were about to have a heart attack — which, given his age, was hardly likely. His adam's apple rose, he swallowed, and once more he emitted that strange acoustic expression of consternation. The little major drummed his fingers on the table, while outside the window they could hear the sharp footfalls of the sentry. The rhythm of his metallic steps and the rhythm of the major's drumming were out of phase. The lieutenant emitted another sound. The Pygmy Devil stopped drumming, gave a short, final, four-finger roll, and then, to Danny's great delight, began tapping his fingers in time to the footfalls. It was a strange duet, almost like African drumming. Again the Pygmy Devil said, "How is this possible?"

By now the veins on the lieutenant's forehead were prominent; drops of perspiration ran down his cheeks and dripped onto his buttoned tunic. The wretched officer gathered all his strength and said hoarsely, "I don't know...."

"What did you say?" squealed the Pygmy Devil. "Are you a sleepwalker? Don't you know what you're doing? How could you abandon your post like that?"

The lieutenant muttered something hoarse and inaudible.

"Are you a sleepwalker?"

"No."

"Then how is it possible that you abandoned your post?"

"I don't know." The lieutenant's voice sounded desperate.

"How can you stand there and say, 'I don't know'?"

Silence. The lieutenant, whose complexion was now as dark as a glass of Malaga, cleared his throat, but all he could say was another "I don't know."

"Are you an officer? Can't you speak? Can't you face the consequences of your actions? Well? Answer me!"

"Yes," said the lieutenant.

"Yes what? Can you or can't you?"

"No."

The little major went into another fit of rage. "Yes or no?" he screamed.

"Yes," mumbled the lieutenant, and then, as though afraid he'd given the wrong answer, he quickly added, "No."

"Comrade Lieutenant, I am not here for your personal amusement. Have you any idea what lies ahead for you? Have you any idea what you've just done? Or don't you?"

"Yes," said the lieutenant.

"Yes you don't? So you don't know?"

"No," said the lieutenant quickly, but as soon as the word was out, he hurried to correct himself. "I mean yes."

The major was about to shout at him again, but instead he took off his cap and set it on the table. He took a big khaki handkerchief from his pocket and wiped his forehead, and began again, forcing himself to be calm. "Look here, Comrade Lieutenant. Just tell me, slowly and calmly – what led you to abandon your post?"

Lieutenant Malina swallowed. The Pygmy Devil's face twitched, but he waited for the answer. The lieutenant gathered his strength to reply; a rough sound emerged from somewhere deep in his voluminous chest and, with some effort, Danny could distinguish the words "Comrade Babinčáková".

"So," said the major. "A woman, in other words. Tell me, comrade, do you know what a soldier's greatest enemy is?"

"No," sighed the lieutenant.

"Women," said the major. His voice was hard, the voice of experience. "I'm not referring to our own women, at home, whose security we are safeguarding here. I mean other women. Do you know the kind I mean?"

"Yes," admitted the lieutenant.

The major snorted, pushed his cap back on his head. "Women like that lead a soldier astray," he said, in the voice of a disciplinarian. "They weaken his vigilance. They make him inattentive to his duties. They encourage him to reveal military secrets. Consciously or unconsciously, they make a soldier the conscious or unconscious agent of the enemy, do you understand me? And the same things apply to Sergeant Babinčáková."

"No!" the lieutenant blurted. The intensity of his protest surprised the Pygmy Devil.

"What do you mean, no?" he said.

Malina blushed until his complexion was almost black, then swallowed and said in a croaking voice, "She didn't want me to – to – reveal any – secrets. It's true I wasn't being very vigilant, but all she wanted was – was – " He stopped, groping for the right word.

"Come on, out with it."

" – just – "

"She just wanted what? Answer in a complete sentence."

But the lieutenant didn't answer in a complete sentence. With an overpowering sense of shame, he mumbled something scarcely audible, something that sounded like "sexual intercourse".

"And you can stand there and say this, just like that?" said the Pygmy Devil, as though he couldn't believe his ears. "You're a perfect example of what's wrong with this army. Oh, I know. You think that because your term of service is over in a few weeks, you can get away with anything. But you're wrong, you're terribly, terribly wrong. It won't be a few weeks now, comrade, but a few *months*. This kind of dereliction of duty must be severely punished, or pretty soon we wouldn't have an army at all, we'd have one big brothel. You ought to be ashamed of yourself, Comrade Lieutenant."

The Pygmy Devil stood up and his cheeks were flushed with red. "You, a son of the working class, who put you in a responsible position, and this is how you behave. This is unforgivable, Comrade Lieutenant. This is treason against the working class. Are you aware of the implications of your disgusting, loathsome, and filthy act? Are you aware that you deserve the strictest possible punishment?"

"Yes," said Malina meekly. In civilian life he had been a cook, and he had hoped to be one in the army as well. But because he'd been a good cook from a once unemployed family, his positive vetting report was excellent, so he was destined for greater things. Thus Malina became the commander of a tank troop, and in the mess he was compelled to eat the disgusting fare served up by a recruit who in civilian life had been an accountant with a tailoring co-operative.

"And you, Comrade Tank Commander," added the Pygmy Devil. "You blithely undo your belt, lay aside your weapon, and allow this kind of thing to go on."

"I was obeying orders," Danny protested.

The major exploded again. "Do you know the regulations?"

"Yes, I do."

"Do you know that you are within your rights to refuse to obey an order that goes against the interests of the people? I would say that is precisely the case with the orders that Lieutenant Malina gave you."

"No," said Danny impudently. "First I have to obey the order, then I can lodge a complaint."

The major was suddenly unsure of himself. Was there really a regulation about not obeying orders, or was it just wishful thinking? Finally he concluded that he must be right, since he was the officer.

"You don't know the regulations very well," he said. "You do have such a right. Why didn't you exercise it?"

"I intended to lodge a complaint."

"When?"

"When I came off duty."

"Don't tell me fairytales!" shrieked Borovička. "I know you, I can just imagine you lodging a complaint. But don't think we don't know all about you. You're relying on your cleverness to get you through, but you're making a mistake." He hated NCOs with university degrees. He knew they were laughing at him inside, and it was too much. "You're making an *enormous* mistake," he exploded. "Our People's Democratic Army will expose you to the light of day! We know who the class enemy are! And we will make short work of them! We'll show them where their true place is! And it's not here, Comrade Tank Commander, with the guard unit. Enemies of the people do not belong here."

"Comrade Major, I'm going to lodge a complaint against you," said Danny, surprised by his own pluck.

"A complaint?" The major turned as black as Malina had been a few moments ago. "You go right ahead and complain, Comrade Tank Commander. You will be entirely within your rights. But don't think you're going to use those rights to undermine the fighting spirit of our People's Democratic Army. The two of you make a fine pair. But we've been watching your battalion and its strange morale for some time now, and I can tell you, we're not going to leave it at that. Your men are shiftless, negligent, and insubordinate. They read trash and worse. But we will take measures, comrades, and I assure you they will be harsh measures. Bolshevik measures. And then you'll regret it. But by that time it'll be too late."

The Pygmy Devil stood up and straightened his uniform with an abrupt gesture. "When you go off duty, both of you will report to your superior officers," he said brusquely, and marched out of the room.

When the sound of the major's boots had died away in the courtyard and the night had swallowed up his tiny, malevolent spirit, Malina turned with an embarrassed smile to the tank commander and said, "There's going to be hell to pay."

"It won't be so bad," Danny reassured him, although he knew it would. He felt sorry for the frightened lieutenant, and wanted to put his mind at ease.

"Why didn't you come and get me?" asked the miserable officer hopelessly.

"It was impossible. He was in here before I knew it."

Bamza walked into the room. "Whoo-eee," he said. "There's going to be hell to pay!"

And then, with the generous, easy grin of someone who is too unimportant for anything to happen to, he turned to the lieutenant and asked with genuine interest, "Well, Comrade Lieutenant, did you at least get laid?"

4

THE ARMY

CREATIVITY CONTEST

Danny did not report to his commanding officer as ordered. It was late Friday afternoon, and he felt the tug of Prague. Not only was Lieutenant Pinkas spending the weekend at home with his family, but Danny had read in an army newspaper that in the auditorium of the Nth Division there was going to be a gala evening that night for winners of the Army Creativity Contest. The winner in the poetry division was Robert Neumann, Lizetka's husband, so it was clear that he wouldn't be home with his wife. And though the tank commander was now under the spell of a new and quite different poetry – the poetry of tracer bullets and stars above the shooting range – he didn't want to waste this new chance to try the marital fidelity of that strange woman, Lizetka.

To avoid possible complications with Captain Matka, he used the underground railway that the men of the Seventh Tank Battalion usually took to freedom. As soon as his shift in the guardhouse was over, he went straight to the attic in battalion headquarters where the wardrobe was kept, donned his walking-out uniform, determined from the duty officer that the CO was at supper, picked up an exit permit from the duty officer, forged the captain's signature on it, then called on Private First Class Dr. Mlejnek, the battalion scribe. Using a skeleton key, Dr. Mlejnek opened the steel strongbox containing the unit's official stamps, and took one and stamped the falsified document, thus confirming its authenticity. Then the tank commander took refuge in the gathering dusk along the path that led among the barracks to the railway station. Despite the splendid forgery, he left the base not via the main gate but by a less hazardous route across the small park behind the baths, and through a hole in the fence below the tracks. He crossed a shallow stream and, sticking close to the hedgerows between the fields, finally reached the highway to nearby Lysá.

It was evening now and growing dark, and trucks from the base drove past him. He could have hitched a ride, but there was plenty of time before the train left for Prague, and he felt like walking. The road led westward towards the town over a ridge of undulating hills. The evening was warm and full of colour, like the recent night when he'd carried the basket of plums home for the lieutenant's wife. Like every autumn night for the past ten or fifteen years, this night held a poetic enchantment that was related as much to his glands as to the weather. His mind was buoyed by his success with Janinka, but, rather than being filled with tender thoughts of her, he felt charged with a dynamic sense of determination to press his luck with the tantalizing, exasperating Lizetka.

When he reached the first houses on the outskirts of town, night had fallen and the streets were dimly lit by a few isolated streetlamps. A military police jeep was parked in front of the Žižka Inn. Beside it, two abject and rather drunk soldiers were just being relieved of their passes by a lieutenant in a smartly pressed uniform. A corporal wearing a service armband stood discreetly in the background, trying to convey to the victims through body language that there was nothing he could do about it. The lieutenant tried to catch out the tank commander, but wilted when he saw that all the signatures and stamps on his papers appeared to be in order. He merely told Danny to straighten his tie and tighten his belt, then drove off into the darkness in search of further victims.

Thus Danny was able to board the Prague express, and at half past eight he was ringing the doorbell of Ludmila Neumannová-Hertlová, known to all her suitors as Lizetka.

* * *

There was a rich variety of faces on the stage. The voices orated and declaimed or mumbled and whined. Some authors, adopting the parade-ground manner of a sergeant-major, bellowed their poetry into the smoke-filled hall, while others were barely audible and were lost in the creaking and scraping of chairs.

The voices and faces varied; the subject matter displayed greater discipline.

I'd rather walk with you on Petřín Hill
And tell you of my love and my fidelity –
But, so that you may bright and peaceful live,
I and my gun stand guard o'er your tranquillity.

The form was as regular as any medieval sonnet or ballad. The first two lines expressed genuine longing, and the next two lines an offering, a libation, to redeem the social irrelevance of the longing in lines one and two. The private who had just delivered this variation was so fat that he could only be guarding the tranquillity of his loved one from behind a typewriter in the office of some command post or other. He left the podium to a smattering of indifferent applause.

The next contestant was a corporal with thick glasses, who, in a deliberate but penetrating voice, made this claim:

A young girl's kisses are sweeter
Than the powder the cannon reek of;
But the world is divided, did you know?
And the enemy his chance does seek, love.

The soldiers and officers gathered in the divisional auditorium listened to all this with Christian patience mixed with military restraint. They were, after all, the army's intellectual elite. Some of them rested their foreheads in their hands, feigning intense interest in the poetry and the lessons they might derive from it and apply in their daily work. Others lounged casually on their chairs and leered at the members of the Women's Army Chorus in their attractive, well-fitting uniforms. Some whispered comments to each other after every poem, others remained silent, fending off sleep.

My hand is frozen hard to the steel
And the icy frost bites into my cheek.
For all our loved ones around the world
I guard our border, week after week.

These lines were murmured in a scarcely audible voice by an engineer who looked like a fly on spider's legs. When he'd finished, an officer with two brightly polished medals dangling from his chest, the Fučík Badge and the Badge of Physical Fitness, leaned over to Robert Neumann and said, "Feeble, wouldn't you say?"

"Good beginning, lousy ending. No juice," said Robert expertly, and he was saved from making further critical comment when an exhausted member of the chemical warfare unit behind him fell asleep and tumbled off his chair. The bemedalled officer turned around reproachfully, leaving Robert Neumann to his thoughts, which were coloured by a strange mixture of his habitual gloom and sudden bursts of euphoria over his own poetic triumph. But the more he listened, the more the gloom began to predominate. A triumph in this competition, he realized, would be of questionable value indeed, especially in the eyes of Ludmila. He watched the next contestant on the podium click his heels together, thrust his chest out, and begin to recite rapidly:

> *You write me letters, darling mine:*
> *When will you come home to me?*
> *And I stand here on watch, and guard*
> *Our future and a better time.*

To Neumann, the future appeared bleak indeed. That morning he'd received an anonymous letter from a colleague of Ludmila's, Jarmila Králová. Last week, at twelve-thirty in the morning, Králová had seen Ludmila on the steps of the Golden Well nightclub, with a man who had his arm around her waist. The man was Dr. Karel Budulínský from the Ministry of Domestic Commerce. Robert knew Dr. Budulínský. He considered him a family friend, and in Ludmila's presence he would read him his real poetry, not the verses he composed for the army. The letter made him feel doubly bitter, for he now knew with more certainty than ever that any husband of Ludmila's must necessarily be a man without male friends. Surrounded by masculine camaraderie, he felt oppressed by loneliness.

This feeling remained with him even during a convivial speech delivered by the National Artist Josef Bobr, a fat novelist whose words, so full of cordial sincerity, glorified the present and, somewhat illogically, attributed to an even more glorious future a feeling of envy that it couldn't have been that glorious past. The National Artist droned on, reading from notes, and the loudspeakers turned his voice into a hollow, soporific monotone. In the back of the hall, the body of the soldier from the chemical warfare unit fell off the chair and again crashed to the floor, and the decorated officer whirled around once more, ready to admonish.

The National Artist went on to glorify the literature of the present, which would preserve for that happy future a truthful and undistorted picture of the breadth, depth, and colour of the age, whose palette appeared to him — again somewhat illogically — in various shades of salmon-pink.

Finally, ogling the female comrades in the Army Chorus, he called out: "Thank you, comrades, thank you, soldiers, for the beauty and strength your poetry pours into our souls — into us, your readers. Thank you for the encouragement and the inspiration with which you endow us, poets and writers. Thank you and hurrah! Hurrah and thank you, comrades!" And the women from the Army Chorus, their nylon knees gleaming below the hems of their skirts, began to sing a song of praise for the armoured assault units, in professional four-part harmony.

★   ★   ★

Lizetka lived in a modest family house her parents had built during the Depression. The door was answered by her father, a stage manager at the National Theatre, who said, "Come in, Mr. Smiřický. Liduška's not at home."

He led the tank commander into an overheated kitchen where Lizetka's mother was listening to Radio Free Europe on an old console radio. The device was sputtering and squawking unpleasantly, but through a screen of mechanical noise induced by the jamming station a distant, piping voice could be heard announcing the failure of Communism to collectivize the villages.

"Good evening," Danny said, and the woman nodded pleasantly and flashed him a gold and white smile. For two years now, this soldier had been instigating her daughter to commit adultery. The mother's generation might well still believe in platonic adoration, but the mother herself had sprung from the bosom of the working people, who had never seriously entertained such notions. "Please sit down," she said, "and listen to this."

Danny sat down and listened. Mr. Hertl lay down on the settle under the window, put his muscular arms under his head, and began listening too, trying to follow the weak voice through the grating noise of the jamming. Sometimes the voice was drowned out altogether, but then it would become stronger, almost comprehensible. Bored by what was obviously a nightly ritual, Danny watched the restless canary in its cage. "The Communists resorted to repression," the voice was saying. "Any farmer who did not give to the Communist authorities the quota of goods set by the Communists...." Then the voice faded.

Mrs. Hertlová nodded vigorously. "That's exactly what they did with my father's farm."

She looked at the tank commander and he nodded in agreement.

The voice was now entirely submerged in background noise, and the buzzing increased until the speaker began to pulsate dangerously. Mrs. Hertlová turned down the volume. "Communist swine!" Mr. Hertl muttered from his couch.

The jamming faded slightly. "They were defenceless," said the voice. "Communist thugs in leather coats with revolvers in their pockets drove around the villages on motorcycles and terrorized...." The voice faded.

"The bastards! The sons of bitches!" came the voice from the settle.

"A dirty business," agreed Danny.

"Just like in our village," said Mrs. Hertlová.

A loud crackle surged out of the apparatus and the voice of Radio Free Europe thundered around the room. "Did the confiscated grain end up in Czech bakeries? Was it turned into bread for the Czech people? Not at all, dear listeners at home in Czechoslovakia. The rye harvested in Hana, the wheat grown from the golden soil of Bohemia, were turned into perogies for the fat Communist cats in Soviet Azerbaijan...."

Another loud crackle and the radio set trembled with a new, aggressive wave of jamming. Mrs. Hertlová turned down the volume again, so that silence framed the bitter cry from the settle: "Those Commie pigs are stuffing their faces!" The stage manager's own face, inflamed with rage, rose like an angry moon above the edge of the table, and he stared at Danny with bloodshot eyes. "Where the hell are we living?" he roared. "Mr. Smiřický, I ask you, where are we living? Is this what we end up with? Is this what we've busted our gut for?"

"They're a bad lot," said Danny gently.

"They're thieves!" cried Mrs. Hertlová. "Stealing from people — *that* they know how to do."

"Mr. Smiřický!" The stage manager's face radiated despair. "Think about it, just think about it. Is this what we wanted? Is this what we spent twenty years building a country for? And we call ourselves a nation!" He fixed his burning eyes on the tank commander as though he were accusing him personally of the disaster that had descended upon their well-tempered state.

"You're right," said Danny.

"Shut your mouth, Mr. Smiřický." Mr. Hertl scowled ferociously. "We're all guilty! We've done this with the nation of Jan Hus and T.G. Masaryk and Jan Žižka! That's the kind of whores we are. Drop the H-bomb on us. Drop the cobalt bomb on us!"

"It's true, we've gone to the dogs," said Mrs. Hertlová. "We've abandoned God, and now you might as well write us off." She sighed. "Before, when the – "

"Do you hear that, Mr. Smiřický?" said the stage manager, interrupting his wife. "And now they're always searching your flat to make sure you haven't stolen anything."

"It's a miserable business," said Danny.

"It's a bloody *crime*, that's what it is," yelled the stage manager. "But just you wait. This can't go on for ever. And then heads will roll, friend or foe. What, I'll say. You say you're my friend, I'll say. Maybe you were once, but not any more. String him up, I'll say. I'm a Christian, Mr. Smiřický, but without the slightest compunction whatsoever, Mr. Smiřický, I'll hang every Commie I can get my hands on. And I know who is and isn't a Commie. I'm in charge of dues in our Party cell, and I've got the goods on everyone. No one will be able to deny he was a member, and I'll show no mercy, Mr. Smiřický, I swear I won't."

"That's exactly what they deserve. Show no pity," said Mrs. Hertlová.

"That's a fact," said Danny. "By the way, do you know when Lída's coming home?"

★　★　★

The merciful and impenetrable Originator of All Things did, after all, grant some solace to Robert Neumann, for into the half-circle of svelte young ladies in the chorus stepped a beauty with bright green eyes. She was welcomed by spontaneous applause, for she needed no introduction; she had starred in several movies that everyone had seen, usually playing a sexy young bricklayer or lathe-operator. Now, in a honeyed voice, she announced that she was going to read the grand-prize winner in this year's Army Creativity Contest – a poem by Sergeant Robert Neumann called "Farewell to the Army". Neumann felt a ripple of exultation.

His winning entry had been inspired not, as the poem pretended, by the approaching end of his army service, but by despair. The actress seemed to sense that its melancholy was of an intimate rather than socio-military nature, for she endowed the verses (Ludmila had called them "fripperies") with a warm, moist fog of practised eroticism. Into the microphone she whispered:

Beneath my footsteps rustle leaves
And the bony crackling of icicles.
Like flakes of winter, two glittering butterflies,
Tears flutter into your eyes.
Your tenderness silences the boys....
How much better, comrade, do I understand
All that we once banished with pleasantries.
But after we leave, and put on other garments,
We will still and always be as once we were
In those years when, rifle in hand,
We stood guard for our Czech land.

At the guardhouse, intent on our love,
We wait, the first time without belt and badge,
And shyly we will lead her
Through an autumn of burnished copper:
The earth her comely luck will yield,
And we become her shield.

Robert Neumann was moved to real tears by his own sentimentality. The rest of the audience was drawn to the speaker herself. Not all of them, though; during the performance, the weary member of the chemical warfare unit fell out of his chair a third time, and on orders from the decorated officer he was escorted from the hall by the soldiers on duty.

Somewhat later, all the winners were sitting around a long green table laden with food and drink, in the small salon in division headquarters, listening to the head of the division's cultural program.

"And so, comrades," said the colonel, whose name was Vrána but whom the men called Colonel Dryfart, "the artillery made an especially strong showing this year, both in the number of awards and in the number of poems submitted. And that is a special reason for joy, comrades, because our aim is to cultivate, not outstanding individuals, but a reliable collective. Our slogan was, is, and will always be 'The masses, above all!' "

A private at the end of the table shouted, "Hurrah!", but the rest merely looked at him and his battle-cry hung in the air in an embarrassing silence. The speaker was so surprised by this unexpected interjection that he stopped talking. Everyone looked down. Finally, a lieutenant from the Army Song and Dance Ensemble said, "Wonderful! Wonderful work, cannoneers."

"Yes indeed!" said the National Artist. "So the artillery muse was the most creative of all?"

The colonel laughed. "That's right, comrade," he said. "Out of sixty-five poems received, thirty-eight were from men in the artillery. And of the twenty awards, twelve were given to artillery men!"

"Including the laurel wreath of victory," interrupted a major from the Song and Dance Ensemble, "which was won by a cannoneer as well." He smiled at Robert Neumann as though he owed his high rank to him. "I'm particularly pleased by that since I was originally a cannoneer myself."

Neumann smiled too – at the major with his mouth, and at the actress (who returned his smile) with his eyes. They had been introduced after the concluding ceremonies and she was now sitting next to the prize-winning novelist. Neumann had already succumbed to the ancient fallacy that one can compensate for bad luck with one woman in the company of another woman without making matters worse.

"And what about poetry from the armoured division, Comrade Colonel?" said a sergeant with tank corps insignia.

"What about the engineers?" roared a large man on the other side of the table.

The colonel examined a sheaf of papers. The prize-winning novelist looked over his shoulder while stifling a yawn with a pudgy hand. He smiled apologetically at the actress; she smiled back at him, then shifted her smile to Robert Neumann, who flashed a flirtatious smile back at her.

He had decided that, should the opportunity present itself, he would sin that evening, at least in word and thought. He wasn't quite ready yet, he realized, to sin in deed.

Then someone invited the National Artist to tell them what he thought of the competition in more detail than he had been able to provide in his speech. The novelist settled into his chair like a lump of jelly and began to speak. "I must say, comrades, the level of the competition astonished me. I had certainly not expected to find such a wealth of young talent."

"What did you like most about the competition?" the Song and Dance major asked humbly.

"What did I like most?" The National Artist was silent for a moment. He was the kind of writer that people in reactionary literary circles liked to call "an old whore". He understood literature, but he didn't place a great deal of importance on his own integrity, and therefore literature, even genuine literature, no longer gave him any pleasure. Gazing around the table, he declared in a voice of thundering authority: "The spirit of the competition, comrades! What a beautiful and joyous picture this competition gave us of the spirit of our young soldiers. In that torrent of genuinely fresh young poetry – and most of it, to a certain extent, was relatively very good poetry, almost – there was not a hint or a suggestion of the self-indulgent melancholy, the despair, the lack of faith, even the disgust, that used to be the main subject of young poets in the old bourgeois times."

Both high-ranking officers continued to nod, and a diminutive lieutenant rescued Bobr from having to expand on that observation. "I agree, comrade," he said. "I've observed that in our own unit, with every passing year, the comrades who come to us are somehow better, somehow – well, new socialist men. What I mean is, it seems that work is continually becoming, well, more and more – joyful – somehow."

"Yes, yes," said the National Artist quickly. "You've put that well, comrade." The lieutenant flushed with pleasure. "Work is indeed a more joyful thing nowadays, both for you in the army, and for us in the Union of Writers. When I think," and the novelist settled his blob-like body more comfortably into his chair, "when I think of the situation in literature in this country back in the bourgeois, capitalist republic – well, it's shameful even to talk about it." For a moment he appeared to be dreaming, and he was – about those balmy days when, as the star writer of a private publishing house, he had been given the cushy job of editor, with the duty of working once a week for three hours and being paid three thousand pre-war crowns for the privilege. He heaved a sigh that could have been interpreted as sorrow, and went on: "The things people wrote then — and published!" He waved a paw in the air to fill his rhetorical pause. "It was vile. It was the deliberate, programmatic dehumanization of man. Poets just mucked about with feelings, and they were petty feelings at that. It was pure existentialism!" He pronounced this with the same kind of disdain Lysenko had used in denouncing the fruit-flies used in genetics experiments. "Ah, but today, in our socialist fatherland, when I hear the variety, comrades — this poem is about love, that one about work, or about standing guard — I am delighted. Truly delighted."

The colonel stopped nodding his head and said, "I think I speak for everyone present when I say that your praise has deeply touched and warmed us all. But now, perhaps Comrade Bobr would like to give our soldier-poets some more detailed pointers — "

"Why of course, naturally, comrades," said Bobr quickly. "That's what I'm here for." He cleared his throat. "It goes without saying that your work has its weak points as well as its strong ones." And with that, he plunged into a list of the negative aspects of the poetry submitted. For a long time he spoke without being specific. Then he focused his remarks on the work of a corporal who, so far, had managed to be inconspicuous. "Take these lines, for instance, comrades," he said. "*You footlockers, beacons of Hope! Soldiers adorn you with the faces of women.* This is not a good line. *You footlockers* — yes, it broaches an interesting subject, a novel subject. But — *beacons of Hope*? Hope? What hope? And hope for what? Can you feel, comrade, how vague, unoriginal, and unrealistic that expression is? It completely spoils the line. Learn from our classical writers like Jan Neruda, or from foreign comrades such as Pablo Neruda, comrade."

He fell silent and the Song and Dance major seized his opportunity. Poetry fell within his area of competence, after all. "Would you allow me, comrade?"

"By all means," said Bobr scornfully.

"I only want to add to what the Comrade National Artist here has said. This matter has to be looked at politically, too. We must realize, Comrade Corporal," and the major turned to the non-com, whose hollow face radiated undisguised terror, "we must realize that such a poem will fall into the hands of many comrades, right? And that poem will have an influence on them. Words too are weapons, comrade, and we who work with the masses must make sure they are good weapons, useful weapons, well-oiled weapons. And this is what you write: *You footlockers, beacons of Hope.* As the Comrade National Artist pointed out, it is a non concrete, naturalist image. And I would add to what the comrade here said, comrade: from the political and ideological point of view it is a very suspect line." The major glared at the corporal so disapprovingly that the young man's head sank and his hollow cheeks flushed crimson with shame. "It is not at all a politically correct line!"

★　★　★

Danny was still waiting for Lizetka at twelve-thirty, long after her parents had gone to bed. Her boudoir, with its intimate lighting, reminded him of the disarray of a soldier's bedroom just before reveille. A large icon of the Virgin Mary and a period etching of Henry the Eighth stared down with dead eyes on the messy pile of books, dresses, underwear, fruit, and cigarettes strewn on the round, glass-topped table, and on the rumpled couch under the window, where she slept. There was an open clothes closet in the corner of the room, and a summer dress and a crumpled petticoat lay casually across a chair.

Several nylon stockings and a sluttish blue satin bra hung on the armrest of another chair. Various other items were scattered on the floor. Everything was exactly as it had been since her husband was called up.

The tank commander opened the door to the next room. There, everything was stiffly tidy. The corner couch was reflected coldly in the glass doors of the bookshelves. If Lizetka's nature was reflected in the shambles of her den, here was a picture of the soul of her poor sod of a husband.

He went back to her room, emptied one of the chairs onto the floor, and pulled a few letters from the pile of things on her bedside table. He took one and began to read it:

> *My darling,*
> *I keep wanting to write you but I can't. You have to understand that, surrounded by all this emptiness, one simply doesn't have the courage; one fears everything. I've composed so many letters to you in my head since you left, but so far not a single one have I written down. I have often thought – not without understanding – of your special saintliness and decency.*

Yes – a saintliness called frigidity, a decency called narcissism. He didn't bother to look at the signature; his experienced eye judged the letter to be the work of the first of his successors, Kurisu, a student of Japanese. *So she didn't put out for him either,* he thought with satisfaction. *At least I have dubious precedence in that, as a* primus inter pares, *I was the first to demonstrate to her that a Catholic marriage need not exclude platonic infidelity, in the hope, of course, that with a little help from a Catholic devil, her platonic infidelity would one day become actual, physical infidelity. I haven't managed to bring her to that point,* he sighed, *but on the other hand I*

have been able to turn her into a perfect little platonic whore.
He began reading the next letter:

*Lizette, it is rather awful. I write you, and my worst prob-
lem is a chronic illness of the soul called boredom. There
is no escape, there is no way out except the one along
which we walk, but that, perhaps, has neither beginning
nor end.*

The quasi-existential sentiments betrayed the writer as
Maurice, another of his colleagues in platonism, who had
grown up in Vichy France during the Second World War.

*Do you think we may have met sometime in another life,
my wise queen? I write you, Karina, and I don't know if
you are alive.*

Well. He reached for another. This one wasn't a letter, just
a crumpled piece of paper. On one side, drawn in an artless
hand, was a crude red heart with a red arrow pointing at it,
and beside it, in shaky English: *It is your heart and beats only
for me?*
Beneath that, in Lizetka's hand: *Yes!!*
And the response: *It is not difficult to love you – you most
charming girl!*
And below that, from Lizetka: *Attention! My man see you!*
Well, here was someone new. He sounded like a real jerk.
Why didn't he learn decent English? On the other side of the
paper, however, they reverted to their mother tongue. *Didn't
I put that rather cleverly? And my husband didn't suspect a
thing.* Beneath that: *You're the Beauty and he's the Beast.* And
then: *That's why I have to sweet-talk him all the time, otherwise he'd leap out and eat you, Budulín.* And with that the dia-

logue ended. Perhaps Budulín had, in fact, been eaten at that point. If he had, a willing replacement would certainly have jumped in.

Danny rummaged around in the pile of papers and came up with a small notebook. He opened it at random and read:

This afternoon, went into town and arrived at the Adria an hour late. Maurice was there, annoyed. A long walk to Barrandov. Maurice teed off at first, then pleasant. Tells me about his problems. Wonderful supper, then we dance. Maurice talks about divorce. Walk down the hill to the trolley-stop. I'm awfully sleepy. Maurice sticks with me all the way to Radlice. In bed by about two.

Tuesday: Rise at 7:45. Terrible rush. Mother has words again. Half-hour late for work, but the Queen wasn't there yet, just Lexina. We gab a bit, talk about Pecka. The Queen arrives about ten, carrying some cakes. We all indulge, feel sick. Then to lunch, and a gentleman starts talking to me, tell him I went to school in Switzerland and he starts talking French to me. I get embarrassed and tell him it was a German school. Says he desperately wants to see me again, he's from the Min. of For. Trade. So we make a date for next week. Then in the Church of the Little Jesus of Prague I pray for Robert and for myself, and for the strength to stop being this way. Back to work about two and I go straight for a bath. I lie in the tub and downstairs they're playing records with a Jewish cantor singing. They're wonderful. I try reading a book called The Egg and I *in the bath, but I get it wet and stop. Out of the bath at four. The Queen didn't show up at all this afternoon. Milan calls, Lexina brings me the telephone in the tub. Then Budulín calls and I go to his place and we drink absinthe.*

So Budulín didn't get eaten after all, Danny thought glumly. He put the notebook aside and wondered what he was doing waiting there. *I suppose it's because I love her. Well – more likely because she never came across. So it's either vanity or it's love. And what about Janinka? Ah, Janinka.... I guess it must be because Lizetka didn't come across.*

In which case it's probably love, too.

Pleased with this reasoning, he succumbed to military weariness and fell asleep.

★ ★ ★

The disgraced corporal's name was Josef Brynych. In civilian life he had been a clerk in a tobacco warehouse, and he had never written poetry before. The poem about the footlockers had occurred to him one night when he was on guard duty. The guard post was a wooden shack with a single bench of rotting planks, and the corporal couldn't sleep. Bored to savagery with the four-hour pause between rounds, he read the only material allowed in the guard post – a two-week-old copy of the tank division daily, *Armoured Fist*. He ploughed through everything, from an editorial entitled "How to Continue Mass Cultural Work while Fulfilling the Summer Plan for Target Practice with Heavy Machine-Guns" to the masthead – everything, including the phone numbers. As he scanned those four printed pages again, in the final stages of terminal desperation and believing that he had read every single letter, something caught his eye, something he would normally have ignored altogether because it promised even less amusement than he dared to expect from the people's democratic press. It was a brief text arranged in short lines of unequal length – in other words, a poem. Exhausted by insomnia, irritated by the snoring of the other guards on the bench, tired of trying to lure an over-experienced mouse out of its lair with a piece of bacon, and crushed by the sight of the guard commander, who was going against regulations by sleeping on the table, Corporal Brynych was driven to read the item, titled "Poem Written on a March" and signed with the name Lt. Jan Vrchcoláb. He read:

> *The merry song flies up like a raptor*
> *and falls, strumming the heavens.*
> *What could be apter?*
> *Our platoon*
> *marches, singing a tune.*
> *I sing and think of you,*
> *My heart's captor.*

His tired brain stopped for a moment to consider the line *and falls, strumming the heavens.* He involuntarily tried to imagine what the merry song of an infantry platoon would sound like strumming the heavens. He imagined something soaring, then rubbing against a firm but yielding substance, then tumbling down to earth again. Then he tried to remember the last time his platoon had sung at all, let alone merrily. He reconsidered the poem and discovered that along with the rhyme *platoon* and *tune* he could add *saloon.* The possibilities began to interest him. He cast about for an appropriate line until he found one. The poem, written by Jan Vrchcoláb and improved by Corporal Brynych, now went like this:

> *The merry song flies up like a raptor*
> *And falls, strumming the heavens.*
> *What could be apter?*
> *Our platoon*

Marches, singing a tune.
I sing and think of you,
And of our favourite saloon,
My heart's captor.

The corporal's imagination was stimulated. After some thought, he transformed the poem yet again, so that it now read:

Grey boredom flies up to the heavens
And falls directly on you.
Our platoon
Couldn't give a sweet fuck.
I yawn, think of you,
And curse my luck.
Somewhere, in a warm saloon,
Some young buck
Is making you swoon.

He found this highly entertaining. He looked through the other verses of Vrchcoláb's poem, and his eye fell on a notice printed underneath it announcing that the deadline for the divisional round of the Army Creativity Contest was July 15. He decided to enter something. He pulled a filthy diary out of his pocket and began to think about a subject. The first thing that came into his head, God knows why, was his foot-locker with the picture of Blaženka and the village square in his hometown inside the lid. Then he thought that this awful boredom would soon be over, and he imagined himself sitting again in the aroma-filled kitchen in Blaženka's house, grinding coffee in the antique coffee mill while Blaženka, in a blue apron, made supper, and her mother, Mrs. Jarošová, called him Mr. Pepa, and Mr. Jaroš winked at him and said, "Some gal, eh? Sugar and spice, she is!" And Blaženka would blush and glance at him, her blue eyes dancing with the promise of pleasures to come after the wedding, and the wedding would be right after Christmas. Thus filled with poetic thoughts, Corporal Brynych produced the first four lines of his poem:

> *You footlockers,*
> *Beacons of Hope!*
> *Soldiers adorn you*
> *With the faces of women.*

He sent off two copies, one to *Armoured Fist*, the other to Miss Blaženka Jarošová, Sales Clerk, c/o Pramen Grocery Enterprises, Modřanky, p.o. Rakovník. From Blaženka he got an enthusiastic letter, and after some time a notice appeared in *Armoured Fist*. Among the poems given an honourable mention in the divisional round of the Army Creativity Contest was one by Corporal Brynych, Josef. And now he was sitting here while the officers tore his poem apart.

★ ★ ★

The rattling of a key in the main door woke Danny, and a few moments later Lizetka was standing in the light from the table lamp. She was wearing a nylon jacket and a slightly rumpled checked skirt. She smiled, but it wasn't a warm smile. "Ahoj, Lízinka," he said.

"Well, company," she replied. "Greetings, Comrade Tank Commander. You haven't come to see us for some time. What's up?"

"Nothing," he said. "Isn't it more like there's something new here?"

But she'd already put him out of her mind. She went to her writing table and began leafing through some papers. He felt as useless as a wax statue.

"So tell me, my friend," she said absently. "What's been going on at the base?"

"I got into some trouble before I came," he said mechanically, looking intently at her bottom in its checked skirt. Was it vanity or was it love? Sex appeal, most likely. He started telling her the story of Lieutenant Malina and Sergeant Babinčáková. Lizetka went on leafing through her file.

"Are you listening, Lizetka?" he asked, irritated.

"I'm listening."

"It's a strange kind of listening."

"I'm paying attention."

"I'll bet you don't even know what I'm talking about."

"There was this Sergeant Babinčáková in the guardhouse and you had guard duty – no, prisoner escort duty – and Second Lieutenant Malina went to bed with her in her cell."

"Well, all right," he said grudgingly, and continued the story. But he had no taste for it. Lizetka began writing something in the file.

"Líza, couldn't you at least pay attention to me?"

"I told you, I'm listening."

"Then couldn't you look at me while you listen?"

She turned to him. "You want me to come and sit in your lap? For God's sake, Daniel, you sound just like Robert."

The tank commander felt anger rising in him. Coming from Lizetka, there was no greater insult.

"If this is how you make him feel, I'm not surprised."

"Not surprised?" she said, raising her eyebrows. "There was a time when you were surprised."

"There was indeed," he said harshly.

"And those times are gone?"

He said nothing. As always, harshness had no effect on her. As always, Danny was the first to soften.

"In that case," she said, "thank God I didn't marry you."

"Don't say that."

"I repeat: thank God. I only regret I married anyone at all."

"Last time, you said that if Robert got killed while he was in the army, you'd marry me."

"That was last time. Not now."

★   ★   ★

"Hope, Comrade Corporal? Hope for what?" the major was asking. "And on top of that, you gave it a capital 'H'. Now, when a young comrade reads a line like that, what is the first thing that occurs to him? We know soldiers miss their loved ones and those close to them. But we mustn't reinforce these tendencies at all. In fact, Comrade Corporal, these tendencies must be wiped out. We don't want soldiers to spend their evenings sitting on their footlockers and mooning over photographs of their girlfriends and sighing. We want them in the mass cultural activity room, singing our mass songs and dancing our mass dances, right? This poem of yours, comrade, does not make our task any easier. No indeed, comrade. In fact, comrade, this poem of yours defeats our purpose." The major's head was tilted threateningly towards Corporal Brynych, and every "comrade" sounded like the salvo of a firing squad. The tobacco-warehouse clerk felt cold sweat dampening his back. Jesus, he hadn't asked for this.

"But otherwise, comrade," said the National Artist, who obviously felt sorry for the young poet, "your poem isn't bad. You know it's not because it got honourable mention, after all."

But the tobacco-warehouse clerk didn't care about the poem; what he was worried about was the report he'd take home from the army. So he just nodded mechanically at the novelist, while glancing anxiously at the major, his heart gripped with fear that mostly had to do with whether Blaženka would still want him if he had to leave the tobacco warehouse and work in the mines.

Corporal Brynch was just opening his mouth to apologize, to explain that he hadn't done this intentionally, when a notorious poetic hack of the Seventh Tank Battalion named Sergeant Maňas spoke up.

"Since we're already on the subject of the political impact of the work we heard tonight," he began, "allow me to draw your attention to one thing. The comrade corporal here was quite correctly and justifiably taken to task because the political content of his poem was different than he may have intended in his possibly, indeed perhaps undoubtedly, sincere effort. In this regard, I should like to draw attention not so much to the first four lines, but to the conclusion of his poem, comrades." He stopped talking and turned his eyes thoughtfully towards the ceiling, where not long ago a soldier who had been a sign-painter in civilian life had rendered a fresco of rosy-cheeked soldiers embracing rosy-cheeked miners, smelter workers, farmers, and the working intelligentsia, whom he had painted wearing white lab coats and glasses; a private in a trooper's helmet was being given bread and salt by a rosy-cheeked but unembraced girl while, seated in a cloud, the Commander-in-Chief of the Czechoslovak Armed Forces, General Čepička, looked benignly down.

Sergeant Maňas took a deep breath, tore his eyes away from the joyous apparition on the ceiling, and went on: "Just take the two concluding quatrains, comrades.

You footlockers,
When tears of rain come down
Upon your cracked paint
Outside the barrack gates,
We will carry a piece
Of life home in you,
And autumn will swallow us
In a grey curtain of rain.

"This captures one thing very well, I believe," Mañas said. "The mood of nature in autumn. But suppose we enquire after its political impact. What is the final impression? Is it happy? Optimistic? Is there a sense of pride in being a soldier? Joy at the prospect of returning to civilian life? I don't think so. I think the basic tone of this poem is melancholy. And it is an unjustified melancholy, one that is consistent neither with the attitude of our soldier to his basic military service, nor with his attitude to his private life. In short, it's a melancholy that has no place in the psychological armoury of our units."

Others now jumped into the debate. A corporal remarked that sometimes melancholy was simply one of the undeniable facts of life, to which the Song and Dance major replied that, if this was the case, then they had to struggle against it. One poetic soul declared that the feeling of melancholy carried within it a kind of vengeful power, and that all revolutionaries were melancholy. Mañas easily deflated that heresy by labelling it an idealistic error and challenging anyone to name him any melancholy revolutionaries – and if anyone did, to prove that they had been melancholy. A politruk from the tank division declared that the comrades in his units had no reason to be melancholy at all. A Sergeant Pankůrek began to develop the idea that, besides its intellectual content, a poem had values that might be called cumulative – that is, they enriched life and created a treasury of variegated emotions. To this the Song and Dance major replied that life was now rich and variegated enough without melancholy. By this time Corporal Brynych was so terrified that he no longer noticed what was going on around him.

When the debate finally ended, in absolute victory for Sergeant Maňas and his opinions over Sergeant Pankůrek and his, the debaters suddenly remembered the person whose versified creation had started the discussion in the first place. But when they looked around, they discovered that Corporal Josef Brynych was no longer among them.

He was on the asphalt road leading back to his barracks, and he was composing in his mind a pledge he would make that, upon completing his basic military service, he would volunteer for work as a miner in the brown-coal mines of Kladno.

★ ★ ★

"I still love you, Líza," said the tank commander. When he said it, he was convinced that it was absolutely true.

"Don't talk nonsense, darling," said Lizetka. "Don't try to make a fool out of me, all right? When was the last time you were here?"

"That has nothing to do with it. We've had weekend manoeuvres two weeks in a row."

"And how many letters have you written me?"

He felt a pang of alarm. It was an odd thing: since that night above the shooting range he had completely forgotten his romantic correspondence with Lizetka.

"I haven't had the time," he said weakly. "I was dog-tired after all those manoeuvres. But I love you, Lizetka. I always have and I always will."

"Baloney," she said. "This Corporal Babinčáková or whatever her name is has got your head spinning. Or is there someone else?"

"Lizetka, I swear to you the only reason I haven't written is those manoeuvres. I can prove it."

"What are you going to do, bring me a note from your CO?" she said.

"Lizetka, get a divorce and marry me!"

"What a catch you'd be! Besides, I can't get a divorce."

"I know, the Holy Mother Church won't allow it."

"Don't blaspheme."

"Jesus Christ," groaned Danny. "Are you that afraid for the state of my soul?"

"Yes."

"And for yours?"

"That too. But that's my worry. I don't want you on my conscience."

"And what if I kill myself because of you?"

"You?"

"Yes, me."

"You're far too much of a momma's boy for that."

"Jesus Christ."

"And don't take the Lord's name in vain. That's a real sin."

"Mortal or venal?"

"If you do it over and over again, it's mortal."

"And what about you? Don't you sin over and over again?"

"What?"

"You know, all those guys you keep stringing along — Maurice, Kurisu. Somebody called Budulín. And don't forget me — "

"I don't want anyone to be sad. And you were the one who started it. I couldn't turn you down, and from that time on I haven't been able to turn anyone down. It's all your fault."

"Oh, sh – " said Danny, and then caught himself in time. He wasn't on military turf now. "You think you don't make me sad?"

"Do I?"

"I sure don't get what I want."

"You know I can't do that. But I do everything I can." She yawned. It was a cruel thing to do. "Come on, Danny. What you suffer from is foolishness. I mean, is it so important? It doesn't matter who you do it with. You can do that with Babinčáková. The important thing is the soul – isn't that what you always said?"

Danny was trembling. *You bloody fool*, he said to himself. *You stupid bloody fool. She's damn right, and you're a bloody fool. Isn't it nice with Janinka? Nicer than this damn purgatory? God, God, God! God damn!* But the only thing he could think to say was, "Lizeta, let me stay with you."

"Oh no," she said. "Take this eiderdown and go next door."

"Let me stay with you. I won't do anything."

"No, no, darling, I want to sleep. You'd just annoy me."

"I wouldn't."

"Oh, yes you would. I know you."

"I really wouldn't, Lizeta. Believe me."

"No, no. Here's the eiderdown. Now, go take a walk."

He took the eiderdown and carried it into the next room. He again remembered Janinka. *My God, is this me? Am I the same guy who made love to Janinka? Fuck it!* he thought – for in spirit the whole world was military turf.

He threw the eiderdown onto the shiny couch and went back into her room. She was still in her skirt, but her jacket and blouse lay on the chair. She let him stand there while she changed into her pyjamas, using a whole array of sly disrobing techniques so that he didn't see much of anything. Perhaps her problem was not so much frigidity as exhibitionism. It was clear that, after this striptease, his only possible goal was to sleep with her.

"One sin after another," he said bitterly.

"But none of them mortal," she retorted. Her eyes were indifferent, but they were also bright with some kind of... desire? Oh God! She slipped under the covers and turned off the light. He tore off his tunic, his trousers, and his shirt, and crawled in after her.

"No, Danny, go away."

"Lizeta! Let me stay with you!"

"No. You'll touch me and I don't want that. I really don't."

"I won't," he said, and he could feel her body through the pyjamas, as hot as an iron. "I won't touch you – or if I do, just a little," and he slipped his arms around her and felt her soft breast in his hand.

"See how dumb you are?" she said angrily, and turned her back on him.

"Líza!"

"Leave me alone and go to sleep."

He knew nothing would come of this. He certainly couldn't rape her – he'd tried it once and it had got him a two-week stay in the eye department of the army hospital. So he just snuggled close to her and placed his hand on her smooth, round shoulder. *It can't be any worse in that hell of hers. This heartless, indifferent body beside me will drive me mad.* He heard her regular breathing. She had fallen asleep. *I'll go mad, I'll go mad.*

But he didn't go mad. He fell into a light sleep, and in it he committed that sin with her. She, of course, took part immaterially, being a dream, but as far as his glands were concerned, the act was physical. He wondered why so much inconsequential stupidity surrounded something so simple to cure. He wondered if she and the sanctimonious religion she espoused were right after all: to become spiritual, to liberate oneself from.... And then he too fell asleep and became a liberated spirit and it was like a sweet death — sweet because, in his sleep, he didn't know that from this death he would soon awaken.

★　★　★

Robert Neumann paid no attention whatever to the entire controversy. In the cluster of bodies that formed after the discovery that Corporal Brynych was missing, the actress threaded her way expertly through the crowd and addressed him in a sociable voice:

"I wanted to congratulate you once more. Your poems read so well, did you know that?"

He wanted to reply that he didn't, or rather that he did — he couldn't make up his mind which — but before he could say anything, she went on, "I'll bet you recite them out loud as you write them, am I right? Poets don't often do that, and that's why their poems don't read very well. But yours read wonderfully well. I mean it."

As she was taking a breath, he managed to slip in a remark. "It's mainly because of the wonderful way you read them."

"Thank you, but I still think that's how you can tell real poetry — it reads well out loud. Isn't that so?"

Before he could say what he thought, she went on, "Won't you give me some more? I'd like to recite some on my road trips, with your permission, of course. You will? That'll be superb. You know, we tour a lot to army units outside the city, and it would be wonderful if I could read some of your poems. Do you agree?"

He could only manage a nod.

"The air's very close in here, don't you think? It's beautiful outside, almost summer weather. Wouldn't you like to go outside?"

He went, of course. In less than a minute (and he hadn't committed a single sin, in thought, word, or deed) they were sitting on a bench beside the wide asphalt road, bordered by a mosaic of white stones that shone a message into the starry night: FORWARD TOWARDS AN EXEMPLARY FULFILMENT OF THE AUTUMN EXERCISES. Despite the actress's garrulous interest in Robert Neumann's poetry, she soon had him talking about his private life. He found relief with her – not physical relief, but the kind that, in theory, the confessional was meant to provide. The difference was an important one. In the confessional, you accused yourself. Now, without even knowing how, Neumann suddenly found himself accusing his wife, and instead of undoing the buttons on the actress's Chinese silk blouse somewhere in the thick bushes across the road, he provided her with the unhappy history of his marriage with the much-admired Ludmila. It felt like a great miracle of compassion, like balsam on his wounds applied by a sensitive and understanding female soul.

In fact, Alena Hillmanová was cleverly exploiting the frustration of the progressive Catholic poet to gain an interesting insight into the love-life of her far too tight-lipped cousin, Daniel Smiřický.

★   ★   ★

The far too tight-lipped cousin was awakened next morning, in the bed of the technically faithful Ludmila Neumannová-Hertlová, by a loud noise. It was the father greeting the new day with a shout: "Goddamned Communist swine!" But the presence of a man who had every appearance of being the lover of his married daughter didn't bother him. Danny, however, was not Marxist enough for the world to appear to him as a simple problem, resolvable through easily graspable laws. He listened calmly to the angry door-slam that marked the stage-manager's departure for work. Ludmila was sleeping like a baby, her fists clenched and her mouth, which seemed so sensual awake, now puckered as if ready to draw milk from a mother's breasts. He got up, put on his clothes, and shook her gently.

With great effort she opened one eye.

"Lizetka, when will I see you again?"

"Come to the office," she mumbled, and closed her eye again.

He tiptoed out of the bedroom and the house, and spent the morning introducing himself around at a new and very large state publishing house where his cousin, the actress, had connections. He discovered that while he had been in the army, intellectual inflexibility had invaded publishing to a greater extent than he could have imagined, with disruptive results. In filling out the questionnaire for the post of editor of Anglo-American literature, he listed Hemingway among his favourite authors, but omitted to mention Howard Fast. In his final year at university, Hemingway had still been considered a progressive author whose only sin was to have crudely distorted the truth about the Spanish Civil War and vilified its real heroes. Since then, as the rather grave man who was interviewing him pointed out, Hemingway had been promoted. He was now a spy and an American intelligence agent. Danny reflected gloomily that this would probably ruin his chances for the job, but the grave man went on to inform him that everything evolves, including people and their opinions, and that no doubt he too, influenced by the female comrades in the Anglo-American "collective" (this was how they referred to editorial departments now), would develop and change. After being introduced to the comrades in question, he had no doubts about it either. One of them, a blue-eyed blonde with a round face, could single-handedly ensure his evolution in any direction she might wish.

That afternoon Danny went to see Lizetka. She worked, or more precisely was employed, in an office called Cultural Enterprises of the Capital City of Prague; Danny never did manage to find out what the organization actually did. During his visit, an old man with the title of Head of the Chess Circle stopped by, but he was quickly swept out of the office.

The office was located behind a glass partition in what had once been a vaudeville hall. Ludmila sat behind a large desk displaying a huge appointment book with almost nothing in it, an empty notepad, and a telephone. She shared the office with a peroxide blonde of about thirty called Mrs. Králová, whose husband was about to be appointed to the permanent Czechoslovak mission to the U.N. in New York. She was supposed to be Ludmila's superior, but in his relatively frequent visits to the glassed-in office Danny had almost never found her in. Today was an exception, however, and perched on Králová's desk (which had *two* telephones) was the third employee of the organization, a slender, pretty, impudent-looking girl by the name of Lexina. A man in a pale blue business suit slouched in the corner staring at her, but he had nothing to do with the affairs of the office. When Danny walked in, Králová was just speaking.

"Naturally Vašek was teed off," she said, "so he goes to the section chief, who's fed up with him, but Vašek and Čepek from Security are hand in glove, and Čepek is in solid with Kopejda, so the section chief promises to arrange it for him, and before Vašek makes it back to the NV a telephone order's

already arrived that Budárek is to take over the Karlín operation. Budárek isn't a bit pleased, and oh, by the way, Vašek
set this little surprise up for him through Mikulka, so Vašek
seemed to be out of the picture. Budárek doesn't even blink,
but he checks himself into the General Hospital with kidney
trouble or something, because the head doctor is somebody
called Šofr who Budárek once did a favour for, and now he's
waiting to see how the thing shakes out. Naturally, Vašek was
teed off – "

Whatever this outfit did, relationships between its employ-
ees were clearly very complex. It turned out, Králová said, that
someone called Pecka was about to get the sack because there
was ten thousand missing from the till, which under normal
circumstances would have been replaced by grants, if only
Hampejz hadn't been after Pecka's job. And Hampejz was in
hot water because of those missing French originals, so he had
to leave the SD though he'd only been there three months,
but he'd certainly push Pecka out because Vosáhlo was keeping an eye out for Pecka, except that now they'd demoted
Vosáhlo, so Pecka was up the creek and would probably end
up in the DO instead of Čuříková, who got involved with Milič
and the word leaked right up to the minister, who was Milič's
wife's father....

As the tank commander listened to all this, the fellow in
the blue suit was shamelessly eyeing Lexina, and Lexina was
shamelessly letting herself be eyed, while popping choco-
lates into her mouth from a box on the table. Danny felt as
though he'd just awakened from some idyllic, pastoral dream
in which simple, uniformed shepherds were herding simple,
uniformed sheep and then, two years later, driving them back
into the terribly complicated world where human beings were
locked in a constant struggle for good, better, and still better
jobs. This complex new society was criss-crossed, it seemed,

by a fine network of friendship and hostility, of favours rendered and owed, of sympathy and antipathy, of kinship and
relationships that reminded him of nothing so much as a
bloody family feud. He was astonished at how much mental
effort went into calculating the possible combinations and esti-
mating strengths and weaknesses, and how much depended
on knowing things that might serve for blackmail. And all
of this was, for some inscrutable reason, financed from the
state treasury.

As Králová talked and talked, the tank commander watched
Lizetka. Her skirt beneath the table was high enough for him
to see under it. He also looked at the long legs and pitch-black
eyes of Comrade Lexina, and the usual mixture of thoughts began tumbling around in his head, most of them ill-humoured
and sullen. The world, it seemed to him, was no more than a
few points of light drowned in a dark mush of displeasure.

At last the fellow in the pale blue business suit looked
at his watch, straightened up, and announced that he had to
be going.

"Jeepers!" said Comrade Lexina, checking her watch.
"Five-thirty! Darling, would you put me down for two hours'
overtime?"

"Now look, Lexina," giggled Králová, "just get out of here.
It was only an hour and a half, and that's what I'm going to
put down. You won't catch me stealing from the state."

★   ★   ★

Lexina and the fellow in the pale blue suit were barely out the
door when the telephone rang for the first time since Danny
had arrived. Králová picked up the receiver and said in a tired,
official voice, "Králová, CECC." Then her eyes opened wide.

She winked at Ludmila, covered the mouthpiece with her hand, and whispered loudly, "Kustka!"

She spoke in her official voice again: "Comrade Kovářová has just left."

A thin voice could be heard speaking on the other end, and then Králová said, "I don't know where. She left by car with Comrade Dr. Hillman from screenwriting." As she said this, she kept looking at Ludmila, her eyebrows dancing a strange routine, while Ludmila's replied in kind. "Would you like to leave a message?" she asked sweetly, and when, instead of an answer, there was a sharp click in the receiver, she hung up and said, "I guess not," and both women burst out laughing.

"Lexina's going to have to deal with that one," said Králová.

"I keep telling her he's going to lay into her some day."

"It's just what she needs, my dear. She's almost as big a bitch as you are." Králová took a sidelong look at the tank commander, then stood up, still giggling, and said, "Well, I'm on my way, young people."

The tank commander suddenly realized that the fellow in the pale blue suit was his cousin's husband, whom he'd never met. He stood up quickly and said goodbye to the affable boss of his platonic mistress.

As soon as she'd vanished through the door, Lizetka said with great feeling, "The cow! She's a real swine, isn't she? She's all giggles and honey, but she stabs me in the back every chance she gets."

"Why would she do that?"

"Why? How should I know? What kind of question is that, anyway? You talk like you've just come from the moon."

It was exactly how the tank commander felt. He said goodbye to Lizetka (she had to go somewhere to arrange something, but she declined to say what and where) and they agreed to meet again at ten-thirty in front of the Ministry of Culture. She was in a good mood and had invited him to something she called a "special screening for study purposes".

★   ★   ★

The special screening for the minister, his girlfriends, and their lovers, and for a narrow circle of film experts and their mistresses, featured an American film called *The Valley*. The screening was held in a tiny rococo salon in the Wallenstein Palace which had been painstakingly restored in brilliant gold leaf and pink wallpaper. There were silver candelabras with flickering orange electric lights turned low, and as soon as Lizetka and the tank commander had taken their seats in the beige and pink armchairs, the lights were extinguished and the credits began to roll across the screen.

The minister preferred musicals, since he liked young women, but sometimes, perhaps to whet his appetite, he declared a fast and showed westerns instead. Such was the case today. A lion filled the screen and, wreathed with the slogan ARS GRATIA ARTIS, roared out his ancient invitation to entertainment. The audience, however, had come to study.

The movie was about a stagecoach travelling through Monument Valley, where it was attacked by a marauding band of Indians. It dealt with the relationships between the people on the stagecoach, and showed the Indians as creatures with a raw animal thirst for blood. Intellectually the film was extremely reactionary, but the direction was outstanding because it offered the specialists in the audience a whole range of wonderful formal ideas. The acting was pure naturalism.

The film experts, who had come to the late-night screening directly from the première of a new Czech film called

Heroes with Callused Hands, studied these elements intensely. In the dimness of the salon, they stared wide-eyed at the crude charm of the love scenes. A famous director, his brow furrowed in concentration, smacked his lips audibly at an original close-up shot looking straight down the barrel of a Colt six-shooter whose cylinder slowly revolved on the screen. Danny was the only one who simply let himself be carried away by the story. The hoofbeats of the horses thundered and the stagecoach lurched and rattled among the rocks, pursued by hordes of red men dressed in feathers and armed with bows. Despite a long-cultivated skepticism, Danny felt deeply anxious about the fate of the beautiful girl in the stagecoach, and Lizetka obviously felt the same, for when the redskins let loose their first salvo of arrows, she grasped his hand. This brought him back to reality. When the need is greatest, he thought bitterly, divine intervention is usually close at hand – in the movies, at least. Then a cluster of men in U.S. Cavalry hats popped up on the horizon. Danny squeezed Lizetka's hand and she returned the squeeze. "After them!" yelled the minister joyfully, and the prize-winning director added, "Hip! Hip! Hip!" "After them!" roared several experts, and Lizetka jerked her hand out of Danny's and added her voice to the swelling expressions of partisan support. Now the shots came rapidly: horses' hoofs crashing like hammers on the stone-hard ground, pistols firing, terrified faces inside the stagecoach, and the painted faces of the Indian cut-throats were rapidly intercut with the determined Yankee faces of the cavalrymen. The salon thundered with applause and the stamping of feet. The specialists rose whooping to their feet, the women shrieked, the minister clenched his fists and emitted incomprehensible but energetic grunts. A sharp, piercing falsetto rose above the hellish pandemonium: "Hurraaaaaaaaaaaaaaaaaaaaaah!"

Danny got to his feet, kissed Lizetka's indifferent hand, and walked out of the projection room. He had to catch the night train that would get him back before reveille the next morning. He was already facing one disaster – the one in the guard-house – and he didn't want to add to that another breach of the orders set for the army by the people who were the source of all power, and the only ones who enjoyed all the rights and privileges of the state.

5

THE AUTUMN INSPECTION

OF POLITICAL AND

COMBAT READINESS

A s it turned out, the tank commander was rescued from the consequences of his dereliction of duty by a stupid idea advanced by the army's general staff. Orders had come down from headquarters that the officers in charge of monitoring the annual autumn inspection of political and combat readiness in the Eighth Tank Division would be arriving two weeks ahead of schedule. This change threatened to disrupt the quiet process of manufacturing illusions about the real state of readiness in the division — something that in army slang was referred to as movie-making. The Pygmy Devil was so upset at the news that he completely forgot about the night-time escapades in the guardhouse.

At a special course for officers, the division CO, General Helebrant, was just taking up the matter of patriotism and treason raised in the past year by the case of Slánský and his ten henchmen. He enjoyed mulling over the question out loud. Those eleven gallows had lent the problem a boldness and clarity dear to the hearts of military pedagogues, and besides, just the day before, a young lady the general had been trying to win over for at least a year had finally agreed to marry him. She came from a good Communist family with connections in the Ministry of Defence. The general's voice was full of warmth and enthusiasm.

"One's mind – not to mention one's political conscience, comrades – boggles. Slánský was paid" – and he paused – "at least thirty thousand a month, and yet he betrayed his country. I – and you too, comrades – none of us makes half that, yet we will never – what?"

"Betray our country," said the eager-to-please Lieutenant Hezký, with feeling. At that instant the general's adjutant burst into the room. The dispatch from the general staff office had come while he was negotiating with the commander of the local detachment of the political detainees unit for the free transfer of some lumber from the site of the future football stadium to the site of his future weekend cottage. The general scanned the dispatch quickly, blanched, and, with the courage worthy of a tank commander, went to the telephone and postponed the wedding that had been arranged only the day before. Then he rushed to the division's political department.

There Major Sádlo was slowly turning the handle of the duplicating machine, reproducing a top secret and rather unreadable (and unread) document called "Instructions of the Divisional Political Department for the Political Backing of the Preparations of the Autumn Inspection of Political and Combat Readiness". Captain Vavruška was putting together the monthly summary of the mass cultural activities of the Eighth Tank Division, based on reports passed to him by the leaders of the individual regiments, who in turn had assembled their reports from material passed to them by the leaders of the individual battalions, which were compiled from memoranda written by the political officers of the individual squadrons, who had conscientiously fabricated these reports in conformity with the program of mass cultural activity invented a month before by Major Sádlo and Captain Vavruška and sent to all units in the division.

The general entered the room, sat down heavily on his

chair, and informed the officers of the impending visitation, which had rendered instantly obsolete the beautifully thought out system now being duplicated. Stencils were torn out of the machine and replaced with new ones, the duplicator began cranking with unaccustomed speed, and the new orders, reformulated as a series of thinly veiled threats, were soon on their way to all units, where they in turn provoked typewriters into a flurry of unaccustomed efficiency.

★ ★ ★

The orders hit Captain Matka of the Seventh Tank Battalion like a bolt of lightning. He had just been watching with great pleasure as Sergeant Filip clandestinely assembled a sophisticated radio receiver for him out of spare parts, while hiding behind the grille of the secret document depository, and the bad news ruined his satisfaction at seeing a job well done. Feeling sorry for himself, he gave his duty officers a brusque order to round up his staff, regardless of where they were, and assemble them in five minutes. When they arrived, he gave them all a thorough tongue-lashing rich in military imagery, like "I'll make your tonsils sit up and beg for supper!" and "I'll make your hams cry out for mercy!", and then marched off to the meeting at divisional headquarters, feeling that his forceful performance had helped lay the proper groundwork for the upcoming inspection and perhaps even guaranteed that the men would do well.

★ ★ ★

In the meantime, Captain Matka's chief of staff, First Lieutenant Pinkas, had assembled the commanders of the four squadrons and their political officers. In a brief and somewhat listless fashion, he informed them of the tasks that lay ahead (as usual these were beyond their capacities) and then dismissed them without offering a glimmer of hope. Next, his face more a mask than ever, he went to the depository for top-secret documents, threw out Sergeant Filip and his unfinished super-radio, and began drawing up an elementary set of orders. This was really Captain Matka's job, but – as usual – Captain Matka was incapable of doing it, and so, using his power to delegate work, he had ordered Pinkas to do it. Lieutenant Pinkas also had the power to delegate, but none of his subordinates, with the exception of some of the enlisted noncoms, was capable of carrying out such an order either. So the first lieutenant, trapped in one of life's conundrums, locked himself in the depository and didn't emerge for two weeks. He even slept there, and sometimes, before dozing off for two or three hours among the secret documents, he thought about his wife, Janinka. Pinkas was an old front-line soldier, and his logical brain told him it was improbable that Janinka, surrounded by so many young men, had remained faithful to him. The thought would inspire momentary fits of jealousy, but in the end he would be too tired, and too wedded to his duty (his military duty, that is), to do anything about it. He would sink back into his uneasy sleep, all thoughts of her round breasts and her delightful mound adorned with those delicious little curls forced out of his mind by the unresolved problem of how to execute a flanking manoeuvre with the indirect support of the artillery. And then, as trapped as his wife (though differently) in the Kobylec army base, he would rise from his improvised field cot, make himself a cup of black coffee, and sit down again to his maps.

And towards morning, Danny would slink along the alley

of chestnut trees, the raindrops rustling the russet leaves, and sneak past the discreet sentry to catch an hour of sleep before reveille.

★ ★ ★

The eager-to-please Lieutenant Hezký, CO of the First Tank Squadron, trotted briskly into his office and enthusiastically tried to stir up some activity. The third-year men were prudently absent, and when he tried to find enough men to tidy up, he could only find a few first-year recruits. Then he came across Tank Commander Smiřický in the cultural centre, in the middle of writing something which he slid under a fresh copy of the army daily, *Defence of the People*, when the lieutenant walked in. Normally Hezký would have asked the tank commander what he was hiding, but today he was preoccupied with grander designs, and merely gave an order. Within fifteen minutes, Danny was leading a ragtag formation of greenhorns across the base and up the hill towards the long shacks that stood near the woods and served as classrooms for the Seventh Tank Battalion. "In view of the upcoming inspection of combat readiness," ran the order, they were "to remove from the desks and latrines all politically inappropriate graffiti."

The camp was humming with unusual activity. Several indignant platoons (all passes had been cancelled because of the tests) were crowding the asphalt roads, sweeping them with brooms which they got (or stole) where they could. Columns of smoke curled into the sky from bonfires as they burned the dry chestnut leaves swept from the roadways or plucked from the unruly trees to which they still clung. Soldiers with artistic talent were assigned to rake the little plots of grass by the entrance to the barracks, and to use sand, smooth stones, coloured glass, and artless wooden models of the T-34 tank to construct displays that looked like ancient grave mounds, decorated with reddish stars made of crushed brick, mosaic portraits of Generalissimo Stalin and General Čepička, and strident slogans like EVERY TANKIST AN EXEMPLARY SOLDIER. A chorus of hoarse singers could be heard from one of the cultural centres, trying to master the rigours of two-part harmony in a thrilling song called "Forward with Čepička". The wind wafted away the hoarse cantata, and groups of men in dirty coveralls slouched along beneath the columns of smoke to the hangars of the 117th Tank Brigade, where the doors were rattling open and the motors thundering into life. The armoured division was awakening from a year-long slumber and, prodded by the officers, was trying to achieve in practice what the officers had achieved in their reports.

When Danny's demolition squad turned past the barracks of the Second Battalion, they heard someone calling out to them. The voice seemed to come from the sky. They looked up and there, fifteen metres above the ground, they could see the figure of Corporal Müller leaning over the edge of the roof. When Danny yelled up to ask what he was doing, the corporal's voice, made fainter by the distance but clear enough all the same, came back: "We're washing the birdshit off the roof."

Perhaps the officer who had given that order was trying to cover himself in case God showed up in person to carry out the inspection.

★   ★   ★

Tank Commander Smiřický led his squad up to the battalion

classrooms, which stood beneath a sandy slope with pine boughs swaying overhead. The door was locked, but after all four of them pounded and kicked at it so long that an inexperienced person would have given up, the sleepy face of Private Semerák appeared in the window. Semerák had a weak heart and had been declared superintendent of the classrooms. He lived up here like a hermit and was therefore practically exempt from standing orders.

Semerák's workplace had a soporific effect on people. As soon as the squad stepped inside the door, they immediately lay down; by the time Danny had managed to prepare a tin of green paint for the desks and a bucket of tar for the latrines, they were all sound asleep. It took a good deal of shouting and shaking to wake them up.

"Now, boys," he said, "we're to look for dirty graffiti and anti-state slogans. Report them to me and we'll paint them over, and then we'll take a break."

Since this was more attractive than a lot of jobs, the team abstained from the usual complaints and spread out through the classrooms. Soon there were requests for the tank commander to come and carry out inspections. He did so with relish.

Our heartfelt thanks
To Lady Luck.
We'll soon be home
So who gives a fuck?

This quatrain, in the motors classroom, was written on the drum of the left clutch of a motor, painted silver, that was used for classroom demonstrations. The classroom itself was a sunny place filled with beautifully constructed teaching aids that recruits had spent many days making. They were so well made, in fact, that they were never used, but stored away carefully for special occasions like the annual reviews, inspections by generals, or visits by Soviet advisers.

On a chrome-plated cylinder head that stood under a picture of a terrible battle, these words were gouged into the metal for eternity:

> *I'm warning you right now, sarge,*
> *Though I may be just a recruit to you,*
> *If you don't get out of my way, sarge,*
> *I'm going to put the boot to you.*
>
> *I'll turn your balls into bookends*
> *And tie your guts in a noose;*
> *So you'd better get out of my way, sarge –*
> *I warn you, you better vamoose.*

When they had eradicated what they could, and had left the classrooms bereft of anything aesthetic, the squad went out to the latrine to complete their work of demolition.

★　★　★

The latrine was a breezy structure with no doors, a row of round holes in a slanted board, and a sloping gutter that reeked of tar, urine, and dehydrated lime. The enormous wall above the gutter, bearing the words YES, SIR! drawn in large, bold strokes in whitewash, provided unlimited opportunities to the muses of military life. Among the gallery of drawings rendering a wide variety of male and female sex organs were clusters of slogans and verses displaying a remarkable range of expression, from the poetic to the political and pornographic.

There was even a special corner, scribbled with incomprehensible verse, reserved for soldiers of Hungarian nationality.

Beside some notices that were essentially want-ads, such as *Big dick seeks slick chick*, a die-hard ideologist had written: *Exploitation must be eliminated!* Beneath the traditional assertion that *Nothing beats a good shit, especially with the wind blowing up your ass* (the truth of this observation was confirmed by the sound of the wind constantly wheezing through the holes in the seats, sounding like an old, worm-eaten pump organ), some reactionary hand had inscribed: *Death to bloody Bolshevism!*, but the last word had been struck out by a progressive hand and replaced with the word *capitalism*. And right below the slogan *Screw orders! Give us women!* a lascivious poet had carved the following lines on the wall, enclosing them inside an enormous, hairy female pudendum:

Annie, Annie, what you doin?
They told me you was only foolin.
Never mind, I make you a big one
Out of a giant wienie bun.

I don't want your stale old bun.
I use it once and then its done.
Make me one of ermine skin;
Feels so nice when I slip it in.

The soldiers went to work more slowly here. The wealth of graffiti gave them the idea — essentially a cultural idea — that they should preserve at least part of this treasury for posterity. And so they pulled out notebooks and slowly, in halting letters, copied the best of them onto smudgy, dog-eared pages. Danny sat on one of the empty holes and stared at a strip of wall illuminated by the sun, which had just broken through the clouds. A Slovak soldier had written here a brief ode to joy:

> *Get ready, my dear, to open your sweet honeycomb*
> *Cause tomorrow, girl, this boy is comin home.*

And the tank commander began thinking, and then day-dreaming. People – or rather the People – are poets without knowing it, some realistically inclined cultural worker had once told him, and he thought about this, or rather rolled his usual vague ideas around in his head, mixed with thoughts of Janinka's curly garden of delights and questions of ideology which he cynically ridiculed yet secretly wasn't so sure about, and these became mingled with the round face of his blonde future colleague in the big publishing house, and the green eyes of the unconquerable Lizetka. His thoughts were complicated by the terrible burden of life, which he only really escaped when he played sarcastic syncopations on a slavering alto sax in the regimental show band, satirizing the joyous tone of the awful tunes they had to play for members of the local collective farms around the Kobylec base.

Finally he got up and ordered his squad back to the class-rooms, where they arranged the furniture as comfortably as they could and spent the rest of the day, until lights-out, sleeping.

★　★　★

Meanwhile the other members of the Seventh Tank Battalion had swept the roadways and rooftops and cleaned the oil stains away with brushes and hot water. Next, the Pygmy Devil had herded them all into the Park of Relaxation, and there, until late at night, they had spread fresh yellow sand on the walks and picked up scrap paper and pine-cones. Then they scrubbed the barracks and tidied up the store-rooms until two in the morning, and there was still time left over to polish the copper kettles in the battalion kitchens. They also brushed down their walking-out uniforms and carried them up to the freshly tidied attics, lest the uniforms become dusty when they refilled their straw mattresses (the next task on the list). Until the dust settled and the barracks could be used once more, they repaired a picket fence around battalion headquarters and painted it green. When they finally went to bed at five in the morning, the rooms were well aired and they (like the tank commander, who was just returning from Zephyr Hill) still had a whole hour to sleep before reveille.

★   ★   ★

The autumn inspection of the Seventh Tank Battalion began with a test in the theory of gunnery. The anxious officers and phlegmatic men were assembled in a classroom equipped with a model of a battlefield, with little wooden tanks that could be pushed about with pointers. A rather portly one-eyed man with gigantic epaulettes of undeniable Soviet taste and czarist provenance stood with Captain Matka on one side and Lieutenant Vrabec on the other.

The first to be tested, Sergeant Žloudek, came into the room with a dumb look on his face and was asked to respond to a question that, for pedagogical reasons, was formulated in highly graphic terms:

"Your tank is speeding through burning streets, with the smoking ruins of walls tumbling all about you. The city is under heavy fire from enemy artillery. Your machine-gunner has just taken out an American soldier armed with a bazooka, but others may be lurking behind any window or pile of rubble. You look through your sights and suddenly you see a Sherman tank enter the square and swing its cannon round to bear on you. Your response?"

Sergeant Žloudek opened his mouth but nothing came out. The lieutenant raised his voice a half-tone and continued, with the aid of vague gestures: "The Sherman is coming nearer. You can make out the white star on its plating. An enemy marine leaps out of the tank and the first shots ricochet off your armour-plating. The church tower collapses in flames. Your response?"

"I open fire," replied the gunner.

"But how, Comrade Sergeant?"

Sergeant Žloudek didn't specify. It seemed that fear had taken possession of him.

"The American tank is coming at you full speed," the lieutenant continued dramatically, glancing around nervously at the Soviet general, who was sitting on a chair beneath a slogan promising eternal loyalty to General Čepička. "From a street behind it a heavy self-propelled gun emerges. How do you respond?"

The desperate gunner looked at his loader, the frowning Private Bamza, beside him. First Lieutenant Vrabec noticed this, and instead of calling on Sergeant Maňas, who was waving his hand ostentatiously, he turned to Bamza.

"You, Comrade Private. How would you proceed?"

Bamza turned his gloomy eyes on the officer as if Vrabec were laying a trap especially for him, and replied rebelliously: "With the cannon. The machine-guns aren't worth sh — I mean, they can't knock out armour," he quickly corrected himself.

"Correct," said First Lieutenant Vrabec, casting an anxious glance at the Soviet general. He, however, appeared to have

fallen asleep. Perhaps this was a consequence of the breakfast served to him in the officers' mess, which had consisted
mainly of vodka. "But how are you going to fire? I mean *how?*"
insisted Vrabec. At last he noticed Sergeant Maňas, who was
longing to show off his knowledge. "Suppose you tell us, Comrade Sergeant. Shrapnel bombs are bursting all around you.
The characteristic barrel of an anti-tank bazooka emerges from
a bombed-out doorway. The self-propelled gun stops and aims
its 250mm navy gun straight at you. Your response?"

"Using the sector method, I estimate the range of the
enemy vehicle," said Maňas. "From the known height of the
Sherman tank, and from the assumed velocity of the shell in
a straight line, I apply the formula

$$D = \frac{s \times 0.75}{v}$$

where 'D' is the distance within the limits of the gun's range,
's' the estimated speed, 0.75 the formulaic constant, and 'v'
the velocity of the anti-tank shot. Then, making the necessary
adjustments to the sights, I set up on the third scale on the
left, which is for armour-piercing projectiles, the distance that
has already been calculated, give the appropriate order to the
loader and the driver, and fire."

First Lieutenant Vrabec looked around proudly at the general, but he was still sound asleep. It didn't matter anyway, for
he didn't understand a word of Czech, and Captain Matka –
acting on the politically correct but linguistically dubious
assumption that these two fraternal armies spoke practically
the same language – hadn't provided him with an interpreter.

★   ★   ★

About an hour later, the men of the Seventh Tank Battalion sat in their war chariots on Zephyr Hill to demonstrate in practice what they had learned in theory. On the opposite slope there was a group of green mockups ranging from small mounds meant to indicate an enemy soldier wielding a bazooka, to an enormous piece of stretched canvas painted with a picture of a camouflaged bunker. The committee again included the one-eyed Soviet general, but thanks to the cold autumnal wind he was now fully awake. They all stood on a wooden reviewing stand near the married officers' quarters, holding onto their caps. The bitter wind was blowing with such force that it seemed to drive the tracer bullets spewing out of the advancing tanks right off their course.

Sergeant Žloudek consistently scored bull's eyes, perhaps because here he was not subjected to horrific battle scenarios. Every soldier perks up the moment he gets his hands on live ammunition, but those instincts were particularly strong in his case. Tank Commander Smiřický sat in the turret, holding the handgrips tightly, and left the commands to the gunner. Private Bamza, whose instincts were similarly aroused, flawlessly loaded the copper-headed ammunition into the breech. "Driver, halt!" came Žloudek's voice in the tank commander's earphones. Corporal Střevlíček's foot hit the brakes; the tank stopped abruptly, rocked, and came to a halt, and with a satisfying thump the round flew out of the barrel. Through the gunsight in the turret the tank commander saw the enemy anti-tank gun on the yellowing slope opposite fly into pieces. When they advanced again and turned to look at the observation post, a red flag was flying above it, indicating a direct hit.

They attacked five times in all, destroying five targets. Then they drove back to the observation post and got out of the tank. As Danny was sliding down the armour-plating to the ground, he almost knocked over a tubby gunner covered by an enormous helmet who was just getting ready to climb aboard. From under the padding of his helmet a pair of panicky eyes appeared, and the gunner's face was chalk-white. The order came, and the helmeted gunner scrambled up on the turret and slipped inside.

"It's Maňas!" came Bamza's voice. He was standing behind Danny. "Let's hide in the bunker. Come on!"

It was indeed Tank Commander Maňas, who had done so well in the theory of gunnery, but Bamza's urgent suggestion was not illogical. To one side of the observation platform, where the general's epaulettes were sparkling in the red rays of the sun, stood an abandoned bunker built for reasons that had long since been forgotten. Bamza, who was not known for speed, practically ran towards it. Danny hesitated; Střevlíček and Žloudek were leaning defiantly against the observation platform. But caution triumphed, and the tank commander followed Bamza into the bunker. There, over a fire fed by wood acquired by chopping up a newly constructed latrine, soldiers were playing cards and drinking something from a filthy bottle. Danny stepped up to the gun-slot and looked out at the range.

The tank was just setting off. On the far hillside, which was covered with mangy patches of rusty autumn grass, a thin line of flame was advancing; one of the tracer bullets had set the grass on fire. Beautiful white puffy clouds crept slowly along the crest of the hill as the rattling tank lurched forward.

A pleasant sense of peace prevailed, awakened by the natural beauty of the place, the approaching end of army service, and Danny's knowledge that somewhere close behind him, in one of those pre-fab apartments, Janinka might be looking out the window — Janinka, who hated tanks but not the men who ran them. A raven circled above the growling tank, clearly see-ing it as an enormous animal that would leave large amounts of nourishing waste behind. At that moment the steel machine stopped, rocked slightly on its springs, and settled.

Danny was now completely alert. What should have fol-lowed was a burst of flame from the cannon's barrel and the dry thump of an explosion – and indeed that was what hap-pened. The barrel obediently released its invisible projectile and, on the crest of the hill opposite, a lone spruce tree was sliced in two. But what came next was completely unexpected. The tank roared forward and the turret began to rotate slowly, flashing intermittent fire. The familiar chatter of a machine-gun echoed across the valley. Steel fragments ricocheted off the concrete sides of the bunker, and the hand of Private Kobliha, which was just about to slap down the ace of spades, stopped in mid-air. The barking of the machine-gun continued and Danny, crouching by the gun-slot, stared in amazement as the tank began a slow turn back towards the observation platform. The turret was still rotating rapidly and tracer shells were flying in all directions. He looked at the observation plat-form. The one-eyed general was just jumping off it, followed by his cap with its red and gold band. Under the platform, Střevlíček and Žloudek were flattening themselves to the ground in textbook fashion, and behind them a window on the third floor of the officers' quarters suddenly exploded into a geyser of glass and smoke. Shards scattered in all directions, glittering in the autumn sun like a fistful of diamonds tossed into the air.

At last the ammunition magazine was empty and the rag-ing monster fell silent. The tank came to a halt directly below the observation platform, and the limp form of Tank Com-mander Maňas was extracted and carried off. Blood was flow-ing down his face and he was sobbing hysterically.

★   ★   ★

That evening the intellectuals among the non-commissioned officers found out what had happened, at a seance held by Lieutenant Dr. Sadař, who had tended Tank Commander Maňas's wounds. When Danny arrived much later (he had remained on the hill to make sure the wild salvo hadn't injured the first lieutenant's wife and, having so determined, had stayed on to comfort her) they had also received a report from divisional staff. That afternoon, Maňas, the most active cultural worker in the battalion, had found himself in a T-34 tank for the first time in his life. Up until then, he had mastered all the military arts purely by theory. He was the bravest sloganeer, organizer of voluntary brigades to harvest potatoes, speaker for all occasions, and contributor to the divisional newspaper, *The People's Army*. He had also written a sonnet to General Čepička, which had got him an audience with General Helebrant, who had appointed him to the divisional committee of the Czechoslovak Union of Youth, where he had been put in charge of creating model billboards. He might have completed his compulsory military service without ever seeing the inside of a tank, had not his excellent results in gunnery theory so impressed a general who'd been seconded to Kobylec from another base to chair the autumn inspection that he insisted that Maňas, although a tank commander, take part in the practical gunnery test. No one, not even Maňas himself, could come up with a plausible excuse to get him out of it. So he took his place in the gunner's seat and grabbed hold of the cannon lever, and they set off. When the tank stopped – not on his orders, but because the driver was used to the routine – Maňas lost his balance and grabbed the trigger by mistake. The cannon went off, the noise made Maňas jump, and he slipped off his seat. Falling with his arms out-stretched, he grabbed the machine-gun trigger with his right hand and the lever to rotate the turret with his left, setting off both mechanisms. Deafened by the explosions and dizzy from the rotation of the turret, he kept a firm grip on both levers until he finally fainted away.

The non-coms seated around the stove in the doctor's infirmary lifted their cups of tea and drank to the memory of the gallant brown-noser. Then Sergeant Krajta pulled out a brand-new number of the divisional magazine, which, as it turned out, contained an article by the newly fallen hero of theory. It was called "Farewell, Faithful Friend".

The wood crackled in the stove and an aroma wafted up from the cups – an aroma from the liquid in the filthy bottle, which had managed to find its way from the bunker to the infirmary, though no one could say how. Sergeant Krajta read aloud from the article in a cracked voice:

So today is the last time. What a pity! I've become so accus-tomed to you. Though at first I didn't want to know you, though I was even afraid of you, I have fallen in love with you over these two years, so warm and close to me, like my best friend. I have learned to know you and understand you, and I recognize your foibles. Often I have devoted all my free time to you, and often part of my nights as well. And the wonderful times we have spent together! Do you remember that marvellous, warm, quiet evening during manoeuvres when I lay beside you in the bushes, guarding the security of our beloved country? A spirited buck and his mate leapt by us, and I so much wanted to feel some-one's caress – so I caressed you, my faithful companion, my lovely T-34!

At this point Sergeant Krajta spat to one side and announced that it was generally known that Tank Commander Maňas had carried on zöophilia in the stable with the regimental mule – and just then a hospital orderly called Beránek stood up and opened the door leading to the infirmary, where Maňas was recovering from shock and from his wounds. When he saw Maňas, Beránek shouted into that warm, wonderful night – just the kind the hapless tank commander had described – "Hey, we've just been reading how you fucked a T-34."

★   ★   ★

Despite this and other misfortunes, the Seventh Tank Battalion and its commanders finally made it through to the review parade before the Commander-in-Chief of the Armoured and Mechanized Army. Exemplary Tankist medals were to be distributed and, as a grand finale, the title of Master Tank Driver was to be awarded to Sergeant Očko of this notorious battalion. That decorative bandage was to salve the scarred soul of Captain Matka, to heal the wounds inflicted by having men so ignorant that they got lost behind enemy lines with a whole squadron of tanks, or didn't know which direction Prague was, or could name only a handful of the thirty-seven incumbent government ministers during a political readiness exam.

Captain Matka invited Očko to his office so that, with the assistance of Růžička and Hospodin, he could help the sergeant prepare himself morally and ideologically for the great honour. He guessed that such preparation would be especially appropriate in Očko's case, for the driver had a habit of peppering his language with expletives that had no place in the vocabulary of the new socialist soldier. Later, Sergeant Očko – who was sometimes called "Fuckinočko" – gave a laconic report of that two-hour session in the captain's study.

"Fuck me, man," he said, unwinding his smelly puttees, "they shouted at me for two fuckin' hours, the pigs, and they told me I should be fuckin' proud of the fuckin' honour and stuff like that, man, and when I asked them how about some fuckin' leave, you know what the fuckers said? They fuckin' said I should fuckin' wait till I'm fuckin' back in civvies, man. I mean, fuck that."

★　★　★

The glorious day finally arrived. The entire division assembled in dress uniform on the football field for inspection. It felt like a real autumn day; a cold wind was blowing, the flags were flapping on the roof of the reviewing stand, and the men of the Seventh Tank Battalion stood in immaculate new white underwear that had been issued that morning, and had been inspected and found spotless by a group of generals. At almost the last moment, Captain Matka was afflicted by what he hoped was the final disaster during this inspection: one of the battalion's political agitators, Sergeant Mácha, was found to have immoral tattoos on his body, and in a notebook kept by Private Mengele the committee found a sketch of an unfinished trip around the world, indicated by a thick double line against the background of the two hemispheres. The double line was divided into seven hundred and thirty little squares, each representing a day of army service. Most of them were already filled in with red ink. The sketch clearly had an international significance, because the Russian general understood what it meant without being told, and Major Borovička sentenced Mengele to ten nights' detention in the guardhouse on the spot.

But these additional lapses by his subordinates no longer had the power to shake the already shaken Captain Matka. He stood tall and erect at the head of his officer corps, the grey clouds overhead reflected in the polish of his riding boots. Birds circled beneath the clouds, flocking together for the trip south, and beneath them the chairman of the examination committee delivered a grand speech. Proudly he affirmed the splendid achievements of the proud Seventh Tank Battalion, for in the overall evaluation it had been given the proud mark of three, which meant good. But we must not conceal from ourselves, he went on, the fact that alongside these proud achievements we must also think about the prou – that is, the considerable shortcomings yet to be rectified. And while he had spoken only vaguely about the successes, he now began to enumerate an almost endless list of very specific faults.

When the general had exhausted his supply of critical remarks, the division commander stepped onto the platform and declared that military service was a rugged experience, just as the Soviet tanks themselves were rugged, and that soldiers had to be rugged too, and that tank soldiers had to be the most rugged of all. The flock of birds circling under the grey clouds was still trying to decide whether to quit this charming autumn land while General Helebrant expressed the conviction that, should a war occur, military service would be even more rugged than it was now, yet today his soldiers had shown that the tough fist of our People's Democratic Army would come crashing down on the enemy and – under the leadership of the supreme commander, General Dr. Alexej Čepička – bring him to his knees. Overcome with military emotion, he declared that he would be satisfied if the soldiers of the tank corps could always overcome all the obstacles of civilian life with a brave tank-corps "Hurrah!" on their lips.

How they could do this in practice was something no

one could imagine at that moment. But, following the Soviet model, the troops shouted out their "Hurrah!" on the parade ground, at least, and the general took over and moved on to the climax of the program, the decoration of Sergeant Očko.

From the tannoy came the order "Troops – atten – SHUN!" The division became still and heard the general's thunderous voice – "Sergeant Očko!" – coming over the loudspeakers like the sound of a trumpet heralding Judgement Day, and then, in contrast to this roll of electronic thunder, the thin, unamplified voice of Sergeant Očko, "Here!" and finally the Jovian order to approach.

Sergeant Očko set off on his triumphant pilgrimage across the parade ground, marching in a somewhat non-regulation step. He mounted the reviewing stand and presented himself to the general in a rather slap-dash manner. The general removed the gilded medal from its case and pinned it on Očko's chest. As he did so, his godlike voice boomed out over the tannoy: "Comrade Sergeant, by the powers invested in me by the Minister of National Defence, General Doctor Alexej Čepička, I name you Master Tank Driver."

This was followed by a gurgling sound in the tannoy which was presumably supposed to be the regulation response "I serve the people!" and which could only have been pronounced by Sergeant Očko himself. At this point the general, who was a rare bird – an officer with experience at the front – forgot himself. Moved, perhaps, by the wind-bitten rural face before him, and recalling other such faces which in times of war had surrounded him in the tanks – faces so unlike the faces surrounding him now at the ministry – he made an unfortunate miscalculation. Sergeant Očko's red, bearlike hands suggested to him that his mastery of the art of tank-driving was real, not just theoretical, like so many of the skills he had witnessed during the few days of inspection, and the emotional war veteran asked kindly, "Well now, Comrade Sergeant, how did you learn to drive a tank so well?"

His words were carried clearly over the tannoy, and were immediately followed by the no less clear voice of Sergeant Očko: "No fuckin' sweat, Comrade General. Like, in civilian life I drive a fuckin' cat."

Behind them, in the ranks of the officers, the legs of the CO of the Seventh Tank Battalion, Captain Václav Matka, gave out under him, and his political officer had to hold him up.

And the flock of birds in the sky finally made up their minds, fell into formation without an order being given, and started the journey south, to more hospitable climes still ruled by the class enemy.

★   ★   ★

The Defence of the People, the army daily, began running editorials aimed at political officers, with headlines like "Towards the Correct Evaluation of the Work of Political Workers" or "Towards Political and Moral Assistance to Soldiers and NCOs Leaving Active Service" or even "Towards Making Farmers Out of Reservists". Inside this popular paper, articles appeared in which soldiers of the Nth unit sang the praises of two wonderful years spent in the good, manly camaraderie of the People's Democratic Army so that loved ones could sleep peacefully at home. There was even something by a young greenhorn who couldn't possibly have joined up yet, because it was too early in the year to draft recruits, but who was already trying to gain favour by reassuring those going back to civilian life that he would take up their weapons so that they could go on building socialism in peace. Soldiers and NCOs of various divisions bade tearful farewells to their rifles, tanks, cannon, mortars, engineering instruments, and poison gases, in articles so brimming with heartfelt emotion that Private First Class Dr. Mlejnek was moved to submit — under the pseudonym Pravomil Poslušný — a piece called "Towards Extending Our Beloved Service to the Motherland", arguing for a return to the seven-year compulsory military service that had prevailed under Maria Theresa. The article wasn't printed, but the soldier actually bearing that unlikely name was summoned by the military secret police and later, on his return to civilian life, sent to prison for seven years for insulting the people's democratic system.

Obliging soldiers — those who, to the very last moments of that happiest period of their lives, had remained afraid of the political officers — decorated the clubrooms and bulletin boards for the last time with slogans urging the fresh new defenders of the peace to walk in the footsteps of the famous Nth Battalion, to emulate the great traditions of such-and-such a unit. Official photographs of exemplary tankists, looking unusually bellicose in their tank helmets, were displayed to inspire new recruits with the appropriate feistiness. Although it was never said, it was assumed that most of the recruits had girlfriends in civilian life, and thus one of the most effective ways of encouraging military zeal was to promise the recruits photographs of themselves wearing tank helmets, which they could then autograph and mail to their loved ones. Unfortunately, no zeal was necessary to have one's picture taken in a helmet, for the local photographer would rent a helmet to members of any unit whatever, for a price. When Lieutenant Hospodin eventually discovered this little sideline, the photographer was given ten years in prison for sabotaging the psychological readiness of the men.

As far as Danny could remember, *The Defence of the People* had never been read so closely — at least, not in the

circle of intellectual NCOs — as it was now. An employee of
the Office for the Advancement of Labour arrived in camp
and held a big meeting and variety show in the auditorium to
encourage soldiers to sign up for work in the mines or in heavy
industry. If the event was well attended, it wasn't because the
men were drawn by the promise of fresh opportunities to build
socialism, but because they were tired of hiding all day from
officers who wanted, in the little time remaining, to exploit
their unpaid labour in improving various facilities, both on
the base and in their private homes. This was work which the
soldiers refused to do, both out of laziness and on principle
(the greenhorns would be here in a few days anyway); they
preferred to wander through the woods on the edge of camp,
hiding from the officers' search parties in shell and gre-
nade craters on the shooting range, eating salami stolen from
the mess, and using the gigantic straw-stacks near the infantry training ground for short-arm practice with Sergeant
Babinčáková, her two colleagues, and a girl from the Youth
Union whom Private Semerák had smuggled into camp in the
back of a milk truck.

But even such evasions and diversions soon became tiring,
and the soldiers turned up in large numbers for the recruiting
campaign. It was a beautiful afternoon, and fresh air wafted
through the windows, promising repose. Some of the men
fell asleep right away, others listened to a long introductory
speech by the divisional political officer, Major Sádlo. Then
an employee of the Office for the Advancement of Labour
used attractive statistics to sketch out the advantages of min-
ing and steel production as a means of building socialism.
The program concluded with a poem read by Sergeant Bivoj
Balík, from his new collection. Those who hadn't already
fallen asleep now arranged themselves more comfortably
in their chairs and, in the hopes that it might induce re-

freshing slumber, listened to his opening lines:

> *Today, we say goodbye with thanks*
> *To guns and puttees, mines and tanks;*
> *At the threshold of work our women stand*
> *And place red roses in our hand.*
> *Two years we've lived here, like real brothers*
> *We swear we won't forget each other.*
> *Our steely tenderness of you's a part*
> *We'll carry you with us in our heart*
> *And swear*

The poet took a deep breath to give the oath its proper emphasis and pathos, but at that very moment, through the open window, the distant sounds of a song drifted into the room. At first, neither the melody nor the words were discernible.

> *that if we're called to stand*

continued the sergeant,

> *We'll give our lives for our dear land.*
> *All of us here are prepared to fight*
> *To show the enemy our might!*

Just as the poet made this assertion, the words of the song, carried on the evening breeze, became audible:

> *Roll out the barrel,*
> *We'll have a barrel of fun....*

Those in the audience who were drifting off to sleep were suddenly aroused as the drunken voices sang on:

Roll out the barrel,
We've got the blues on the run....

A hum of excitement went through the hall and here and there voices joined quietly in the melody, while the unknown minnesingers outside continued with great verve:

Zing boom ta-ra-rel....

As long as we live, our wrath will guard
This holy oath within our heart!

cried Sergeant Balík, and the voices from outside commented:

Ring out a song of good cheer....

Prepared to live that happy life! The sergeant tried to outshout the singers, but his voice was drowned out in the crescendo —

Now's the time to rooooll the barrel

— as the hall joined in, softly at first, and then in an increasingly loud voice:

For the gang's – ALL – HERE!

With this song on their lips the men rushed out of the hall, and in the next quarter of an hour they filled all five pubs in the neighbouring village to capacity.

★   ★   ★

By about eleven o'clock that evening, the blood alcohol of almost everyone in those five pubs had gone well past the level officially permitted by the army's chief health officer. The squad of sentries at the gate, who sent every conspicuously noisy or unusually quiet soldier under escort to the infirmary for a blood test, had good hunting. The military police who tried to restore order in the Jan Žižka Inn fared less well. They were insulted by a foul-mouthed corporal who boasted, "You shithead gumshoes, you better roll your fat asses out of here or I'll kick them so hard you'll be eating shit for a week," and when they tried to apprehend him, the crowd pushed them out of the pub and threw them down the steps into a muddy ditch.

With true tank-corps grit, they cleaned the mud off themselves and went back to work in the Angel Pub, where they apprehended Sergeant Kobliha for illicit trade with civilians. He had sold his Exemplary Tankist medal for fifty crowns to a civilian who later turned out to be the district secretary of the Czechoslovak Union of Youth, and then spent the money on a bottle of alcohol called Devil's Brew.

At the next pub, The Magistrate's Arms, a first-year recruit in a fit of despair over the long year of civic duty still ahead of him went temporarily mad and attacked Lance-Corporal Lakatoš, who had ridiculed his misery and called him a one-year wonder and a dumb turkey. The clash climaxed in a knife fight, and only the pubkeeper's intervention prevented bloodshed.

But the bacchanalia reached its ideological nadir in the back room of an inn called The Hedgehog and Apple, occupied for the most part by NCOs of an intellectual bent. At eleven-thirty, a hollow plaster bust of an important statesman made the rounds. It was inverted and filled with wine, then drained to the singing of a song that sounded very much like a funeral march:

The whole world knows it, and every grunt and churl:
Kobylec is the asshole of the world.

They emptied the bust at precisely a quarter to twelve.
Then, having painted a pair of spectacles on its face, the non-
coms put it back in its place and marched briskly, in an optimistic mood, back to the gates and crossed into the camp
seconds before their passes expired.

⋆   ⋆   ⋆

That night, the guardhouse couldn't handle the crush of soldiers who had managed to get themselves "accommodation
with a blanket", or what the regulations called "off-duty detention". Danny, who was once again on duty as a prisoner escort,
had to push the exhilarated offenders not only into common
cells, but into practically every available space.

Then he sat down in the escorts' room, where Private
Bamza was once again snoring on the couch and the ironshod
footsteps of the guard could be heard from out in the courtyard. He opened a drawer in the table, pulled out a thick notebook, and began to read with great interest.

The notebook contained something he'd been working on
for almost a year. He was immensely proud of it. It was in the
nature of a military/pedagogical treatise and service handbook,
and bore the title *A Training Course in Bullying*, and the sub-
title *The Art of Chewing Out, for Officers of the Czechoslovak
Armed Forces*. The first page displayed a motto: "A soldier
without a sense of humour is a mercenary – J.V. Stalin." (The
tank commander had made this up in case the opus fell into
the unauthorized hands of an officer.) The next page was a
table of contents dividing the material into a number of sec-

tions: "Bellowing", "Chewing Out", "Bullying", and so on, and each of these sections was in turn divided into chapters. At the end of each chapter was a brief summary modelled on *The History of the All-Union Communist Party (Bolshevik)*.

The tank commander read his work fondly, lingering over the concise but apposite chapter headings. The first, "An Historical Introduction: The Origins and Development of Bellowing", promised information about "Julius Caesar and His Importance for the Classical Theory of Bellowing", and those that followed examined the theme throughout various historical eras, paying detailed attention to "Bellowing in Feudal Armies", with a special subsection on "Bellowing at Mercenaries", then "Bellowing in the Capitalist Armies", and finally "Bellowing in the Red Army and the Czechoslovak People's Army". Next came an analytical passage that looked at "Bellowing Classified by Types", where a good deal of space was devoted to "Bellowing in Churches", with subsections on bellowing in Catholic, Protestant, and Orthodox churches ("with special emphasis on the peaceful mission of the Orthodox Church"), and in synagogues ("with special emphasis on the reactionary essence of Zionism"), and finally, to round it off, "Bellowing in Atheistic Shrines, Prayerhouses, and Churches".

This was followed by "Reflections of Marx–Engels–Lenin–Stalin on Bellowing", interspersed with many unknown quotations; an instructive article called "Soviet Bellowing – Our Model"; a legal-cum-philosophical treatise called "The Dialectics of Bellowing: Can One Bellow at One's Superior Officers? The Consequences of Same"; and, in conclusion, a brief recapitulation with a message: "How to Be a Better Bellower". Other sections of the work analysed such complex issues as "Bellowing at Privates, NCOs, and Officers in the Women's Army Corps" and "Bellowing at Service Animals".

There was a well-researched historical essay ("Hannibal

and the Decline of Bellowing in the Carthaginian Armies");
the author's class approach to the material was always correct,
as in "Spartacus – the Father of Democratic Bellowing"; the
intellectual aspect was of a high calibre ("Bellowing as an
Instrument of World Peace"), and the breadth of material
testified to the author's erudition and to his sense of the practical side of things ("Hints on How to Be Decorated for Exemplary Bellowing").

The tank commander leafed through the notebook a while
longer, making some changes, additions, and improvements,
but he was soon overcome by exhaustion. He lay down on the
couch by the opposite wall and fell asleep. He dreamed that
officers behaving in precisely the spirit of his treatise had
dragged him in front of a drumhead court and there, using
his handbook as evidence, had condemned him to death for
betraying military secrets.

★   ★   ★

In the main cell of the guardhouse, where the dusty overhead light had long ago been extinguished, the men were still
awake, sitting on the wooden benches around the walls and
chatting in the dark. By this time, a sentimental mood had
overtaken them.

"It's been two and a half years, gentlemen!" Sergeant
Vomakal sighed reproachfully.

"What'd they chuck you in here for tonight, Bohouš?" said
a voice from the darkness.

"Same as you, man," said Vomakal. "I got pissed in The
Hedgehog and Apple."

"Now, how could you do a thing like that, Bohouš?" said a
voice belonging to Private First Class Dr. Mlejnek.

"You'd of done the same fucking thing, man, if you'd been stinking up the joint for two and a half fucking years like I have."

"I understand," said Dr. Mlejnek. He was not one of those who had to serve six additional months. An unfortunate accident had landed him in the army despite a weak heart, which of course made him even more bitter than the others. Correctly guessing that his political profile wasn't much of an advantage, he had decided to make a good impression on the draft board by uttering the politically correct greeting "Honour to work!" when he appeared before them. When he didn't know, and could not have known, was that the chairman of the board was the former owner of a highly profitable abortion clinic which, after the Communist takeover, had been subsumed by a public health centre in Prague. The chairman and his fellow draft-board member, a young doctor from a good bourgeois family, had decided to apply a remarkable set of criteria to declare a draftee fit or unfit for service. If the future defender of the nation greeted the board with the Communist greeting, he would be declared "fit with no restrictions". On the other hand, anyone who mumbled something vague, suggesting that he could neither bring himself to utter the politically correct greeting nor say anything expressly reactionary, would be classified as "fit for service, but not to bear arms". Finally, bourgeois greetings like "Good morning" or even expressly Christian greetings like "Praise be to Jesus Christ!" would earn the classification "unfit for military service". Poor Dr. Mlejnek, who had just managed to squeak through his final examination on *The History of the All-Union Communist Party (Bolshevik)*, which marked the academic apogee of his legal studies, had thus become the author of his own misfortune.

"Two and a half years, gentlemen!" This time it was Sergeant Mácha who broke the silence. As kitchen inspector, Mácha had taken a floor rag, breaded it, and fried it to a golden brown so that it looked like a piece of wiener schnitzel, and then put it on a plate near the kitchen door from which First Lieutenant Kohn regularly stole a few pieces for his Sunday dinner. For this he'd been given three nights in the guard-house. Now he was lying here waxing sentimental. "Two and half years, gentlemen, and it's all vanished up the asshole of time."

"Did you say 'up the asshole of time'?" said Sergeant Krajta in his raspy voice. "Up the asshole of time, boys. Do any of you know the Tale of the Mysterious Asshole?"

"No," came several voices at once.

"Tell it, man," said Vomakal.

Krajta lit a cigarette and leaned back comfortably against the bent legs of a private lying behind him. Krajta was a chemical engineer and he'd made a name for himself as the organizer of an unusual form of mass activity which sometimes took place on long Sunday afternoons. As soon as it got dark, the soldiers would turn out the lights, pull their pants down, and lie face down on their beds. Soldiers who were ready would give the order "Fire!", and Sergeant Krajta would hold a lighted match as close as he could to their rears. The resulting explosion and blast of flame as they passed wind was remarkably like the cannonades on Victory Day – especially since, to produce the longest, clearest flame, the participants would eat as much warm bread, onions, and garlic as they could steal from the mess-hall at Sunday lunch. On the activity schedule of the political department, this amusement appeared as "Organized Free Time", although there was no mention of it in the moving description of "A Tankist's Sunday", from the pen of Sergeant Maňas, printed in *The Defence of the People*.

Now Krajta stretched his legs out on the wooden bench

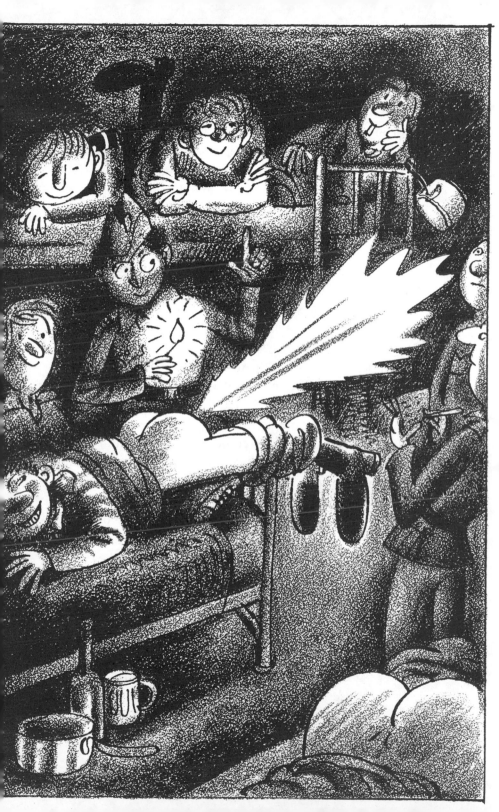

in front of him and, in his pleasantly rusty voice, began to tell the story of the Mysterious Asshole.

"Once upon a time," he began, "ten thousand years after our present era, the axis of the earth shifted, making the evenings long, dark, and boring. Granny would gather all her grandchildren around her and the grandchildren would say, 'Granny, tell us a story, Granny!' 'Well then, what story should I tell?' Granny would ask. And the children would reply, 'The one about the mysterious bum, Granny, the one about the mysterious bum.' 'Very well, then, I'll tell you the story about the bum,' said Granny, nodding her wise old head. 'But as a matter of fact, it was a very, very, very big bum, so it wasn't really a bum at all, was it, children?' 'No!' cried the children. 'No, indeed,' said Granny, 'it was — ' 'An asshole!' the children shrieked in delight, 'the mysterious asshole. Tell us the story, Granny!' And Granny would pull her shawl around her shoulders and begin to tell the tale.

" 'Once upon a time, terribly long ago, when people still had to trade little pieces of coloured paper for things that now, in this era of real Communism, we just go to the warehouse and take home for nothing, like sausages and television sets and women and other things — in those days there were wretched, miserable people who had almost none of those pieces of coloured paper, and they went around dressed in crude clothes that all looked the same and at night they were locked up in sad-looking shacks and in the daytime they had to walk around in straight lines and drive around in stinking metal boxes that they couldn't properly see out of. And all day long they were shouted and yelled at by stupid men with little gold stars on their shoulders, but they weren't allowed to answer back, they had to click their heels together and say, "Yasser, yasser, yasser," and when those mean, loud men weren't around they said other things, but what they said has never been put down in writing. And in the evenings these poor, wretched people sat around in rooms they couldn't leave, and thought about their loved ones, and were very, very sad.

"'Outside the settlement where they lived, there was an enormous mountain, completely bare and bald. And every month when the moon was full, these sad people in their sad uniforms would gather at the foot of this mountain and wait. They'd watch until the moon came up, and after the moon emerged like a big fisheye, they'd watch, waiting expectantly, while it moved slowly across the sky, shining down on the earth. And they'd watch it, trembling in anticipation. Finally, when the moon stood right over the mountain, the earth would begin to tremble and rumble deep inside, and the mountain would open up, and a huge bum would emerge from it and stick up into the sky. And the full moon would fall straight into the bum, and the sad people would rejoice and they'd all of them shout, as one man: "Another month up the asshole of time!" And then the bum would once more retreat inside the mountain and the sad people would return to their sad settlement and be sad once more, until a month later they returned to the mountain and there was a full moon again, and the big bum appeared again, and the moon fell into it again, and they all cried out, "Another month up the asshole of time!" and wept for joy. And all in all, children, the big bum had to emerge from the mountain twenty-four times before those sad people could leave that sad settlement and be happy once more.'"

The tale was over and the room was quiet.

"Yeah," said Sergeant Mácha. "But in my case it had to disappear up the asshole *thirty* times."

The soldiers chuckled. Sergeant Krajta stretched out to go to sleep. Some others went on talking and telling off-colour jokes, but the evening had exhausted them and soon they too fell asleep.

It wasn't long before a great and just silence spread over the entire guardhouse, disrupted only by the full voice of Private Mengele from a distant cell, singing a soldier's bedtime ballad to his three cellmates:

It's a da-hark and lo-honely ni-hight
A-hand the sky-hi is black as pi-hitch
A-hand everyone is gone to slee-heep
Bu-hut that dirty old su-hun of a bi-hitch
My captain....

But even the private fell silent, then fell asleep, and only the footsteps of the guard measured off the remaining hours of those last wonderful moments before their return to life.

A MASS CULTURAL

FAREWELL TO ARMS

The evening before the Seventh Tank Battalion held its
farewell party, First Lieutenant Růžička and Lieutenant
Hospodin learned that Major Borovička and Major Sádlo were
to honour the event with their presence. This sent the two
political officers into a feverish whirl of activity. The affair had
originally been meant as an in-house event; it would now be
a public test of the battalion's mettle. The celebration, in
which the soldiers would bid farewell to two (or two and a half)
years of basic service, would have to demonstrate what they
had learned in the moral and intellectual sense. Military songs
of a mass nature, military and folk dances, recitations and artistic performances, puppet shows and storytellers and magicians
would come together in a demonstration of popular creativity. It was such a display that the two political officers set
about, diligently but belatedly, to cobble together.

Fortunately, they had Tank Commander Maňas to call
on. This mythical hero of the Seventh Tank Battalion had survived his débâcle on Zephyr Hill, despite the fact that General Helebrant had demoted him on the spot by tearing off his
epaulettes even as they were carrying him away from his tank
on a stretcher. The general had resorted to this dramatic gesture to neutralize the unfavourable impression the tank commander's performance had made on the Soviet general, who

had sprained his ankle when he jumped off the observation platform. But the former sergeant, now a private, had resorted to an equally dramatic counter-move. When he had partially recovered in the infirmary, he sawed most of the way through a beam in the latrine, put around his neck a web belt (also mostly severed, just to be on the safe side), and hanged himself from the beam, plunging with a great racket into the toilet. Thanks to the noise, he was discovered almost immediately, and was admitted to the psychiatric section of the infirmary, where he was visited by General Helebrant. The general was merely showing due concern for a subordinate, but Private Mañas fell on his knees before him and he softened and, after a private meeting demanded by the divisional officer of the military secret police, promoted Mañas back to his former rank. This valuable soldier (and secret collaborator) then made a rapid recovery, and returned to his unit just as the two political officers were frantically searching for a program to demonstrate the results of their educational activities.

As always, Mañas displayed a ready political awareness, and offered his services. He would, he said, recite his own poem, "Farewell to Our Second Home", read his own humorous story, "Private Pimlas's Accident", and perform in a one-act play written by himself on condition that the political officers get him a co-actor and a girl to play the female lead. He was also, he said, willing to perform several card tricks (if he could remember them), organize a game called "A Test of Political Knowledge", and, to round out the evening, perform a satirical piece called "Hypnosis and the Power of Suggestion". This would give them a complete evening of performance, a kind of one-man show, and under normal circumstances the political officers would have been delighted to accept.

But now, after the crushing news from division headquarters, they weren't sure the notoriously fault-finding Major

Borovička would be satisfied with Tank Commander Maňas reciting a poem by Tank Commander Maňas, reading a humorous story by Tank Commander Maňas, appearing in a one-act play by Tank Commander Maňas, and doing card tricks and a funny skit all starring Tank Commander Maňas. Thus, of all his suggestions, they accepted only his poem, his one-acter, and his story-telling act, since that was a role he traditionally played in the division. Next they set out to track down a singing circle which, in the vague memory of Lieutenant Růžička, had been formally established long ago but had never actually done anything. The trail of the singing circle was so cold as to be almost non-existent – in fact, the only trace they could find was a guitar belonging to Sergeant Kobliha – but they decided they could build an emergency group around that. Oddly enough, Sergeant Kobliha was willing to lend his art to further their aims.

Following up on an inspired idea from Lieutenant Hospodin, they locked the mess hall just when the Seventh Tank Battalion was working its way through one of its final army meals, and Růžička called upon the trapped soldiers to form a singing group and rehearse a few songs. Resistance was fierce, but the negotiations dragged on until a compromise was reached: all those present would learn one song, provided the whole process didn't take more than half an hour. While this was being carried out under Růžička's guidance, Hospodin set out to find the puppet theatre that had been donated to the unit by a local factory some time ago, when the lieutenant still had illusions about the practicability of mass cultural activity *per se.*

He searched the attic of the barracks, the special room set aside for mass cultural events, the living quarters of all four squadrons, and the CO's rooms, until finally he found the remains of the puppet theatre in the cellar, partly chopped up for kindling. As for the puppets themselves, the earth seemed to have swallowed them up. (Later, when most of the men had returned to civilian life, they turned up in a green map-case that First Lieutenant Pinkas had taken with him on tactical manoeuvres.)

Crushed by his failure, he quickened his tempo and ran about battalion headquarters with no clear purpose in mind. On the second floor he came across Sergeant Omámený, a gunner who was famous for his extraordinary diligence in political education classes, and for the extraordinarily poor results this diligence brought him. Of Hungarian-Slovak nationality, he was the embodiment of servility; although he had been in the army for thirty months and was about to return to his native village, he saluted Lieutenant Hospodin without being reminded. This so astonished the political officer that he asked Omámený if he knew any folk dances.

"I surely do, Comrade Lieutenant."

"Which ones?" asked the lieutenant quickly.

"The one about the brigand and the cop with the *federpuš*," Omámený declared, in a combination of Hana, Glatz, and German dialects.

"You're going to dance it tomorrow," the lieutenant decided.

"*Charasho*," replied the sergeant in Russian, and saluted Lieutenant Hospodin, who disappeared down the stairs before the soldier could remind him that he needed music in order to do the dance.

"*Jebemte hegedüss!*" cursed the victim, in a combination of Polish and Hungarian vulgarity. Then he went back to the barracks to polish his shoes.

Hospodin rushed down the stairs and ran along the corridor to the exit. In the doorway he bumped into Sergeant Krajta, whom he had last seen locked up in the mess hall with the others.

"Comrade Sergeant, why aren't you practising with the choir?"

"I had to make a bowel movement," said Krajta.

"I want you to tell an interesting story at the farewell event," the lieutenant told him, encouraged by the lack of resistance from Sergeant Omámený. He had a vague memory of a long-ago evening on one of their exercises when he had been hidden under a tank, and had heard Sergeant Krajta speaking through a hatch in the floor and telling an infantry corporal, who had sought refuge from the rain inside the tank, the contents of a pornographic book. At the time he had thought (with some envy) that Krajta was recounting a personal experience.

"I don't know any stories, Comrade Lieutenant," said Sergeant Krajta.

"Krajta, you're lying."

"But all I know are dirty stories – "

But the lieutenant was already hurrying somewhere else, so Krajta only heard him shout over his shoulder, "Then tell a dirty story."

"What's a body to do?" said the sergeant to a greenhorn who was on duty in the corridor. "An order is an order." And he retired to the latrine to spend a pleasant half-hour reading a sadistic detective novel called *Kill the Killer*, borrowed from the private library of Dr. Mlejnek, which was doing more business than the official Gottwald Library.

*   *   *

The lieutenant ran on around the building to the offices of the political department and, in a mood of desperation, set out to put together a program. After five tries, he managed to type it with a minimum of typos and spelling mistakes.

FARWELL EVNING
for the men and NCOs of the 7th Tank Batallion
CULTURAL POGRAM
1. Marsh of the Tank Corps – sung by singers cercle
2. Goodby to Our Second Home – a resitation by Tnk.
Com. Maňas
3. Speech by Comp. CO
4. Bandids Dance – by Sgt. Omámrný
5. Beware! The Enemy Is Listening – a play staring Tnk.
Com. Maňas and Lnc. Cpl. Lakotuš and a female comrad
5. A couple of duets – sung by Sgt. Kobliha and Corp.
Pískal.
6. Populer storyteling – Tnk Comdr. Maňas and Sgt.
Krajta.
7. Stalen's Falcons – sung by the singers cercle
After the cultural progam their will be a dance with
Comrades from the Czechoslkvak Union of Youth.
THE END

★   ★   ★

Fate arrived the following day, in the persons of the Pygmy Devil and Major Sádlo. They sat at the head table in the battalion's mess hall. The room was fully illuminated for the occasion, and the tables were arranged in a large U, with space in the middle for the performances to take place. The whole battalion entered the room, in dress uniform, for the last time, to eat the last ceremonial wiener schnitzel with potato salad and wash it down with an official glass of wine (rationed to one per man) and an unofficial, indeterminable amount of hard liquor smuggled in from the village and hidden under the tables.

The married officers brought their wives. Captain Matka came with a tired-looking woman who, in keeping with the moral demands placed on the materially secure officer class, was pregnant for the sixth time. The iron Lieutenant Pinkas was there with his sweet wife, Janinka, in a black dress, with red lips and gazelle-like eyes that constantly drifted towards the table where the NCOs sat. The sadness in those eyes, which had been gradually disappearing over the last few weeks, was there once more. The arrogant First Lieutenant Bobby Kohn, whose leg was still in a cast, came with a very pretty, loose-looking woman. The foul-mouthed First Lieutenant Kámen was there with a plump wife who brought the men a basket of cheese pastries she'd baked herself. And finally, the pips on their epaulettes polished brightly, came the commanding officers of the individual squadrons: the eager-to-please Lieutenant Hezký, clapping members of his squad on the back in an awkward attempt to be friendly and asking them jovial questions in his nasal voice, like "Tell me, then, who's the minister of the wood processing industry?"; the inconspicuous Šlajs, who sat silently at the end of the officers' table and drank, unobserved, two of the bottles of cognac meant for the honoured guests; the smart-alecky Jakubec, who took a seat right next to Major Sádlo's wife and, in the course of the evening, penetrated her defences and arranged a date with her the following Sunday in a Prague nightclub; and the easygoing Grünlich, who devoted all his attention to the food. Finally, there were both the political officers, with faces like the Mask of Conscience from a medieval morality play.

★   ★   ★

Someone tapped a fork against an earthenware bowl until it

cracked, and at the midpoint of the officers' table the Pygmy
Devil stood up to make himself a head taller than the officers
around him. The hum of conversation in the hall died down,
the Pygmy Devil thrust his chest forward, and, while the wiener schnitzel in the kitchen grew cold and the bootleg alcohol
under the table grew warm, he began a rant at the assembled
soldiers in his grating falsetto.

"Comrades! You have gathered here at the order of your
commanding officer so that you may celebrate, in a way fitting
to men, the completion of your honourable service to our People's Democratic Army, a service all the more honourable in
that most of you have served six extra months in addition to
the compulsory twenty-four-month basic training. You did so
with enthusiasm," he told them angrily, "though some of you
did not do so with the kind of enthusiasm we expect to come
naturally to a soldier of the People's Democratic Army. Those
who have not carried out their orders with enthusiasm," and
he raised a clenched fist above his head, "have lost the right
to be considered as belonging to your ranks!" By now, he had
worked himself up into a proper lather and was beginning to
hit his stride: "The people and the working class, the government and the mother Communist Party," he thundered, "will
not permit discipline in the army to be disrupted by subver-
sive elements. You have been in the army for thirty months,
and you must have seen that it is far too short a time for soldiers to learn how to properly operate a machine as complex
as a T-34 tank. A three-year basic training period is necessary!"
His voice had risen to a screech, but since most of the soldiers
in the room were unaffected by this dire suggestion, it failed
to evoke the desired sense of terror — except in a first-year
recruit who was standing by the kitchen door with a plate of
wiener schnitzel in his hands. On hearing the major's remarks,
he began to tremble so violently that he dropped the plate on

the floor. After the excitement had died down and the wiener schnitzel had been taken back to the kitchen to be wiped off with a damp rag used for mopping the floor, the Pygmy Devil continued. "The working people will soon see that a three-year period is utterly necessary, and the people's will is sovereign. Those with the proper political consciousness will go into the army with enthusiasm, and they will spend the whole three years absorbing and mastering the techniques of warfare. There will always, of course, be those who do not do their duty with the kind of enthusiasm expected of a soldier in our People's Democratic Army. But such men will feel the hard fist of the people coming down on them, and it will compel them to carry out their duties with enthusiasm. And if that does not work, they will be ejected from our People's Democratic Army. And they will not be missed, for this will ensure that those who remain carry out the orders of their commanding officers with even greater enthusiasm, and if they don't, the people will deal with them promptly. And the people will soon see that a weapon as complex as the famous T-34 tank requires a three-year training period...." The Pygmy Devil was getting tangled up in the vicious circle of his arguments. "They will go with enthusiasm... there may be such people... will force them to... and if they do not... will get rid of them, comrades," and with these words, or scarcely perceptible variations of them, the Pygmy Devil concluded his ten-minute rant. The officers applauded politely, joined by Tank Commander Maňas and Sergeant Omámený from the rank and file. The only disruption to the mood of serious, disciplined discourse was the drunken voice of Sergeant Líbezný, of the regular army, who responded to the major's threats by bellowing, "Long live the U.S.S.R.!" When Sergeant Krajta yelled at him to shut up, he added in a darker tone: "Long live our great friend and defender, our leader and teacher, and our dear liberator, the humiliator of our hated occupiers, the great, wise, magnanimous and immortal, the one and only Generalissimo Josef Thesonofabitch Stalin!"

Fortunately for Líbezný, his bad pun was lost in the clatter of cutlery and plates and the hum of excitement as the new recruits came fanning out through the hall with trays of wiener schnitzel. The clinking of spoons (except for Tank Commander Maňas, only the officers used knives and forks) grew in volume and the sound rose and echoed off the wooden ceiling, where garlands of dusty paper flowers converged in regular loops on a large red star behind the head table. To the right of the star was a portrait of the incumbent President Zápotocký, and to the left was one of the minister of defence, General Čepička. Both men were in uniform and bedecked with an alarming number of medals, and both were rendered in the kind of fading focus that daguerreotype photographers in the last century loved to use. In the middle of the red star, Sergeant Remunda had pasted a truncated portrait of Stalin. A portrait of the recently deceased President Gottwald hung suspended from the star on a piece of string, for symmetry and hierarchy.

★   ★   ★

While the men of the Seventh Tank Battalion demolished mountains of wiener schnitzel without flinching, the beautiful Janinka pecked away at her cutlet like a sparrow, her eyes lost in distant contemplation. Tank Commander Smiřický failed as a lover by not displaying a similar lack of appetite, but he did observe the rules of eye-play. He felt sorry that things had to end this way, yet at the same time it meant freedom; he was not yet acquainted with the relativity of life. The uncertain promises of Prague beckoned from a distance, and waged an unequal battle with the charms of the first lieutenant's wife.

Neither of the political officers enjoyed his meal very much. They too pecked at the meat like birds, casting nervous sidelong glances at Captain Matka. The captain ate heartily, but his stomach wasn't bottomless, and at last he remembered what they were there for. Belching slightly, he leaned over and pronounced the fateful sentence: "All right, Růžička, how about the program?"

And so, feeling like men mounting the guillotine, Růžička and Hospodin got up from the table and began assembling the remnants of the day-old singing group. They formed them in ragged array in the space between the tables and then, their voices trembling, announced that the mass cultural program of farewell to army service was about to begin. The chorus stood facing the head table, directly opposite the Pygmy Devil, who had spilled dollops of mayonnaise on his tunic and had the demeanour of an angry hornet. The chorus of the Seventh Tank Battalion began singing an atonal rendition of "The March of the Tank Corps", a version of the famous "March of the Security Forces". The result was somewhat absurd, but nevertheless dear to the ears of Captain Matka.

Once again we're marching homeward
From the mountains of the east,
Youthful tankists all assembled
Ready for the imperialist beast.

This is what most of the chorus sang, but the group around Sergeant Krajta seemed to be deviating from the text, something that only the oversensitive ears of Lieutenant Hospodin picked up. Instead of "from the mountains of the east" he thought he heard some of them sing "from the brothels of the east" — but the words were tactically drowned out in a thunder of hoarse voices that could barely carry the melody, let alone deal with harmony.

★   ★   ★

Aside from the musical qualities of the chorus, the song fully expressed the momentary feelings of the singers, and the intensity of their rendition overcame any shortcomings in melody and harmony. Fortunately the Pygmy Devil had no ear for music. Major Sádlo listened, and in the folds of his brain where his centre of musicality should have been, he began to suspect that the Seventh Tank Battalion choir did not quite measure up to the standards set by the divisional choir (called *The People's Fist*, but sometimes referred to privately by its own members as *A Fist in the Face*), which performed mainly at local festivals in the surrounding villages. But he hid his uncertainty behind a firm expression approximating intelligence, and when the tonal torment was over, he applauded politely.

The space between the tables was cleared and Tank Commander Maňas got up and tried to put on a look of inspired enthusiasm, but the effect was marred by his sensual lips and his epicurean paunch, which had grown considerably during two years of activity that had been largely ideological. He struck a pose meant to express confidence, with the thumb of his left hand hooked over his belt and his right hand poised for any gesture that might add drama to the poem. Then he began reciting his creation:

> *Let cannon thunder and let mines explode;*
> *Beneath our tank-treads we will crush the foe.*

The red flag shall above the tumult wave;
The Seventh Tank Battalion's on the go.

Captain Matka responded vigorously. Breaking a second earthenware dish with an energetic blow from his fork, he rose to give one of the serialized talks that had been a source of merriment all year to the decadent elements of his battalion. Růžička and Hospodin both hoped Matka would say something so spectacularly stupid that the glaring inadequacies of their program would pale in its blinding light. But he disappointed them all by speaking unusually briefly and intelligently:

"Comrades," he said. "On the very eve of your celebrations, we have some good news. One of the United States of America, Ecuados, has withdrawn from the American union. Comrades! The imperialist camp is falling apart. The collapse of the U.S.A. has begun! The contradictions inside the imperialist camp are destroying the camp of imperialism!"

This stunning piece of news left most of the soldiers unmoved. Of all those present, only Private First Class Dr. Mlejnek was able to put the news in its proper perspective. As the only regular reader of *The People's Defence*, he alone had noticed a tiny item saying that Ecuador was withdrawing from a pan-American trade agreement on the commercial exploitation of turtle dung. The other members of the battalion, or at least the officers, thought the captain's valedictory address highly successful, ideologically; Major Sádlo decided that he would use the information in tomorrow's ten-minute pep-talk.

★   ★   ★

The program continued relentlessly. An unsuccessful attempt at a Slovakian brigand's dance by Sergeant Omámený was followed by Tank Commander Maňas's play, *Beware! The Enemy Is Listening!* It was a symbolic drama, or at least it made liberal use of symbols. Lance-Corporal Lakatoš, the amiable Slovak who had been cornered into one of the main roles, appeared in a shiny rubber suit borrowed from the chemical warfare unit and a hat with a little brush in the hatband pulled low over his eyes (both the hat and the coat were generally recognized emblems of subversion). Maňas entered from the other side with an exaggerated, cocky step and a flower in the lapel of his uniform (to indicate that he was on leave). As he walked across the space between the tables, he stopped in front of the Pygmy Devil, pulled a lighter out of his pocket, and tried to light a cigarette. The lighter worked, but because it was supposed to symbolize a lighter that didn't work, the nervous Lakatoš stepped up to Maňas and, with trembling fingers, broke three matches before managing to light the cigarette that had already been lit. He said, in a voice that was noticeably strained:

"So how about it, soldier-boy? Taste good? Taste good?"

Troop Commander Maňas shot back curtly and professionally: "Yeah, sure it tastes good."

The dialogue took off from there.

> *The spy:* "I was in the army once, too."
> *Maňas: (crispy and coldly)* "That so?"
> *The spy:* "I swear to God. In the First Republic. Everything was different then."
> *Maňas:* "I'm sure it was."
> *The spy:* "Back then I was issued ten cigarettes a day."
> *Maňas:* "Really?"
> *The spy:* "How many do you get now?"
> *Maňas: (cautiously)* "Enough to satisfy me."
> *The spy:* "You a heavy smoker?"

Mañas: "Depends on what you call a heavy smoker."
The spy: (forgetting his lines) "Uh...."
Mañas: (prompting in a whisper) "Leave."
The spy: "And what about leave – do they give you enough leave?"
Mañas: "We have enough leave to satisfy us completely."
The spy: "Me, I.... Me, I...."
Mañas: (whispering) "Me, I had leave every day."
The spy: "Me, I had leave every day. Well, goodbye."

With this, Lakatoš abruptly brought the first scene to an end. The script was much longer, but he had forgotten the rest of his lines, and decided the audience knew enough already to see what the point of the scene was. So he touched the brim of his hat with his fingers and walked off with a feeling of relief. The point was now supposed to be driven home by a young woman in a blue shirt and a (Soviet-style) movie-star figure, who shyly approached Tank Commander Mañas. He stretched out his arms and cried, "My word! Márinka! Look at you, Márinka, you're as fresh as a tank after a general overhaul."

Mañas had put a lot of stock in that military simile, but he had thought it up long before Hospodin had found someone for the role, and the apt comparison brought a roar of laughter from the audience. The woman blushed deeply and her reply, "Oh horsefeathers, you flatterer!", could scarcely be heard over the noise. The following lines were more audible:

"And where were you last Sunday, Honza? I was waiting for you...."

"I couldn't come, Márinka. I had guard duty at the ammunition dump – you know, the one over there among the birch trees, where that big triangulation point is; the one you can see from town, about fifty metres due west of the wayside cross."

With miraculous ease, the girl extracted from him a precise account of every sentry's sector, the rotation times, information about each unit's location in the camp, the battalion's
emergency plan, the names of the commanders all the way up
to the head of the division, the daily food consumption, technical details about the tank engines, standing orders on how
soldiers were to behave on leave, and the minister of defence's
birthday. Having done so, she gave him an exemplary dressing-
down for his lack of vigilance. In other words, no one was left
in any doubt as to what the play symbolized – not even Major
Sádlo, who was notoriously prejudiced against lack of clarity
in works of art.

Both political officers, glancing sideways at the major's
expressionless face, applauded wildly. The woman, whose face
was now raspberry-red, ran off to the thunderous applause of
the men to join her two friends from the local Youth Union,
and into the centre of the room stepped Corporal Pískal and
Sergeant Kobliha, with a guitar, to sing several "songs for
two voices".

By now the battery of bottles on the officers' table was
almost half empty, and the men could bring out the rest of
their hidden supplies and put them right on the table in front
of them. Luckily, the amount of alcohol consumed by the
officers was greater than their measure of judgement. To the
clinking of glasses, Sergeant Kobliha began to strum his guitar and the duo launched into a song that, fortunately, none
of the officers except First Lieutenant Pinkas (who by now was
too drunk to care) recognized as coming from the very bosom
of the imperialist West:

> *Oh, give me a hoooome where the buffalo rooooam,*
> *Where the deeeer and the antelope plaaaay. . . .*

Kobliha's lewd tenor provided a special contrast to the castrato descant of Corporal Pískal. They held each note to the limit and beyond, and as the plaintive melody and the slow strumming of the guitar rose above the hum of conversation, soldiers and officers alike fell silent and listened. The song carried above the cigarette smoke, above the alcoholic vapours, above the heads of the political officers, and rose to the heights of the mess hall, where the stone-faced portraits stared down, draped in colourless crêpe paper. High on the wall, a sign in blood-red letters proclaimed:

FORWARD TOWARDS OUR HIGH IDEALS!
FORWARD FOR OUR COUNTRY!
NOT A STEP BACKWARD! ONWARD TO SOCIALISM!

Where seldom is heeeeard a discouraging woooord
And the skiiiies are not cloudy all daaaay,

sang Pískal in his falsetto, while Kobliha strummed at his roughly tuned strings and the inner being of the assembled men was filled with emotion. The foul-mouthed First Lieutenant Kámen (a depleted bottle of Chartreuse in front of him) even began to cry, and the moment the song was over, he applauded with loud, explosive claps. Before the Pygmy Devil could respond, the duo began another song, devised in the cultural workshops of the border guards but with the lyrics adjusted for the tank division. Swayed by the response to their first number, they stretched the vowels even more, adding strange guttural noises wherever a short syllable fell on a long note. This added to the ballad's hypnotic charm, and the soldiers' hearts were overcome. Not even the hard heart of Captain Matka was excepted.

Where the Vltava's siiiilver waaaaaters floooow
A young tank driiiiver staaaaands on guaaard,
A stout machiiiine-gun iiiin his haaaand,
To guaard the peeace of ow-er fa-haiir laaaand.

In webs of cuuuunning and deceeeeeit
Our moooother-land is held in thraaaall,
Our tankist bra-havely faces west,
Against our enemi-hies he stands taaaall.

His iron fiiiist comes cra-hashing down
To crush the traaaaitor i-hin his lair,
He fears not daaanger, to-hoil nor woe
Nor e'en to dea-heth his brea-hest to baaare.

A mob of dirty handkerchiefs trumpeted, and moist tears dampened the stubble on many a cheek. Růžička leaned over to Major Sádlo in the storm of aplause that followed and remarked that the soldiers had their hearts in the right place, and that the right kind of song had the power to move them strongly, just as another kind of song could inspire them to greater achievements and nobler deeds. Major Sádlo didn't reply, being no longer in control of his tongue. The songsters went on:

And when at la-hast, his du-huty done,
He wends his weeeeary homeward wa-hay,
Where maiden faaair waits patientleeee,
And by his siiiide she'll fo-hondly staaaay.

The guitarist's hand swept across the strings in an elegant half-circle, suspending in the air a long, lingering, and slightly out of tune chord, sweet and honeyed…and then wild applause, cries of *bravo*, the clinking of glasses, the thud of bodies falling under the table, men crawling along the table-tops, yelling, crying out, weeping. The tough veteran Lieutenant Pinkas collapsed on top of the banquet table, his thinning hair floating in a pool of whisky. First Lieutenant Kámen embraced the Pygmy Devil and, in his determination to plant a kiss on his cheeks, prevented the major, who was as moved by the song as he would ever be by anything, from making any remarks. Janinka caught Tank Commander Smiřický's eye and gave a slight nod of her head towards the door, and he slipped quickly out of the room.

Inspired by the preceding performance and by the state of the officers, an improvised quartet consisting of Sergeant Krajta, Sergeant Vytáhlý, Private Bamza, and Corporal Střevlíček came together between the tables and began gaily singing a tune of complaint. Hospodin and Růžička, lulled into a belief that everything would turn out well, stiffened as if struck by lightning when they heard the words:

T'was nineteen hundred and fifty-one,
The year that I was drafted;
I'll kill the man who took me in,
The dirty rotten bastard!

Out of the corner of his eye, Lieutenant Hospodin saw the Pygmy Devil, still immobilized in Kámen's embrace, suddenly come alert and begin to scowl. With the corner of his other eye he saw Matka prick up his ears.

They brought me here to Kobylec,
This shitty one-horse town,
I wish to God we'd shelled the place
And burned it to the ground.

Captain Matka shot out of his chair with unusual energy, but instead of intervening like a commanding officer, he shouted:

"Now boys, let's sing our own song, that good Bolshevik tune. Kámen, fall in beside me!"

Oddly enough, Kámen, who was usually slow to obey orders, released the half-choked Pygmy Devil from his grasp so that he fell with a thump onto his chair. In an instant both the officers were singing a martial song:

> *We are Bolsheviks so red*
> *And we're better red than dead;*
> *And we'll never go to bed*
> *With capitalist dogs,*
> *No, we'll never go to bed with capitalist dogs!*

Kobliha came up to them with his guitar and, quickly picking up the half-familiar tune, began to accompany them loyally. The officers put their arms around each other's shoulders and joined in:

> *They call us ruddy terrorists,*
> *The dervishes of Gottwald;*
> *We'll pay them back for their attack,*
> *We'll build a mighty scaffold.*

Carried away by the exuberance of their interpretation, several drunken privates joined in, and soon after, timidly at first, the two political officers. The final verse of the song of battle – which appeared in none of the army songbooks – rang through the smoke-filled room:

> *When Gottwald sends his orders*
> *From the castle up in Prague,*

We'll take the bourgeois by their necks
And throttle them like dogs.

As most of the soldiers were aglow with excitement, and the convivial influence of the alcohol took the edge off class hatred, the performance of the officers was received with applause. But Sergeant Krajta's quartet was not about to be upstaged. The officers' revolutionary song had come from the pre-Communist days; they now sang one from their own era:

The working class, they gave us guns
And showed us how to use 'em;
But now we sit with broken hearts
And wish we could refuse 'em.

It was a provocative ditty and, surprisingly, it even provoked a sense of honour in First Lieutenant Kámen. He put his arms around Captain Matka's neck, pulled Lieutenant Hospodin close to him on the other side, stomped the floor with his riding boot to establish the beat, and then, accompanied by Sergeant Kobliha on the guitar, began to sing a fatalistic song:

When the boys come over from the U.S.A.
They'll hang us all within a day,
They won't let nothing in their way,
Oh, they'll hang us all within a day.

Sergeant Krajta's quartet overlaid this with a sprightly, optimistic tune that had a danceable rhythm. Everyone who wasn't too drunk joined spontaneously in the refrain:

When we joined the army, boys,
A song was on our lips,

We thought no one could touch us,
We didn't know from shit.
Oh, the army is a bugger
And the army is a whore,
The army breaks your balls and has
You crawling back for more.

The sharp crack of a pistol rang through the room. Everyone froze, terrified. The Pygmy Devil was standing on the officers' table with a smoking revolver in his hand. A small cloud of white dust descended from the corner of the room, where the bullet had gone into the ceiling, and the startled singers felt bits of plaster hitting their heads. Speaking into the shocked silence, the Pygmy Devil waved his pistol and screamed: "Soldiers! Dismiss to your barracks at once!"

He left a dramatic pause, but it was filled by a rising hum of anger. He shouted again: "I will not permit anyone to insult our working class, our country, and our People's Democratic Army. It seems to me, comrades, that two years of political schooling has not been enough! Is *this* how you fulfil your responsibilities, Comrade Lieutenant?" And he turned to face Lieutenant Růžička. The politruk turned green and felt a swoon coming on.

"*This* is the respect you have for the wonderful opportunities our People's Democratic State has given you, comrades?" the Pygmy Devil went on, turning to the soldiers in the room. "*This*... is supposed to be an evening of farewell to the most sacred duty of a citizen of a people's democracy? You've shown yourselves in fine colours, comrades. You've behaved like a gang of the wickedest reactionaries."

The hostile buzz in the hall grew. Soudek stepped out of the crowd with a bottle in his hand. "What kind of bullshit is this, you little runt? Who the fuck are you calling reactionary?"

"Tomorrow you report to your commanding officer!" the little major screamed. Then he stopped and corrected himself. "To the division commander! And you too, Comrade Captain!" and he turned to Matka. Matka clicked his heels together and replied in the only way he could think of: "Yes, sir."

"And now – *dismiss!*" screeched the Pygmy Devil. The tempest of voices rose, and once again Soudek's was the loudest: "Throw him out!" he cried.

"Kick his ass!" shouted Private Bamza. The voices grew louder, and a dangerous circle formed around the little major. Hospodin and Růžička, both of them deathly pale and almost fluorescent with fear, shielded him with their own bodies.

But the Pygmy Devil didn't wait for a hero's death. He shook his fist and shouted at the crowd: "You will all bear the consequences of this!" and then turned quickly and rushed out through the corridor and into the darkness of the night.

★　★　★

When Tank Commander Smiřický found himself outside in the night air, he walked quickly across the road and into the shadow cast by a tall tree with a wide crown. Clusters of distant nebulae were shimmering in the sky, like sparkling cuttlefish swimming through an inky sea. The stars looked down on the army base, on the chestnut trees where the last leaves were rustling in the night breeze, on the network of roads radiating in all directions. On each road, somewhere near the end, stood a guard who let no one pass, though he cared not who the traveller was or what his business; he had been given his orders. The stars also gazed down on the silent training field, on the parachute landing pits filled with white sand and the high wooden towers from which the trainees jumped. A confusion of voices, snatches of song, and bursts of laughter came from the window of the mess hall. Danny leaned against the wooden wall of the equipment shed and gazed at the entrance to the dining hall, a dark rectangle in the white wall.

Suddenly a young woman appeared in that rectangle. The faint white glow from the sky mixed with the darkness of the night to suffuse her face and flow down her black dress. On her bosom a dark green tear flashed and disappeared. She looked around and the emerald on her dress ignited again, then went out, ignited and went out.

She stepped out onto the road, into the full light of the night, and looked around uncertainly. Several steps, a movement, as though someone in the dark of the night had whispered a favourite verse, and in his heart the lieutenant's wife triumphed, temporarily, over the seductive aroma of civilian life and the attractions of Prague. It was as though a floodgate had opened up in him and released his river of sorrow over thwarted longings, over the weakness of longings fulfilled, over the pathetic way life was set up.

"Janinka!" he called out quietly.

She ran across the road and pressed herself into his arms. He looked at her.

"Danny!" she whispered. He kissed her. The spark in the emerald went out when his shadow fell across it.

"Come on." He took her by the hand, and they went into the exercise field and stood at the edge of the jumping pits. She pressed against him but said nothing. He needed to speak, but in the shadow of the equipment shed, where ropes hung like nooses from an enormous gallows, he felt a constricting anxiety.

"Let's climb up here, Janinka."

She looked upwards, towards the sky, and laughed. "We aren't monkeys, are we, Dr. Smiřický?"

It was a poor attempt at humour, and her voice broke. "Damn," she said, "all right. Go ahead. Go ahead, Danny. And give me your hand. It's going to be wonderful, we'll be right under the stars."

Wanting to show off, Danny swung vigorously onto the first rung of the tall ladder. It was as high as her head, and he reached down for her. She put one of her hands in his, and grabbed the rung with the other and tried to swing herself up.

"Wait a moment," she said. "I'm going to take my stockings off."

He watched as she turned around and pulled up her skirt, first on one side, then on the other. The ceremony aroused an agonizing hunger in him. Two grey clouds of smoke floated down on the white sand, and she clambered up to him, her pale knees sparkling. Then they quickly climbed up the wooden ladder together.

It was quiet on the platform. The roads winding beyond the buildings and snaking around the exercise field looked like lines on a map, and under the phosphorescent cuttlefish in the sky rose the dark outline of Old Roundtop, theatre of such glorious tank battles. The breeze blew lightly on their cheeks. The lieutenant's wife snuggled up to the tank commander. She crossed her bare legs and they swung in the darkness, glimmering in the night air like two lighthouses on the shores of sleep, her tender little toes pointing towards the white landing pits.

"So it's the day after tomorrow?"

"Yes."

"And then we won't see each other again."

"Sure we will," he said. "We can meet in Prague. You'll be able to come, won't you?"

"I don't know."

"Why not? Your husband is always on duty. He won't even

know you've been away. You can take the morning express – "

"Why did you have to come into my life, anyway?" she interrupted him. There was a sad desperation in her voice.

"What do you mean?"

"Why did you show up is what I mean, damn it," she said unhappily, and looked away, across the camp to the black mass of Old Roundtop, and past that, past the sentries pacing away the night, past the borders of her lost world named Kobylec. "There was little Honza, and the canteen and the officers and movies three nights a week, and a little flat in a new married quarters, and the boredom and the emptiness and at night the tanks on the shooting range and the beautiful tracer bullets in the air, and everything was just as it should have been. And then you came into it. Why, for the love of God, why?"

"Janinka," he said, "don't be sad. The way it is now is just the way it should be. Now it's really the way it should be."

"What's the way it should be? That I don't care about my husband any more? Is that the way it should be? That I don't care about all the men who came before you, or about all the men who'll come after you, is that how you want it? That I'll miss you? More than I've ever missed anyone? Is that the way it should be, Danny?"

"Come on...."

"I know," she said. "I'm just another hysterical woman. A dumb officer's wife who probably gets talked about a lot, right?"

"But – "

"No, no, don't say anything. Keep your precious, beautiful, wicked mouth shut. I don't want you to lie to me. I know it's true, and you know it too."

"Janinka," he said, shaken by his foolish passion, "I only know I love you. An awful lot. You mean more to me than anything else in the world. Run away with me, Janinka."

"Where to?" she said darkly. "To some dumb sublet in

Prague? Before long you'd be gone in a cloud of dust – just so you wouldn't always have to look at this poor, ignorant Mrs. Pinkasová – "

"But Jan – "

" – who loves you so badly and yet so little that she makes herself a burden to you."

Tears fell from the parachute tower towards the white sand below. Danny took out his handkerchief. He mumbled something.

"So badly," she said in a hopeless voice. "I love you so awfully awfully awfully badly, Danny. I don't know what it is. I'm such a dull woman. Why do I love you so much? I – I've had five other tank commanders before you came along. Yes, it's true, and my husband is an old tank man too, and everything's so awfully, awfully, awfully.... Danny!"

"Janinka, get a divorce," he said, but he didn't meant it, and he suddenly heard the fraudulence in his voice.

"Don't say that, Danny, please. Don't say things like that," she exploded in a tearful rage. "I love you, but I can't do anything, I don't have any skills, books don't interest me – but I love you. Awfully. Oh Danny, don't leave. Stay here with me."

"With you?" he said helplessly, and the idiotic idea came to him that she was suggesting he join the regular army. He stiffened.

"Oh, you don't understand," she groaned. "You're just a dumb, heartless guy, but I love you. I only said that so I wouldn't have to keep saying I love you. Everything I say to you, every single word, means in my language *I love you*. Do you know that, Danny? Do you know that?"

"I know," he said.

"No you don't. You don't know anything. You had to wait until Mrs. Pinkasová, that slut, that Jezebel, told you. You haven't got a clue, you're just a big dope, a goof, my darling.

You have so much to learn, so much. But will anyone ever teach you? Will anyone ever teach you?"

"What, Janinka?"

"Oh — " she said. "I'd — like — I want — but no," she said. She was sitting almost alone, lost above the camp, unhappy tears streaming down her cheeks. "No, it's stupid. It's idiotic. It's dumb. No, I don't want anything. Things are fine the way they are. Things are arranged in this completely stupid way and no one has any right to expect them to be different. It's just the way things are. Come on, Danny," she said, turning to him. "What are we doing sitting here? I can have these stars any time, but I won't have you again. Come on."

She climbed down the rungs on the ladder, her skirt tight against her stomach and thighs, her white knees shining like the stars again. And perhaps that was an answer to everything, the only answer she knew how to give. An answer anyone could have given. He felt gauche and ignorant when he crawled down after her. When they got to the bottom, they went into the equipment shed, where it was dark and the exercise mats were piled up.

★   ★   ★

From then until the members of the Seventh Tank Battalion went back to civilian life, nothing special happened. The joy of this last and greatest event of their army careers completely overshadowed the enigma being investigated, so far unsuccessfully, by the military secret police. Major Borovička, better known as the Pygmy Devil, had mysteriously disappeared. He had never returned home from that final celebration, and the participants in the night's events remained unpunished.

In view of facts that came to light much later, one circumstance seems especially important. But the only witnesses to it were Tank Commander Smiřický and the wife of his superior officer, and Smiřický had long since vanished into civilian life, and the lieutenant's wife kept her silence.

When they had made love in the equipment shed and then walked back across the road to the mess hall, they heard a thud and a splash, and they saw a private – based on the words he spoke, the tank commander guessed that it was Private Bamza – sitting on the ground with his feet in some kind of hole.

"Fucking hell!" said the private angrily. "Those bloody cooks! Someone could fall right into this shithole."

The tank commander and the officer's wife retreated into the shadows. The soldier got up, picked up a board, and grumbled, "Fucking bastards left it open!" And then he covered the hole in the ground with the board.

The hole was the opening of an enormous septic tank, into which all the sewers of the camp drained.

★   ★   ★

It was many days later – the feeling of liberation among the newly liberated soldiers had long since evaporated, and the officer's wife had begun showing up at the battalion offices to appraise the new recruits with her sad eyes, and Dr. Daniel Smiřický was once again preoccupied with the small, meaningless details of life and had completely forgotten Janinka's wise words – when a special vehicle showed up at the Seventh Tank Battalion's septic-tank opening. The vehicle was known to inmates of the camp by the technical term "shitsucker". The driver removed the board from the septic-tank opening, manoeuvred the truck's huge hose into the gaping hole, turned on the motor, then lit a cigarette and accepted a freshly fried wiener schnitzel from the friendly chef.

The machine worked well at first, but suddenly there was a hollow sucking thump and the pump began to whine.

"What did you put in the tank, boys?" said the driver, putting his half-eaten wiener schnitzel down on the fender of his truck. He stopped the motor and began extracting the hose. "Something's clogged 'er up."

The cook came out to help, and together they pulled the heavy hose out of the septic tank. Sure enough, there was a black object stuck in the intake. When they pulled it out, they saw that it was an officer's riding boot, of unusually small proportions.